MY PERFECT EX

CHERRY BLOSSOM LANE SERIES. BOOK 1

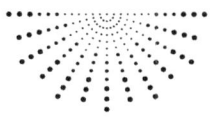

LIZZIE CHANTREE

This novel is a work of fiction. All characters, names, events and places portrayed in it are the author's imagination. Any resemblance to any persons, living or dead, is coincidental. All rights reserved.

No part of this publication may be reproduced or transmitted by any means, electronic or mechanical, including recording, photography, or any information stored in a retrieval system, without permission from the author. The moral right of the author has been asserted.

My Perfect Ex is written and edited in British English rather than American English. This includes spelling, grammar and punctuation.

© Lizzie Chantree 2022

Cover images: ricorico, aqabiz

❦ Created with Vellum

A big thank you to my amazing friends, family and readers (many of whom have become friends), for being part of my writing journey.

Big hugs to my writing buddies, Isabella May, Heidi Catherine, Christine Penhall and Alice Castle. Writing can be isolating, but you all make me smile every day and keep me writing.

To both the reading and writing communities, thank you for your endless support, wisdom and friendship.

Love from Lizzie x

A CHERRY BLOSSOM LANE SERIES

Book 1

CHAPTER ONE

Poppy threw her car keys into the little hand-painted bowl on the hall table. The rattle set her teeth on edge. Her hands were still shaking from the drive home, and the visit to her old school friends. She should have told them her secret. She'd wanted to, but her head had been full of worry about her mum, so it had just been impossible.

If Poppy's mum found out who she was dating, it might send her health spiralling. She'd been doing so well and Poppy wouldn't risk her mother's fragile mental well-being for anyone. The town grapevine would bring her the news in seconds, so Poppy had no choice but to keep her newfound happiness to herself. Their daughter dating Dylan wouldn't ever be a mother's first choice - he'd never settle down! Poppy saw a future for them, but for now it felt easier to keep her relationship status to herself. She was an independent woman and having a gorgeous boyfriend should be gratifying, but currently, it was a bit of a headache.

She wandered over to the couch and flopped down in between her two favourite men, Dylan, her boyfriend, and Billy, her personal assistant and best friend. Dylan immediately wrapped his arms around her and the pain in her head eased. This was her real home, not the place where she'd just been, the tiny flat she'd grown up in. She often felt torn in pieces, coming back here, to the palatial house she now owned. Even the design studio on Cherry Blossom Lane she'd just bought seemed a world away from the tower block she'd come from. She'd bought her studio because it sat on the edge of a pretty little rural village and it gave her mind room to breathe. The fields of wild flowers at the back of the property and the short stroll to the local pub, made it the perfect home for her growing business. Clients could feel relaxed there and Poppy never wanted to feel hemmed in by a town again. The new location set her soul free.

'Did you tell them about us?' Dylan asked her.

'I couldn't,' she admitted, rubbing her eyes with the back of her hand to try and wake herself up at bit. Dylan pulled her feet onto his lap and began to massage them, making her sigh in bliss. The sensation finally broke the tension of her horrible day. Then she giggled and shook him off. 'Ok. What are you up to?'

Both men looked at her innocently and she narrowed her eyes. She took in Dylan's strong arms, in a fitted white T-shirt that still had sawdust on the shoulder, and his blue eyes, framed by thick dark lashes. Her mouth watered at the sight of him. Then she turned to Billy. His blond hair was as immaculate as always, swept to one side in a quiff that he'd told her was bang on trend. He even had a little bit of designer stubble this week. She used to tease Billy that he matched his outfits to what his boyfriend, Ed, wore, but since Ed had left, he was a taboo subject. 'I would wonder how I got so lucky… except for the fact that you are obviously up to something. Spill.'

Billy caved first. 'We thought we'd cook you dinner to

cheer you up...' He started wriggling with excitement, he was such a fidget.

Poppy almost grimaced, but hid it in time. 'Uh... how lovely!' she said over-brightly and pushed herself up, using Dylan's thigh as leverage and enjoying the feel of taut leg muscle against her palm.

This was supposed to be her treat after a difficult day? It was all she needed. Both men were awful cooks. Dylan's mum had never let him inside her kitchen, as she ran a cake business from home and the place had to stay spotless. He hadn't even managed the basics. Billy was just a lazy arse who'd never bothered to learn. His attempts were based on photos in glamorous magazines. He didn't like to follow a recipe in case it 'dampened his creative energy'. The results were inedible. It was becoming increasingly difficult to keep making excuses to leave the table so she could spit it all out. Unfortunately, Billy had decided his new passion, other than their work, of course, was culinary art. The pounding pain in her head was back at the very thought. She took a deep breath and the scent of trimmed roses from her rose garden filled her senses. They were propped in a glass vase on the counter top, and a few soft petals had dropped onto the surface, mirroring her mood.

Then Dylan winked. 'But... I've just decided we're getting a takeaway instead.' The relief on her face must have shown. Billy frowned for a second, but then his eternal optimism kicked in, assuming Dylan was too tired to cook after a busy day at work. Poppy reached over and brushed the sawdust off Dylan's shoulder. 'Do you have to bring your work home with you?' she joked, running her fingers along his shoulder blade.

Dylan grinned and Poppy wandered over to the huge open plan kitchen-diner to fetch a bottle of wine. The floor-to-ceiling windows to the garden were open and the scent of freshly cut grass filled the air. She knew that job must have been done by Dylan, as Billy preferred sunning himself on the lawn, or posing for photos to fill his social media streams.

'How bad was it today?' Dylan asked Poppy.

'Pretty bad.'

He walked over and pulled her in for a cuddle and her body sighed at the contact. She loved the feel of his arms around her and couldn't believe he was hers. With his broad shoulders and tall frame, he caught glances from other women wherever he went. Poppy was used to it now, and she revelled in the fact that it was her that he wanted. She knew she could be annoyingly obsessive-compulsive about her work, downright stubborn and opinionated. She'd had to be, to survive. But he loved her. She could never quite work out how it had happened.

'So what did you say to them?' he asked.

She gently shrugged him off, biting back her irritation. 'It was the same as usual. I wanted to tell them, but the words wouldn't come out.' Her eyes clouded over and her shoulders drooped.

His voice rose slightly. 'You said you'd let them into your new life. How much longer can you go on like this?' He was an easy-going man, but she knew even he had his limits. He took the wine she offered him and sipped the rich red liquid, watching her. Then he reached past her and picked up a small remote control. As he pressed the top button, the television built into the wall began playing soft music and scenes of places Poppy wanted to visit around the world. The views never failed to soothe her.

Inspiring images were a big part of the Poppy Marlowe homes and mood panels she designed. There was a lot of talk in the press at the moment about mental health, but it was something Poppy had always been passionate about. She'd trained night and day to get where she was, and finally her dreams were being realised. She was designing the interiors of homes and helping people. She'd created a certain lifestyle for herself, too, but making others happy and advocating mental health issues, was at the forefront of her work. She just wished she could open up to her three oldest friends… and her mum, about who she was dating.

They still met for lunch in the same place they had for years. Sasha, Demi and Anne, wouldn't even try a new sandwich bar, not that she didn't love the one they gathered in. They were all fiercely supportive of Chris, who ran the café right next to the tower block. Her closest friends would tell her off for risking her heart for Dylan, even though it was going well. Poppy had obsessed about him at school, as he'd attended one nearby with his brothers and they'd earnt the reputations of 'the heartbreak kids'. All of the girls swooned over them. It somehow felt easier to keep her dating status vague, in case everything burnt to ashes around her and Dylan realised she wasn't for him. They'd look at her with pity in their eyes and say they told her so. It was a repetitive theme when they'd been at school. The Taylor brothers were trouble. Her body had quaked with fear every single time she lied to her best friends, but a laser-like determination to prove them wrong, spurred her on. It had started off with her telling a few fibs about what she was doing and who she was spending time with, but the untruths had snowballed. Now she was stuck in her own web of lies. She watched the screen, hoping for inspiration or answers.

Dylan looked into her troubled eyes and then put down his glass. He reached for her shoulders and gently eased the stress away for real this time. His gorgeous face always made her heart pick up speed and he often kissed his way up her neck when they were alone. The combination was intoxicating. Whenever she was in the same room as him, her eyes followed him around of their own volition.

Poppy sighed and turned to face him, noticing Billy eavesdropping from the lounge. 'I couldn't tell them about you.'

'Why?' asked Dylan.

'They'll hate me. I should have just told them at the start, but I wobbled and fibbed.'

'They won't hate you,' he leaned down and brushed his lips with hers. The taste of wine was delicious, but she resisted pouting, or leaning in for more kisses.

'They won't understand. I've left it too long to explain it all now. They think I'm having a casual fling with someone mysterious,' she waggled her eyebrows at him, reaching for humour and failing miserably.

He gave her a measured look and she tried to control the frisson of heat it always ignited inside her. 'Why won't you tell them about me?' he asked.

She couldn't meet his eyes, and pressed her face into his shoulder. 'I told them I'm seeing someone, but I didn't say your name.'

'Do they think you're dating one of your clients? You spend so much time in your studio at Cherry Blossom Lane. Most of your clients are over sixty and have gone grey!'

His own shoulders drooped now and she realised how much it meant to him. She had to tell her school friends about her relationship. She sipped her wine, then chewed on her lip, making it sore. Even the stunning photos on the screen of the trees in bloom, that lined the street to her studio, weren't raising her spirits tonight. She pressed the button to turn them off.

Billy, who had given up eavesdropping and clearly wanted to be part of the conversation, waltzed over and poured himself a glass of wine, sniffing it appreciatively.

MY PERFECT EX

'They think you're sleeping with a client?' He roared with laughter at the idea. Poppy knew she was too uptight to mix business and pleasure – but Billy didn't need to laugh quite so loudly about it.

'They know I've been on some dates,' she chided Billy and looked at Dylan, hoping that might cheer him up, but Dylan's mouth was set and his beautiful blue eyes bored into hers. 'But I didn't say it was you, Dylan. They added me to some dating app ages ago and although I never look at it, I pretended that I've met a few people from there. I'm sorry,' she hung her head in shame. 'They know you. You know them. It's a bit messy'

'Surely that's a good thing?' he walked to stare out into the garden. It was just beginning to get dark. 'And I thought they liked me.'

She rushed over and hugged him, linking her arms around his waist and resting her face on his chest, but he was immoveable. 'Of course they like you. They love you!' she said, carefully omitting that her friends called him and his brothers, Casanovas.

'Then what's the problem?' Dylan said. 'I thought you liked smoulderingly sexy men who are good with their hands?' he joked, smiling – but it didn't quite reach his eyes.

'Sexy?' asked Billy, pretending to look scornfully at Dylan's thick dark locks and impressive arms. Dylan looked miffed for a second, then he and Billy both laughed. Poppy relaxed. She loved it when her two men lightened her mood. When she was feeling down, she sometimes wondered if she was too much like her mum. Then she shook that thought away. They were poles apart.

Her mum, June, had suffered from clinical depression when Poppy was a child. As Poppy grew up, the illness progressed. Poppy had learnt her triggers and had taken on the role of carer at home sometimes. The world had felt like it was closing in on her and she didn't have anyone to turn to. Eventually her mum had needed to have residential treatment and Poppy had coped with that alone too. No one knew how bad it had been for her, or her amazing mum, and she wanted it to stay that way. The slightest upset, or change in routine, could trigger a relapse in her mum's health and Poppy wouldn't risk that for anyone. Her mum was her absolute priority.

June didn't wring her hands in agitation as much, now that some decisions had been taken out of her hands, and she spent her days gardening. She and Poppy had lived in a tower block, so June loved the huge heavenly garden she now had access to and smiled more often, which was promising. She still had dark episodes, so she couldn't return home to the flat. Poppy did hold some happy memories of her parental home, even though it was on the fourth floor of a building that often had a broken lift.

Poppy had been forced to build a career for herself, but was glad of that now. As a teenager it was a miracle that she'd gained any qualifications, as she had barely been able to concentrate at school. It was a blessing things had gone well. She'd been able to move on with her life, though she still visited her mum every week. She also met her old school friends for lunch once a fortnight in the local café, but she had never confided in them about how bad her mother's long illness had been. She'd hidden it from them, even when they'd all been at school together. Now she hadn't dare tell them she was dating Dylan. They'd be furious at her for not confiding in them and for risking it all for a man who would leave her eventually. She wanted to break free of the expectations most locals had about The Taylor brothers. It was ok to date them, but anything serious, not a chance.

Dylan sighed, regaining her attention. 'How was your mum?'

'She's no better. She still can't move back to the flat, or come here either. Not that she would. She feels uneasy in new surroundings and doesn't like change. She'd say I'd taken on too much – and that's not true, but she'd start to worry, regardless,' she said sadly.

CHAPTER TWO

Snuggled up in bed with Dylan a few hours later, Poppy thought back to her lunch with her friends. Was she being too harsh on them? Dylan began kissing his way along her collarbone and she sighed and let her mind go blank. It was a trick she'd taught herself whilst trying her best to care for her mum. Sometimes the pressure had been too much, so she'd learnt to empty her mind for a while as a coping mechanism. Now she put everything else aside and concentrated on the very hot man who was in her bed, and doing extremely interesting things with his hands.

She lost himself in his arms and wondered yet again how she'd got so lucky and snagged a man like him, especially when he'd been the high school crush she'd watched from afar. They'd attended different schools but she'd known exactly who he was, as had most of her friends. Dylan's dreamboat status was a hot topic. He'd swanned around town with his brothers and their group of sexy friends, leaving a trail of broken hearts. He was all grown up now and he didn't seem to want anyone else, which made her excited and confused at the same time. One reason she hadn't told her friends about him yet was that she knew they'd say he would smash her heart to smithereens. Particularly Sasha, who was always so dramatic. Poppy didn't think he would, though. The way his hand trailed lazily up her leg and gazed into her eyes made her mind turn to mush.

She moved around to face him fully and he tenderly brushed her hair out of her eyes. She smiled and her eyes sparkled with mischief. 'What did you do today? I forgot to ask, as I was otherwise engaged,' she grinned, picking the covers up and glancing at his glistening body. He grinned back wolfishly, before pulling her to him, kissing her thoroughly. When they resurfaced, he tucked her under his arm so that her head rested on his chest and he could run his fingertips across her skin. She could hear the beat of his heart and it comforted her. In his arms was her favourite place to be.

'I didn't do much today, to be honest,' he said, finally answering her question. 'I finished that big job yesterday, so I had the morning off. I left everything to my staff. They can handle it.'

Poppy gave him a tight-lipped smile and picked at her shell pink nail varnish. She moved forward in her career every day and his complacency confused her. The incredibly beautiful, bespoke bedside cabinets, in her bedroom, were made by Dylan. There was such high demand for his craftmanship, but he acted as though his small furniture factory could pretty much run itself. 'Why don't you reach out to that contact I gave you? Jared Wright is building ten houses and four stunning industrial barns, on the plot behind this house.' One of the barns was directly behind her garden, but you would only be able to see the apex of glass of the second floor, so she wasn't worried about it at all. The barns were already there, but were being updated, as it had been farmland before Jared acquired it. He was going to offer work-home solutions for local business people. Poppy had been thinking of how to use the land herself, when she heard it was being sold off for more housing, but the price was beyond her reach right now. 'Jared mentioned he was looking for contractors for the interior.'

Dylan, frowned and a warning tone came into his voice, 'I don't need more contracts. I'm happy as I am.'

She took a deep breath and smiled, but it didn't quite reach her eyes. 'Ok.' She kissed his nose, wishing she didn't have to get up so early the next morning. She had a meeting herself with the multi-million pound property developer. Dylan might not want Jared's business, but she'd agreed to go and talk to the man about making bespoke sensory panels for his houses, similar to those she'd designed for depression sufferers like her mum. Mr Wright had read about her ideas in a glossy magazine and wanted to incorporate them into some of his own building projects.

Poppy marvelled at the exciting changes in her business. She often caught herself staring out of the window of her office in Cherry Blossom Lane, at the seemingly endless fields of wildflowers beyond and smiling gormlessly. It was the perfect place to inspire creativity. She just wished that Dylan could see there were similar opportunities for his own work. Jared Wright could be a valuable contact and working with him might help Dylan's business grow very quickly. The problem was that Dylan was content just plodding along. He did well with minimal effort, and that was good enough for him. Poppy wasn't like that. Her persistent motivation was to succeed, to help others who, like her, were carers. She had the determination to grow her business and make it stand out and make a difference. She made a profit, but she also provided a service that eased stress for others. It was win-win in her eyes.

CHAPTER THREE

Poppy glanced at the inexpensive wristwatch her mum had given her for her eighteenth birthday. It was her most treasured possession. It always made her think of her mother and feel close to her. She looked around her office, lined with bookcases, and at the large window with views over the hills laden with wild flowers, and she felt the tension leave her. Walking through the front door every day, seeing the cherry trees that lined the road, swaying in the breeze, taking in the sight of the little flowers, never failed to ease her mind. She'd read somewhere that cherry blossom symbolised love, hope and happiness. She didn't know if that was true, but she loved the thought of being surrounded by such delicately beautiful trees.

She already knew what to say in the meeting with Wright Enterprises later that day and had her figures in front of her. If Jared Wright couldn't see her product was worth the price, then she didn't want to be working for him as a consultant. She'd learnt very early on that creatives were frequently expected to work for free, and she'd had to fight her corner. It was such a competitive world. She'd had plenty of knockbacks, but since hitting on the idea of improving people's mental health through their homes, she'd never been so much in demand.

People usually only got to meet Poppy at the planning stage. She hated publicity, as it had made her quake with anxiety and spend nights tossing and turning in rumpled sheets, but it was essential for business growth. Then the fear of the worry created more worry. It affected her work, so not talking about her family was one of her quirks, and PR companies just had to deal with it. She didn't want strangers to judge her mum when they knew nothing about her history, or what she'd been through. They either focussed on Poppy's creative ideas and got on with it, or they didn't get the interview. When her company was in its infancy, no one had been interested in taking her picture anyway. It was only now that they scrambled to talk to her. She wasn't risking her mental health for anyone. Occasionally, she had to step out of her comfort zone and feature in a very high end magazine, but it wasn't often that her home life or relationship status were mentioned. Dylan wasn't famous, so they weren't interested in him. Someone press-worthy like Jared would be of interest, but she'd just be very clear about their working relationship if it was ever brought up.

Billy loved the limelight, which helped a lot. She'd found him by accident when he'd stumbled into her newly refurbished office, thinking it was a casting agency. She was still tripping over packing boxes and trying to alphabetise her bookcase at the time. She remembered the way Billy had burst through the doors, saying he had an appointment for a casting. After she'd explained the agency had moved on, he'd followed her back into her office, plonked his backside on her desk and proceeded to ask her twenty questions about why she was there. She'd been so taken aback that, for once, she'd spoken about what she was trying to achieve and he must have heard the passion in her voice about her hopes and dreams. He'd paused, misty eyed, for a moment, before his bottom had begun to wriggle in excitement. He hadn't been able to sit still.

When he'd asked where her receptionist or assistant was, she'd made the mistake of mentioning she didn't have one yet. He'd promptly asked for a tour of the premises. She'd been so surprised that she'd got up and explained that there had originally been four interlinked areas on the ground floor of the building. The rooms had layers of dust and mismatched wallcoverings until she'd tackled them, as the agency had left ages ago and moved to a smaller property down the road. Luckily, Poppy had seen the potential of the place. It was in a beautiful location on a long road, that led straight up to a picturesque little village, with views across rolling hills. The whole area was dotted with cherry blossom trees, but her road seemed to be the only one lined with them.

She'd walked him around the space and explained how she had opened up the whole back wall and replaced it with two floor to ceiling windows and a set of folding doors that she'd swung open to let the afternoon breeze drift through and the scent of wildflowers fill the air. Next she'd led him to her favourite area with wall to ceiling bookcases, where a round table was set up for creative meetings with clients. This room also led to a charming private outdoor patio that she'd screened off from the larger paved area, that ran along the back of the building. They trundled up the stairs, to the flat that she might convert at some stage, but she'd mostly left that for now. She'd picked some wild flowers from the fields behind the office that morning, and they sat prettily by the window and drew your eye to the stunning view beyond. Billy had selected the prettiest bloom and tucked it behind his ear, which had made her laugh.

The area was up and coming, so she'd bought at the right time. Everyone along this section of the road seemed friendly and a couple of people from neighbouring buildings had popped by to say hello to the new girl on the block. She'd tried to hide her nerves at being a fairly new business owner, but was determined to push through her insecurities and to wow them with the transformation of her beautiful office space.

When they'd returned to the ground floor, Billy sat at the front desk, tilting his head from side to side and straightening his shoulders, as if deciding whether he'd take her on or not. Then he'd disappeared for twenty minutes. She'd sighed with relief at getting her peace and quiet back, only for him to return with steaming takeaway coffees and two fat croissants, telling her graciously that he'd accept the job.

Thank goodness for Billy. She grinned as she listened to him singing off-key. He was one of the most important people in her life now, and she was so grateful to him. He kept her sane with his endless sunshine and streamlined her whole operation. He organised her world and had turned into her best friend. Billy thought it was hysterical that she hadn't told her old friendship group about her sexy new business acquaintance, or who her hot boyfriend was. He nudged her about it often, but didn't push it too far. He still loved theatrics and was the darling of the local amateur dramatics group, but his new passion was Poppy and her business.

She sat sipping a cool coffee and musing about the meeting with Jared Wright today, curious to find out more about the man behind the company she was visiting. She'd read about him and spoken to him on the phone. The articles she'd studied suggested a dynamic and driven man, whose business was flourishing. He caught on to growing trends and people like her, who created them, and nurtured talent via partnerships. She liked his style. Her business was growing, but there was always room for more. She wanted to employ extra staff and had big expansion plans. It was funny – as a child she hadn't even dreamt of running a business. She'd just wanted to help people like her mum, so other kids didn't have to go through what she'd experienced. She supposed that this was her way of achieving that.

At the moment her business was making a healthy profit and still giving her time to do her charitable works. But she was mindful of overloading herself. She was the chief – and only –designer, though she had a team of skilled artisans like Dylan backing her up, to bring together a beautiful product range. In the long term, she wanted to find ways of making her sensory panels more accessible to smaller households, but for now that would have to wait.

She scooped up the papers she would need for her meeting and tucked them away in a pretty folder, ready for later. She knew her presentation by heart anyway. Her business had seeped into her bones. She knew every inch of her designs and how they worked. The notes were more for her customers. A developer like Jared Wright taking interest was good news. Her usual work on corporate sites, or with small independent building contractors, was exciting, but this was a whole new ballgame for her.

Billy wandered in, looking sharp as usual. His blond hair was slicked back today and he was wearing fitted black jeans and a crisp white shirt, worn loose, with a scalloped edge. On top of that was a tailored waistcoat. It made her smile. Billy never failed to brighten her day, managing to look sharp and sexy at the same time. Poppy didn't have a dress code at work, but usually wore black skinny jeans and a fitted T-shirt with little splashes of colour. She wasn't into designer clothes, even though she could afford them now. Her wardrobe held one or two beautifully-made items, but they were from artists and designers that she'd met along her creative journey. One of her new friends, Verity, had her own tiny boutique down the road. Poppy's feet often took her there without conscious thought. Billy teased her that she needed friends she could be herself with, which was why she kept popping over to check out Verity's latest stock.

'Is that top one of Verity's designs?'

Poppy looked down at herself absentmindedly and nodded.

'You seem to be getting close to her.'

Poppy shrugged. 'She's just a friend. I'm surrounded by them…' she joked feebly.

'Only work ones. Apart from me and Dylan. Everyone else you keep at arm's length. You're as bad as you say your old school friends are. You don't like change! If anyone chats you up, you steer clear of them unless they're a client. They invite you to parties and you always decline. You're a hermit. I know you have a boyfriend, but that doesn't mean you can't socialise.'

Poppy's hand shook. She should have told Billy the real reason she hadn't confided in her friends. It was more about her mum having a relapse from stress if people started gossiping, than Dylan's reputation. Poppy was a strong woman and it would take more than a fractured relationship to destroy her. Causing her mum stress, on the other hand, made her stomach swirl in pain. Poppy had already lived through the consequences of that more than once and would do everything in her power to prevent any breaks in the glimpses of light they saw these days. She knew her mum spoke to one of her old neighbours regularly. Gossip on the estate was rife. 'I don't hide from people!'

'Why don't you mingle with them, then?'

'Why would they want me for a friend? You're right, I'm pretty unsociable.'

Billy perched his bottom on her desk and looked at her with wonder. 'You're an exciting new entrepreneur – and why wouldn't they like you?'

'I don't have time for parties. My work commitments are too demanding.'

He slapped his hand against his forehead. 'You need to learn to network.'

'My business isn't big enough for me to fit in just yet. It's not that I feel intimidated, just a bit… weird. Like I'm the hired help.' Poppy sipped her cold coffee and nibbled on her croissant, leaving a trail of crumbs across her desk. Billy tutted at the sight, then went on.

'People book you months, sometimes years, in advance, to help advise on their building projects. You're a business owner, with staff, keeping self-employed artisans in work by recommending them all the time. You make a fortune. And you still feel you're the hired help? Are you mad?'

She flinched. Billy got up and for a second she thought he was going to shake her, but he just shook his head and picked up her coffee cup to go and refill it for her.

Then he turned, smiling mischievously. 'Do you have a seedy past, something that I don't know about?'

Poppy's eyes glittered a warning, but she just stuck her tongue out at him. 'I do not have a seedy past, as you well know.'

'Then why hide yourself away?'

She sighed and looked out of the window to the soft green hills, watching the birds swoop low as they flew past in the sunlight. 'I'm not.'

Billy walked to the door and turned back to face her. 'You know you are. I'd shout from the top of one of those cherry trees outside if I had as much talent as you.'

'You are such a drama queen,' she said, throwing a pen from her desk at him. He ducked and went to get their coffee. She frowned for a moment, then pressed a couple of buttons. Soft music filled the air, while the daylight lighting hidden in the front of the bookshelves blazed a little more strongly, as though filling the room with sunshine. She took a calming breath and let her mind relax. She moved a file she needed so that she wouldn't forget it for her meeting and settled back to check her emails, all thoughts of troublesome friends and annoying assistants forgotten.

CHAPTER FOUR

*P*oppy wrung her hands in her lap. She tried to think back to the successful meeting she'd had with Jared Wright the day before, but this was even more important. When she finally saw Anne come into the coffee shop, she jumped to her feet and gave a nervous smile. They had been having coffee in the same place every other week for years.

The café hadn't changed much. It still had the same old plastic tables and chairs, while the aromas of bacon and coffee mingled with the chocolatey scent of cakes displayed under domes on the glass counter. It was a weird combination but it was one of the few places that felt like home. She hugged Anne as soon as she saw her and Anne giggled and hugged her back, her long curly dark hair swishing across Poppy's face. Poppy's own blond hair was tied up in a high ponytail, as it always was when she met her old friends. They scolded her to leave it down and show the beautiful cut and colour she now had regularly, which left her hair so glossy and manageable, but she still reached for the hairband and scraped it back. In the end, they had given up moaning at her to change it.

The two women sat down and Poppy waved to Chris behind the counter. He nodded and began to make their usual fare, calling to Terry in the kitchen to make a plate of sandwiches for another customer. Terry's sandwiches were legendary locally, as was Chris's café.

Poppy and Anne liked frothy cappuccinos, but Demi and Sasha, who were going to join them, enjoyed tall glasses of dark hot chocolate with cream and marshmallows sprinkled on top. Chris didn't use the tiny marshmallows she often saw in her own high street, but plonked a huge pink mallow on top instead. He'd been doing that for years and it still made them smile. His eternally sunny nature made it hard to be grumpy around him and he had watched over them since they were in school. He was pretty good-looking for his age, too, with a quiet charm and sparkly eyes. He still asked after Poppy's mum every time he saw Poppy, and he also went to visit June regularly. Poppy had once wondered if he'd had a crush on her mum, as he'd never married, but he'd not voiced it to her.

A burst of noise came from the front of the shop as Demi and Sasha rushed through the doors. At twenty-six, they were both still as rowdy as teenagers. Their faces lit up when Chris placed their drinks and a round of sandwiches on the table. They blew him theatrical kisses and pulled Poppy and Anne in for brief hugs, before sitting down. Sasha grabbed a cheese sandwich as if she'd never eaten in her life and sighed in bliss, her body sagging into the chair. Poppy and Anne exchanged glances and they all stared at Sasha until she stopped eating and looked at them innocently. 'Oh... sorry. Were we waiting for the Queen? I'm famished. My new boss is fit, but he's a slave driver.' She finished her sandwich and picked up another, which made the others dig in before she ate the lot.

'Does he actually expect you to do some work?' joked Poppy. 'That's shocking!'

Demi giggled and Anne rolled her eyes. Sasha was not known for her work ethic. She was too busy daydreaming about the opposite sex.

'Not all of us can be workaholics.' She pointed her sandwich at Poppy, which made the others' mouths twitch. Poppy tried to hide her flush with a sip of coffee.

'At least she's trying to do something with her life and is helping her mum,' defended Anne. 'She can't help it if her clients are tyrants.'

Poppy stopped eating mid bite. 'Um… they're not tyrants, and I enjoy what I do.'

'You work all hours and you don't have any time off. You were always so clever. I bet you don't charge enough.' Anne was in full rant mode now, her dark curls bouncing around her face and her green eyes flashing. Poppy put her food down and touched her hand.

'My clients are amazing. My pay isn't bad at all and my work has potential, so I'm happy.' Poppy drew breath. 'I just signed with a new client.'

'Another client? Have you got enough hours in the day? I know you can afford that posh four-wheel drive car, but weren't you happier with more time on your hands and driving around in your mum's old banger?'

'No,' said Poppy defensively, her stomach starting to hurt and lunch forgotten. 'Anyway, how do you know I collected the four-wheel drive? I was going to tell you about it today.' She pictured Dylan sitting next to her in the new car and blanched.

Anne stared into space and picked up her coffee, sipping it, taking her time. Finally she said, 'I saw a guy driving it when I had a hospital visit with Freddie. You were in the passenger seat. I'm sure it was you. Billy just looked like you described him. He was chatting away and you didn't see me. He was fit, though!'

Poppy started to shake slightly. 'Oh, ok. Yes, that was probably us.' Poppy pictured her beautiful shiny black car and remembered she'd asked Billy to drive, as she was tired from a meeting. Phew!

Now Poppy noticed Sasha watching her. Sasha didn't miss much. Poppy used to tease her about not wanting to progress in her career, but she was actually proud of her friend for doing as she pleased and being happy with her life. Sasha was nobody's fool. She'd kept the group out of trouble for years.

'How is Freddie?' Poppy asked Anne, changing the subject. Anne's face lit up at the mention of her six-year-old son. 'The doctor said he's fit enough to travel. I just can't believe how generous people have been. The fundraising page you set up, Poppy, is almost ready to close. With all the car boot sales, pub parties, bake sales, and other events we've done at the school, we're only a few hundred short of the £20,000 we need, to get the treatment in America. I have no idea where the money has come from, but I'm not knocking it. It's trickled in from all over the place.'

Poppy's face broke into her first genuine smile. 'That's great news!' She leaned in and gave Anne a hug, seeing tears in her eyes, that after years of suffering from a medical condition that affected his immune system, Freddie might finally get better.

'The doctor's know that we're planning to fly to receive specialist treatment that isn't available at home. Even the travel could be dangerous, but the risk might pay off if the treatment works, so they understand it's our best choice,' said Anne. All four women relaxed and held hands across the table, so happy there was hope at last.

'That social media page you set up really worked,' said Demi, brushing her wild curls out of her eyes and grinning. 'How did you get so many followers that quickly, Poppy?' They all turned to hear her answer.

'I, uh, I went round lots of local businesses, and used my contacts book. It grew that way.' Poppy had never bragged about her business and wasn't about to start now. In a way it embarrassed her that she'd done so well, even though she was incredibly proud. It was a weird paradox, or guilt for doing well financially when her mum was stuck in a medical facility.

'The donations from that page were incredible,' said Sasha. 'Lots of small amounts, but they really added up.'

'It wasn't just that,' protested Poppy. 'The bake sales at Freddie's school, and the money people donated instead of drinking in the pub, they brought in thousands, too.' The others didn't look convinced.

'So, have you settled into your new house yet? Isn't it a bit big to rattle about on your own?' Demi asked Poppy. Sasha signalled to Chris for more coffees. He nodded and started the coffee machine up – the old girl took some coaxing these days.

Poppy hesitated. Could she tell them the truth about Dylan? She decided that she couldn't. 'Billy lives in the annex above the garage. It's beautiful, so he's not complaining. I live in the main house and he's nearby if I need him.'

'I bet you need him!' winked Sasha.

'It's not like that. Billy's amazing. He's my assistant. Plus, he's not interested in women.'

'Really?'

'Really.' Said Poppy firmly. 'He never has been. He's just

come out of a very serious relationship and is heartbroken. He was in love and they were together for years.'

'I thought you said he liked to party?' said Anne.

Poppy smiled and pictured Billy dancing around her kitchen and inviting friends to the annexe flat he lived in above the garage at her house. He had so many amazing friends… as did she. She just needed to trust hers more and open her heart, she guessed. Her smile slipped a little. 'He has lots of friends, he's really outgoing, but he's much happier in a relationship. He's a great boyfriend. I'm still not sure what really happened to break them up. He's as confused as I am.'

'It sounds like you confide in each other,' said Anne, with an edge to her voice. Her friends eyed each other. Sasha kicked Anne under the table, but they all felt it as the table wobbled and Anne yelped.

'Are you jealous?' Poppy half-joked. No one answered. 'What's going on?' asked Poppy, looking around the table.

'We want to meet this Billy at last, and we would also like an invitation to your house sometime,' said Anne, rubbing her sore foot. 'Plus you're very evasive about these dates you've been going on. Don't any of them deserve a mention?'

Poppy's face blanched. 'But my place is miles away,' she said, ignoring the dating jibe.

Sasha tutted 'We do have cars.'

'You're all so busy.'

'Not for you, we aren't.'

'It's about time Billy met some of your friends, and we want a chance to find out for ourselves if you have any sort of work-life balance. Can we come to your offices in Cherry Blossom Lane too?' Anne was like a dog with a bone.

Poppy pictured her idyllic little office crammed with noisy women and winced. 'Of course you can. I'm not a workaholic!' she protested, but it fell on deaf ears as they pointedly stared at her beautiful car, which was parked beside the café. She'd worked incredibly hard to afford it. She'd been determined to make a car her first big purchase, as she travelled a lot. She'd had a tiny flat initially, and her hatchback had sat proudly outside. The upgraded glossy four wheel drive, complimented her current home's countryside location. Now she enjoyed sweeping into the driveway in front of her own house, a place she'd designed herself. Anne often joked that she'd never be satisfied. She'd always be looking for the next big thing to aim for.

Poppy chewed on her bottom lip. She was about to use her usual excuse, that the house wasn't ready for guests – but she'd just told them that Billy was a party animal, so that wouldn't wash. 'Billy isn't good with strangers.'

'We won't be strangers if you introduce us, will we?' argued Sasha.

Poppy's skin was starting to warm up and her knuckles were white, she was gripping her fresh cup of coffee so hard. She forced herself to place it down on the table in front of her. 'Um... ok. I'll talk to him.'

'Stop being so timid, Poppy! It's not like you to ask permission from anyone. You're usually in charge of everything. *Tell* him we're coming round,' said Anne, her eyes flashing. Poppy gulped and agreed that she'd try. That seemed to appease them and then things returned to normal. Demi told them about all the arguments between her boyfriend and her dad, who worked at the same garage in town.

'Dad thinks Allan is a waste of space, as Allan doesn't want to end up running the garage. It's too much stress for him. He just wants to do his job and go home and sleep... with me,' she grinned slyly.

'You wear the poor man out!' laughed Poppy. She fleetingly thought about Dylan. 'Why doesn't Allan want to take over? Surely it's an opportunity most people would jump at?'

Demi shook her head. Cute tight curls bounced around her face, and freckles danced across her nose. Poppy loved hugging Demi, she was all soft curves and sexiness. Poppy had longed for hips and a booty like Demi's, not to mention an attention-grabbing body like Sasha's, when they were all growing up. Neither had happened. Poppy's long legs and slim body often felt a bit gangly. Not that any boyfriends had ever complained. Having such gorgeous mates might have intimidated her, but she was proud of each and every one of them. Plus she'd seen them all with spots and braces, at school.

Demi sipped her coffee, and Anne butted in. 'He wants the money but not the paperwork. He likes tinkering with cars – and women.'

Demi looked affronted and Poppy wished Anne would think before she spoke sometimes. Her jokes were often caustic and fell flat. 'He's happy working on the cars, but he doesn't want to know how to run a business,' Demi explained. 'My dad's constantly stressed and the pay jump wouldn't be worth the hours Allan would have to work. Plus all of his mates work at the garage and would rile him for being the boss.'

Poppy could sympathise with Allan on this last part at least. It wasn't so far away from her own line of thinking, with everyone around the table and her own business venture. They didn't understand the dedication it took or why she pushed herself so hard. She frowned. Her stomach rumbled noisily. She hadn't touched the sandwiches. She picked up the one remaining cheese and tomato triangle and nibbled its edge.

'Allan knows his life will change if he steps into Dad's shoes. We aren't even married,' said Demi, looking down. 'Not yet…' That was another touchy subject, Poppy knew. Demi's life plan had always been to get married by her mid-twenties, and to have had at least one child by now. It hadn't happened. She'd been with Allan for years and years, but he still hadn't proposed. It was a bit of a sore point and they all made sure they showed no signs of sympathy or she'd start crying. Demi was known for her long dreamy sighs and romantic longings.

Anne was the only one of the four who had been married, and that had happened in haste. She and Connor had only been together a month beforehand. When they'd split up years later, she'd said she was ok with that. Poppy wasn't as convinced. The ex-couple got on better now than they had when they were living together. Poppy, Sasha and Demi all loved Connor, as they'd known him since school, but he hadn't dealt well with his child being unwell. They couldn't blame him entirely, it had been horrendous for them all, but Anne hadn't walked away. He had – and it was a bone of contention.

'Are you going to your mum's flat today?' Demi asked Poppy – but not before Poppy had noticed her glistening eyes. Poppy gave her hand a squeeze under the table. Demi's smile wobbled and then rallied.

'I am,' stated Poppy. 'Anyone want to come with me?' Everyone looked shifty at this. Poppy went round to the flat and cleaned it every other week, in case her mum ever returned. Sasha had an aversion to cleaning and Anne couldn't understand why Poppy bothered, it was just a little dust. Demi was always non-committal, as she hated being away from Allan for too long. But Poppy was determined to give the place its usual airing. She had also been making changes. She hadn't told them about that, either.

CHAPTER FIVE

*P*oppy smiled at Gladys, who lived in the flat next door to her mum's place. Gladys covered her face in little kisses, in profuse thanks for the bags of shopping Poppy brought each time. Eighty-year-old Glady's slight frame worried Poppy, so she made sure that her shelves were restocked and got her medicines collected once a fortnight.

She turned the old key in the lock and stepped inside, gratified to find the place didn't smell musty. The painting she'd done last time had dried without leaving a lingering bitter smell. The new light panel was easy to use and brought daylight into the flat as soon as she stepped through the door. She could almost imagine that moment when you stepped out of the shade of a tree and were bathed in sunlight, and it instantly lifted her mood.

Gentle music started playing from the kitchen when she walked past the door. Her mother's favourite songs brought a tear to her eye, even though she'd programmed them for her mother's benefit, to make her smile and remind her of happier times. The fact that June still hadn't been back yet was hard to take. Poppy wiped away her tears with the back of her hand and then walked into the freshly decorated bedroom. Billy had painted a huge mural of rolling hills on the back wall. It helped make the small space appear vast and relaxing. Poppy tried to refrain from sagging down on the new bedspread to snooze for a while. Her work days seemed to be getting longer and longer and she hoped her friends weren't right about burning out. Her meeting with Jared Wright had been a ray of light, though. She had wondered how she would summon the energy to get through it, but she'd found herself fidgeting and hundreds of ideas had fizzed through her brain about future projects. He'd asked her so many questions, and his eyes had bored into hers. She didn't think she'd ever met a more attractive man – other than Dylan. She'd been inspired to hear about his plans for expansion and his innovative ideas.

Poppy stepped next door into her tiny bedroom. The memories came rushing back, as they always did. She'd tidied up in here, but many of her childhood mementos were neatly stacked on the two shelves above her bed. She ran her fingers over the duvet and glanced around the walls, freshly redecorated in a soft blue hue that was darker at the base and lighter as it reached the ceiling. Her eyes lost focus and for a moment she could almost imagine being submerged in a watery bubble. It would be so easy to drift off to sleep here. She opened the window and went out onto the tiny balcony. This was where she'd first spotted Dylan. She and her friends had secretly spied on him for years. She picked up the binoculars that still hung on a nail on the textured wall outside, and leaned on the metal railings. It felt so familiar that she grinned.

Movement caught her eye and she accidentally knocked the binoculars against the railings. Dylan was walking out of his mum's house, kissing her on the cheek and hugging her. He looked gorgeous in inky blue jeans and a white cotton shirt with the arms rolled up. Poppy flushed and almost dropped the binoculars, tipping them over the edge, but her quick reflexes saved them. Dylan sometimes teased her about the fact that she used to spy on him, and that she'd always fancied him. She hadn't known he was coming this way today. The thought didn't sit well with her, even though he was just visiting his mum. The local community adored him and she wasn't sure how everyone would feel about him dating her. They'd assume it wasn't serious, as he wasn't the type to settle down and they would worry, or gossip, about her. She was loved by the community too, she knew that, but none of them knew how hard it had been with her and her mum and she didn't want to be the talk of the town now either. She didn't want anyone's pity.

Poppy hung the binoculars back up and looked at the freshly painted rail. She'd placed two big urns out here, one on her mum's side of the balcony and one on hers, even though her mum had stopped coming outside years ago. She had planted beautifully scented flowers in the urns which had their own watering system, and had even added fake grass, to make it feel like a little oasis. It worked. It was tiny, but beautiful. Her worries drifted away when she was there. All it needed was for her mum to come home.

She went back into the kitchen and made herself a coffee, then brought it out to the balcony and perched on the pretty little chair and table she'd set up there. Her mum would have loved this balcony, if it had looked like this when she'd lived here. Poppy had renovated Gladys's balcony the same way, and the old lady told her how much she loved it every time Poppy visited. She said it made her feel like she was in the Queen's own garden, which was a mighty stretch of the imagination, but if Gladys was happy, then so was Poppy. A few of the other neighbours had commented on how nice it was and they had started visiting Gladys more. That was good, but Poppy hoped that they wouldn't all ask her to transform their balconies. She'd used the bare minimum of materials, but there were loads of flats in the tower block and she couldn't afford to help everyone, however much she loved some of them. For now she was happy with them visiting Gladys.

She did wince at keeping this flat empty, when someone could have lived in it. But it belonged to her mum, even though Poppy had taken over paying for it years ago when she was just a teen. She'd worked in the café in every spare moment and helped where she could with the bills. Her mum needed to have a home to return to. She wouldn't stay in the treatment facility for ever. For now, residential care was a necessity, but Poppy lived for the day when her mum would be well enough to come back to her own flat again, without anyone looking over her shoulder.

Poppy recalled all those times when she'd had to sleep here alone. She'd often huddled up in her bed, hugging her knees, and the noises outside would scare her half witless. Those first stays away were short, then, for her mum and she'd always returned bright and sunnier, but it never lasted. The dark cloud always descended eventually. Poppy began to fear it as much as the night terrors she'd developed as a teenager. Not that anyone was there to notice, as her mum took sleeping tablets every evening. Poppy told everyone her mum had a sick sister who she had to visit and take care of, if anyone asked where she was. Over time, they just gave her sympathetic glances, sometimes a quick hug, but mostly she kept her head down and didn't make eye contact with anyone until she was clear of the building, so they couldn't ask awkward questions and she wouldn't have to make up new lies. She was sixteen by that time, and could be left at home.

Now June was in proper care, Poppy could see that the

original place she had stayed at was a bit rough, but they had taken whatever was offered at the time. However afraid Poppy had been, alone in the flat, she'd just been glad that someone was helping her mum.

The problem was that June was always brought home within a couple of days, and a few days after that, the gloom would return. Poppy often felt a punch of guilt for not doing better for her mum in those early stages. She had been young, but she'd already been micro-managing her mum for years by this point, trying with all her might to make June happy, not realising it was beyond her control. She'd always felt that she was the cause of her mum's problems. Poppy stared unseeingly across the town and hoped with all her might that her dream – that her mum would come home – was going to come true.

CHAPTER SIX

Anne wiggled her bottom and looked at the big clock on the waiting room wall again. There were paintings by a local artist on display too, with tiny price tags dangling underneath each one, but she was too distracted to concentrate. She and Freddie had an appointment with the doctor. Although he seemed to be improving, they needed the treatment from abroad to give him the best chance. Coming to these appointments alone made her hands sweat and her skin itch. Connor should be with her, giving her support. Poppy came when she could, as did Demi and Sasha, but it wasn't the same as having Freddie's dad there, holding her hand and telling her it would be ok. Not that Connor had ever done that. He'd scarpered at the first sign that Freddie might be ill. They'd stayed amicable, as they had so many friends in common, but Anne often wanted to kick him in the balls for being so weak when she'd had to be strong. She'd loved him ferociously, but in the end it had meant nothing.

Absentmindedly, she checked that Freddie was still listening to music via his earphones and picked up a glossy magazine. She needed to distract herself and a few hot male models would do the trick right now. Flicking aimlessly, a photo caught her eye and she frowned, trying to go back and find it again. She really didn't like touching magazines in doctors' surgeries, you never knew if someone with a cold had picked them up before you. Germs could be dangerous for Freddie. She'd go and wash her hands in the little washroom by reception afterwards.

Paging back and forward, she finally found the article. She gingerly spread it out on her knees and scanned it. Her mouth hung open for a second as she gawped at the images. *What the hell?* Staring back at her from the pages of the magazine was a very glamorous-looking Poppy and beside her it looked like it must be that guy, Billy. Anne looked again at the front cover of the magazine. Poppy usually told them about every fancy photoshoot, as they made her nervous. Anne bent to take a closer look. Poppy looked exotic and dreamy. She was wearing what appeared to be a designer dress too. She had a huge smile on her face and her eyes were sparkling. Anne read the article again and scratched her head. She couldn't believe what she was reading. Did Poppy have an identical twin? Anne checked on Freddie, whose head was bobbing up and down in time with his music, and she slumped back in shock.

The article said that Poppy was an incredible designer who was in high demand for her work in the mental health arena, which Anne already knew. It said her brand was innovative and ingenious, and that she was a rising star to watch out for, which made Anne puff out her chest in pride. Why hadn't Poppy mentioned the interview to the girls? She knew they liked to read those articles together. It also listed some of her recent work projects. Anne had heard of one of them. It was a flashy hotel chain. It also mentioned her boyfriend, Dylan, a local business owner. Poppy would be fuming. Anne knew he worked on some of her projects, but he wasn't dating Poppy... was he? She pictured Poppy looking shiftily away and dodging Anne's many questions about where she'd been and with whom... and a few things slotted into place in her mind. She knew Poppy hated dating apps!

Anne looked around her furtively and ripped the centre pages out of the magazine. She folded the picture of Poppy's face in half, shoving it into the bag by her feet. An elderly gentleman in the corner of the room had been watching her and tutted, but she kept her eyes on the magazine in front of her in an almost zombie-like state. She wanted to open the article again to find out more about Dylan get a better look at Billy. She'd only seen him fleetingly in the car. She glanced across at the old man, but he was still looking at her disapprovingly. From the date on the front of the magazine, she could see it was a few months old. The facts must be wrong, surely? It was the kind of glossy that was well out of Anne's price range, the sort of thing she'd never usually look at. Perhaps Poppy had banked on that. A strange sensation was filling Anne's veins and her bones felt heavy. Why had Poppy been misleading them all? If she'd slept with Dylan, she'd have gone through pain when she was dumped. They all knew she'd had a crush on him for years. Maybe she was too embarrassed to own up.

Freddie's name appeared on the screen and she picked up their bags, nudged her son, who was still in a trance listening to his music, and wiped his fingers down with antibacterial gel. This was their normal routine. Then she took his hand and headed to the door. She'd have to think about what the hell Poppy was playing at, later. Dating a Taylor brother? That was crazy. They were all heartbreakers! Her blood started to boil and she clenched her fists. Dylan better not be messing with her friend. Anne also needed to call the girls. But for now, she had to focus on Freddie.

After a good meeting with the doctor, who cleared Freddie to fly to America in the coming months, she wanted to pick Freddie up and swing him around and around. She felt her pulse ramp up a notch. Going abroad for treatment was a big decision. But it had to be done and she wasn't about to let her usual fears hold them back.

Poppy had had a hand in that as well. There was no way the funds could have been raised without her tireless work. Anne quickly sent out a text to Sasha and Demi and called an emergency meeting, like they'd always done at school. She threw her phone in her bag, headed to the car with Freddie like a woman on a mission, and started the engine, her mind whirring between Freddie's treatment and Poppy's secrets.

CHAPTER SEVEN

Poppy looked out of her kitchen window and wondered what it would be like to see some workshops and ten houses in the fields beyond. She was used to gazing across a green expanse next to the barns, but Jared Wright had now bought the plot. Ten new Poppy Marlowe houses were being built, although that's not what they would be called. The architect had already drawn up plans and construction was underway, but Jared wanted to add Poppy's ideas and change things up. It would mean extra cost, but he had verbalised how innovative her ideas were without hesitation and was happy to add her growing brand to his.

Although she'd been floored by the offer he'd made, she had refused to be bought out. Instead, they'd come to a working agreement based on supply and demand. She'd had to say yes to more projects, which would mean she would have little time for other clients, but she guessed he knew that. It would also explode her brand. She'd haggled for her company logo to be left discreetly on her sensory panels, even though hardly anyone knew the brand was hers. At the moment her business was too small and niche for the wider public to care, but it would grow considerably in the coming months. The thought both terrified and elated her. She'd be even busier at work and would have to speak to her friends and sort this mess with Dylan out, so that they could come to her house and spend time together there.

She'd agreed to work with Jared and her breath caught in her throat when she thought about it – it was her biggest project to date. It was also a bit too close to home. Only one modern warehouse would back onto her garden, but it would be a shame to lose the view from her bedroom. She did sometimes jump at the slightest noise here, though, after growing up with lots of neighbours. And her garden was vast, so she wouldn't be too overlooked. It wasn't like she was used to prancing around naked out there. She did have neighbours on either side of her house, but as they had big houses with huge plots, they didn't see much of each other.

In her old flat, you couldn't step out of your front door without someone knowing your business. She'd had to learn subterfuge. She'd often sat in the corner of the little lounge and quietly sobbed, her arms wrapped around her skinny legs, when looking after her mum. Gladys and other neighbours had asked after her mum and offered help, but she hadn't taken it, or told them how awful it really had been for her. They must have thought her mum was a bit flaky and antisocial – or even a complete angel, after hearing she spent so much time with her fictitious ailing sister. Poppy had had to wash her own school uniform and make her own lunch for years, and her mum missing school concerts was par for the course. Gladys had quietly spoken to Chris at the café about it one year. After that, Gladys would sit proudly in the front row at school events while Chris delivered fresh bread to her door every three days for sandwiches. Poppy's heart swelled at the memory of Gladys's sunny smile and her deep red lipstick. She never left home without a tube of it in her handbag.

Poppy made a simple meal that evening. Dylan would be staying over. That had been happening a lot more, recently, and she liked it. He had his own flat in the centre of their old town, but he seemed to like the green spaces around her home. They hadn't talked about him moving in, but it was something she fleetingly thought about now.

Dylan walked up behind her and slid his arms around her waist, nuzzling her neck and almost making her drop the plates. He smelt of sawdust and a spicy aftershave, which made her mouth water more than the steaming plates of Bolognese she was preparing.

Billy burst in and made a sick face at their coupledom. Dylan released her and took his plate. Billy immediately went over and sniffed the frying pan, giving a puppy-dog stare to them both. *Perhaps giving Billy a key hadn't been such a great idea.* Poppy giggled and Dylan sighed theatrically.

'Can't we have one romantic meal alone?'

'Nope! I'm bored – and I love Poppy's cooking.'

Dylan gave up and got Billy a plate, knowing full well that Poppy had made enough for him, too. This was a regular occurrence since Billy and Ed had broken up. Thinking about it, it had been pretty usual when they were together too, as Ed was just as bad in the kitchen as Dylan and Billy. Poppy had enjoyed their dinners together, and was determined to get to the root cause of their break-up. Considering Billy usually spilled information on his private life like a carton of milk, on this he was unusually buttoned up.

She pulled out a chair for him and he sat down and tucked in with a sigh of bliss, which filled her with hope. She needed to find a way to explain her relationship to the girls, and get around why she'd fibbed a little. Maybe if they all came over for dinner or lunch, as they'd suggested in the café and saw how happy she was, then they'd want to visit more often. Perhaps she could say her and Dylan were a new item? She squashed that idea quickly. More lies were not the answer.

Sitting down on the couch and watching television into the evening as a trio had also become routine. She laughed as Billy presented them all with matching fluffy socks and they lined their feet up so Billy could take a photo on his phone. They were so glamorous… not! Poppy tried to shove away the little niggle that they had all become a bit complacent, but it scampered to the forefront of her mind.

Dylan was so laid back, he was almost horizontal. She felt the weight of responsibility, not only for these two amazing men, but also for her mum. In her own weird way she'd been trying to steer clear of causing everyone she loved extra worry, in case her relationship or business failed. She loved each of them, but wished someone would take care of her, sometimes. She knew she'd led them all to believe she was fiercely independent, and she was, but now and then it would be good if someone else was planning for the future, so *she* didn't have to.

CHAPTER EIGHT

Poppy took a deep breath and pushed the gate open. She liked visiting her mum at Green Manor, the healthcare facility and sanctuary where June was being looked after, but the last goodness-knew-how-many-years were taking their toll. She'd love to be able to pop to the flat to see June instead, but it just wasn't possible. Even taking her out shopping for the day was hard work. Her mum would start to shake and her eyes would dart around looking for danger. It made them both so anxious that they'd stopped trying.

Looking up at the imposing building didn't give you a sense of what was behind the façade. The big frontage and simple design, with its rows and rows of windows, looked more like a prison. The rooms inside, thank goodness, were light and airy. The living quarters at the back of the building had balconies overlooking the garden. Luckily Poppy had managed to negotiate one of them for her mum in return for the work she did there. Looking out onto the road would have made her mum even sadder. Nowadays Poppy could afford the best room available, but June hated change, so she'd stayed in her little room on the first floor with one window and the tiny balcony, looking out on the garden. She said it reminded her of her balcony at home.

Poppy went round the side of the house into the gardens, knowing she would find her mum there. Her mood lifted when she saw the little pods she had designed on the back lawn. They were dotted about and people were going in and out of them with smiles on their faces. Poppy would have loved to tackle the front of the building, but these pods tucked away were actually making a difference. Each big project that Poppy built meant another pod could be paid for, at Green Manor. She'd manged six so far and it was something her mum was proud of. That meant more to Poppy than anything else she'd achieved in life.

The pods were all different. One was a sensory room, one was a workshop with daylight bulbs and music to work to. Others were for Pilates, yoga or just provided a quiet space to relax and unwind. The staff had reported that they were hugely popular. She had been tentatively asked to meet up with a charitable trust about providing designs for another sanctuary, like Green Manor. She had more work than she could cope with right now and still had to find time to visit her mum, the flat and her school friends. She had always been a bit obsessive about routine, since she'd had to work out a system to care for her mum without anyone finding out, or separating them. She'd basically spent her whole life terrified of being found out and somehow punished for not taking better care of her mother's health.

She took a quick look at her phone, and then frowned. She had about ten messages from Sasha, Demi and Anne asking to meet them urgently. That couldn't be good. She hadn't been planning on meeting her friends today, but as she scrolled down, she saw they wanted to have lunch at the cafe. It all sounded very urgent. That was weird. They did usually meet every other time she visited her mum, but today Poppy had come a day early. She had a planning meeting tomorrow with Jared Wright, which couldn't be missed. She would never normally put her friends off for anything, none of them would, but they all had busy lives. She hadn't thought to reschedule as Thursday was their normal day. It was easier to stick to that than try and fit an extra lunch around all four of their schedules.

She knew Anne had had a doctor's appointment the day before, to check she had the correct paperwork to take Freddie abroad. She hoped nothing had happened to derail that. Poppy loved six-year-old Freddie fiercely and couldn't imagine a world without his cheeky smile and perfect hugs. He always held his arms up for a cuddle when he saw her and she treasured the feel of his cheek next to hers. He was a fighter and she adored him. Freddie had been so much stronger lately. Anne said it was because he now had hope of recovery. Poppy's bottom lip trembled and she stopped and caught her breath before her mum saw. She didn't want her to fret.

Instead, she put on a bright smile. Then she picked up her pace, spotting her mum sitting on a bench by one of the pods and reading her favourite book. She had a soft green jumper over her shoulders and she looked relaxed and happy. Poppy stopped for a moment to sear the image into her memory bank. Then she walked across the grass to sit next to June and take her hand.

Her mum's eyes searched her face for signs of anything worrying, and then her face broke into a smile that made Poppy's doubts drift into the gentle breeze for a while. She scooched nearer so that they were side by side. She rested her head on her mum's shoulder, like she had as a teenager, and her mum opened the book on her lap and began to read.

Pushing open the café door later that day and waving to Chris, Poppy couldn't shake the tingling sensation that something was really wrong. No one had replied to her texts, other than to tell her the time to meet. For all they knew, she could have been busy at work. She tried to bite down on the annoyance at being taken for granted, worry at the forefront of her mind despite her peaceful time with her mum. She saw that the others were already there. They looked up as she approached. Chris walked over and placed a coffee in front of her. The others had already got their drinks and were warming their hands around their mugs. She smiled in greeting, but no one smiled back. She sat heavily in her seat and looked at their faces in turn. They didn't look happy.

'What's happened? Is Freddie ok? How did his doctor's appointment go?' Her heart felt like it was beating out of her chest.

Anne took a deep breath and Poppy's stomach tightened. She was already flinching at Sasha's cold stare, before she'd even found out what the hell was going on. Then Anne bent down to get something out of her bag. She placed the crumpled centre pages of a magazine on the table and flattened them out. 'Freddie is fine. Thank you for asking… but what the hell is this?' She pointed to the glossy photo of Poppy's face.

Poppy's cheeks turned fiery red. She grabbed onto the edge of the table and looked around for support. She found none – just hostility and confusion.

'This is a pretty big mess-up in a very posh magazine, if they've got their information wrong.' Anne said with a really pissed-off tone to her voice.

'Why are they saying that you're dating a local businessman called Dylan?' Sasha demanded to know. Then Poppy could see the lightbulb moment, as Sasha really took in Poppy's red face. Sasha sat back in shock, and waited for the penny to drop for the others. When Poppy didn't speak, she enlightened them. 'You've been lying to us this whole time. Why?'

Poppy tried to pat her cheek with the back of her hand to cool her burning face. 'I didn't lie to you… exactly.'

'What does this article mean?' asked Demi with a frown.

'She's sleeping with Dylan,' said Anne.

'Poppy and Dylan? Don't be daft,' commented Demi.

They all seemed content to chat amongst themselves, so Poppy took a minute to catch her breath. This was a nightmare. She'd hoped to gently explain her reasons for hiding her relationship, to one of them, and make them understand. Then they might have helped ease the way with the rest of them. Facing everyone at once was her worst nightmare. The moment she'd been dreading so long had come.

'You didn't tell us about this article,' said Demi. 'You know we like to read them.'

Anne looked at her sideways. 'That's the point, isn't it Poppy, that we didn't read the magazine?'

'I love the photo,' said Demi, admiring the stunning backdrop to the image of Poppy and earning a dig in the leg from Anne. Poppy gave her a grateful look for trying to change the subject, even though she must be hurting too.

All eyes turned to Poppy, as if she was a complete stranger in their midst. 'So?' asked Anne. 'What is this?' she held up the offending photos. 'Is all that stuff you told us lies? About you working such long hours that you don't have time to date? You told us that the men you chat to on that stupid dating app that are not worth talking about, as you never like any of them!'

'I do work hard,' mumbled Poppy, her face flushing again.

She couldn't meet their piercing gazes. She started picking at her nails until they started stinging. She winced, shoving her finger into her mouth and sucking on it, trying to numb the pain.

'I don't understand,' said Sasha.

'Me neither,' said Anne.

Demi said nothing until Poppy looked up and met her gaze, one set of eyes blazing, the other pained. 'I thought you'd stop me,' Poppy said eventually.

'Stop you doing what?' asked Demi, confusion showing on her beautiful face.

'Dating the Taylor heartbreaker,' she caught her breath and stared at the table.

They all sat back in stunned silence. Poppy glanced up and willed them to understand.

'You'd prefer us to think you're lonely and frustrated?' asked Sasha.

'No! I just don't want your judgement. It's hard enough trying to run my own business and sustain a relationship. Let alone risk my heart by having sex with a Taylor brother.'

They all sat back and gasped. 'We'd have understood,' said Anne, under her breath.

Poppy paused and tilted her head. 'You'd have told me I was an idiot and not to do it,' said Poppy, looking pointedly at Anne, who flushed.

'You would have come round and told me I was deranged and to get my head examined,' she said to Sasha, who went pink as well. 'And you,' she turned to Demi, angry suddenly, 'You'd have said that only an idiot would put themselves in that position. He's not career driven like I am and you'd tell me he'd weigh me down.'

All four women sat in silence. Poppy's face was hot and everyone else's colour was heightened, too.

'Demi wouldn't mean there's anything wrong with Dylan,'

said Anne, affronted. 'It's just that she knows first-hand how hard it is to be successful in business with her dad's garage and Dylan, of all people, might distract you.' She rolled her eyes heavenward, as if speaking to a small child. 'As you said, he's pretty laid back and you aren't.'

'That's the point, though!' said Poppy, banging her fist on the table and making them all jump. Some of her coffee leaped out of her cup and splashed on the magazine photo, landing straight on the image of her face. 'You don't know him like I do.

'Of course we know him. We grew up with the Taylor brothers!' said Anne, her hands gripping the table as if she was about to jump up and turn it over. 'And you're our best friend. Of course we want to protect you. Those boys are bad news.'

'I bet the sex is great though,' joked Sasha, waggling her eyebrows at Poppy, some of her earlier anger seemingly forgotten, until Anne gave her an evil look. Then she flushed and grabbed her half-eaten cheese sandwich, stuffing it in her mouth and munching quickly, looking like a demented gerbil.

CHAPTER NINE

'What about Billy?' asked Anne seriously. 'Where does he fit into this? Does Dylan know you live together?'

'He works for me. I need him close to hand,' said Poppy quietly and winced, waiting for the axe to fall and the deeper questions about her relationship with Dylan to start. 'I told you he lives in the annex.'

'So you basically lied about everything else?' Anne pulled her chair back in and picked up her coffee, but she was eyeing Poppy warily.

No one had punched her yet, so that was a bonus, Poppy thought. That's how they used to work out squabbles at school, until they'd got too big and the punches had started to hurt as they'd all grown breasts.

'Dylan stays with me sometimes,' she finally admitted, hoping for a feeling of release after finally being able to admit her secret, but it didn't happen. Her insides were still tied up in knots.

'We thought Billy might be your boyfriend, at first. You don't really talk about men,' said Demi, grabbing a sandwich before Sasha ate them all, and staring at her victoriously.

'Billy? No. I told you before. Billy had a boyfriend, and they just split up.'

'It does feel weird that you're dating Dylan,' said Sasha, whose face had gone pale. 'I know you fancied him like mad when we were younger, but I thought you were over that ages ago?'

'Dylan's the town playboy,' said Anne. 'You can't be serious about him, surely?'

'Dylan's hot!' said Demi, making Poppy smile and blush at the same time.

'We used to spy on him from your flat,' said Anne 'I remember. Your mum has an old set of binoculars that were your grandad's. So you've been seeing him on the sly and been keeping secrets from us? His parents live across the road. He lives in town!' Anne was in full rant mode now as she pointed to the house Dylan had grown up in and almost hit Chris as he served coffee to the next table.

'I didn't *not tell you*,' protested Poppy. 'I just dodged the subject and left you to assume. We've had so many other things to talk about lately, with Freddie and the fundraising.'

Sasha sat back in her chair and looked at Poppy. She didn't seem happy. 'How long have you been seeing him?'

'Um… about six months…'

'Six months!' they all shouted together and Poppy ducked in case they were going to throw something at her. She swiftly shoved the plate out of reach of the others. It would be sacrilege to waste one of Chris's sandwiches.

'How the hell could you be seeing someone for that long and not tell your best friends?' demanded Sasha, eyes blazing. 'Especially as it's someone we already know *well*.'

Poppy didn't like the inflection of that last word at all. 'I didn't mean to hide it, I just thought you might not approve, as we all fancied him at school.' She looked pointedly at Sasha.

Sasha flushed, but Anne rolled her eyes. 'That was ages ago and I've been married and had a kid since then, not to mention that Sasha and Demi have had a thousand boyfriends.' Demi tried to protest that she'd been dating the same man for years, but Anne spoke over her. 'Don't you think I'd like to know if my best friend was getting some, and from a local sex god to boot?'

Poppy hung her head. 'I'm sorry.'

'Will you be spending every spare minute with him now?' demanded Sasha. Poppy's heart sank. This was the reaction she'd been dreading. She wanted everyone to get on.

'Of course not! I come here every other week to see you all.'

'Well, thanks for doing us all such a favour,' said Anne drily. 'But you led us to believe you were lonely and overworked, when you're actually probably in town every other day and shagging someone from across the road.'

CHAPTER TEN

Anne pushed back her chair and for a second Poppy thought she might actually walk out, but she flicked her hair over her shoulder and went to ask Chris for another round of coffees and hot chocolate. When he came back and placed four cream buns on the table, Poppy knew it was serious. They rarely ordered cakes. Chris caught her eye and winked in sympathy. So they'd told him about the article too! Everyone would know by tomorrow, if they'd told him within earshot of any of the café's regular clientele. Her brain ached and she just about held it together, glancing around the café and seeing everyone staring at her. Dylan might be seen as a womaniser, but everyone loved him and gossiped about him and his brothers incessantly. They were treated like movies stars or mythical creatures. Knowing Dylan as she did, she knew he didn't play around and neither did his siblings, but they kind of enjoyed the notoriety and couldn't be bothered to correct anyone. They dated a lot, but from what she could see, they treated women well.

The fact that they had managed to keep their relationship secret for so long was quite an achievement, even though

Dylan wasn't happy about it either. Now, the whole town would be taking bets on how long she could keep Dylan for and it would pile on the pressure, which was exactly what she'd been trying to avoid. People quickly returned to their own chats, but they were locals and had seen all four girls grow up. They were used to them bickering, today was more than that.

'You told everyone?' asked Poppy, wanting to hide her head in her hands.

'They overheard us asking Chris about the article when we got here. We wanted to know if he was in on your secret, but he wouldn't say. Chris visits your mum, so we thought he might have the inside track,' said Sasha. Poppy flushed again and wouldn't meet her eyes, so Sasha threw her hands up in exasperation.

'You didn't tell your mum either? Poppy. What the hell were you thinking?'

Poppy finally met her gaze and instead of the anger she expected, she saw hurt and bewilderment. 'I'm sorry. You know what Mum's like. She can't stand change. She loves her flat so much she won't let me sell it, even though I can't imagine her ever going back.'

Poppy's bottom lip wobbled. Demi took her hand and squeezed it across the table for a second before letting go. Poppy's heart grabbed this tiny ray of hope.

'We know you've had a lot to deal with, looking after your mum on your own for all these years. Perhaps we should have helped more,' said Demi, her eyes suddenly misting over.

'She wouldn't let anyone help her, because she's a control freak,' said Sasha angrily.

'Sasha…' Anne nudged her knee.

Poppy's heart felt like it was breaking in two. 'I'm not a control freak, Sash. I was just a kid and I didn't want anyone

MY PERFECT EX

to know how bad it had got with my mum. If one of you had told your own parents about my situation, they might have told social services and had me taken away. Not just from Mum, but from my other family... all of you.'

Sasha pushed away from the table and looked at her friend, but it was clear her anger was fading. Now Anne took Poppy's hand. 'I'm sorry you didn't feel you could trust us, Poppy.'

Poppy smiled weakly. 'It wasn't about trust. I've always trusted you with my life. It was about knowing how much you cared for me. If you'd known how bad it was, you'd have told someone to try and help.'

'Oh, Poppy,' Demi got up and pulled her into a hug. 'How bad did it get?'

'She tried to kill herself twice when we were at school.' Big fat tears plopped onto Demi's shoulder and Demi brushed them away and pulled her tighter into her arms.

'I can't believe you kept something like that from us,' said Sasha, the fire back in her eyes. 'Then again, you lied about your boyfriend, so no biggie.'

'Sasha!' said Anne, kicking her this time, so she yelped.

Poppy looked steadily at Sasha and moved to sit back closer to the table, so not everyone in the place could hear. 'I didn't want you to find out about my mum or view me differently, now, just because I'm dating a Taylor brother,' she defended.

'Are you really serious about Dylan?' asked Sasha.

'Honestly, Poppy, you don't have to answer that,' said Anne. 'I just wish you'd trusted us more. We wouldn't have thought you were a sex-starved idiot, or tried to scupper your new... relationship. We've grown up with you. We know you're just a regular idiot.' Demi spluttered into her coffee and Poppy grinned.

'Well, she's definitely proved that,' said Sasha. 'How would you feel, Poppy, if we had all lied to you for so long? You could have told us,' she added. Poppy could see how much her friend was hurting.

Poppy rolled her shoulders and tried to sit up straighter, but she still felt like she was in a boxing ring and she sagged back down. 'I'd have hated it and been really upset. Rightly so. I'm sorry.' She hung her head in shame. 'It was why I put off telling you, after I'd left it too long. I know you'd have been pleased for me, but the business took off quickly and I've been busy making it work and hiding from the stigma that comes with everyone thinking my relationship might fail. Coming here and just being myself meant I didn't have to think about the responsibility I have for my mum or anyone else. I need to earn a lot of money to pay for Mum's fees and the flat, plus business premises on Cherry Blossom Lane and my staff.'

'That's what I was saying about Allan! He doesn't want the stress of running the garage. I've seen from my dad how hard it is.' Demi jumped in, and Poppy could have kissed her.

'Exactly. Starting something new and putting yourself in debt to build it up is scary. You'd have told me not to get involved with Dylan at the same time.' All three women looked shiftily around for a moment. People were still eavesdropping with interest, but Poppy decided to give up worrying about what they thought. 'Working every hour I can is exhausting, but I'm succeeding and I now have a profitable business and a gorgeous man.'

'So he's officially your boyfriend? Not a casual fling in between meetings?' asked Sasha, but Poppy brushed off that question. 'You promised you'd slow down a little bit and maybe employ someone new.'

Poppy sipped her still-warm coffee. 'It's still just Billy and me, but I do hire freelance contractors and artisans. There can be up to a hundred working at any time.'

MY PERFECT EX

Sasha's mouth dropped open in surprise. 'I didn't realise your company was getting that big,' she said, admiringly. Poppy smiled gently, but Anne gave Sasha a pointed look that said she was giving in too easily, which she ignored. 'All of this time you could have been introducing us to some hot artists,' Sasha added, smacking her lips together, and Demi smothered a giggle.

Then a lightbulb seemed to go on in Anne's brain. 'It was you who organised the fundraiser for Freddie. You ran it. Did those amounts that you said came in regularly really come from other donations, or directly from you?'

'Um... some of them.'

'So you are basically paying for Freddie's treatment?' Anne looked horrified, exactly as Poppy had known she would.

'Look, Anne. Many of the donations have come from business contacts of mine, but of course I'm helping as much as I can. He's family!'

Anne sat back in stunned silence and Demi's eyes were as wide as saucers.

'So I'm indebted to you?' Anne finally asked.

'Of course not! There were lots of donations. I added what I could afford. I would do anything for Freddie.'

'So would we,' said Sasha, defensively.

Poppy stood up abruptly, her chair hitting the floor with a bang. Everyone in the café turned to look. 'Listen, I was at the quiz nights and bake sales. I gave my time as much as you all did.'

'Did you make those cakes, though, or did Dylan's mum make them? She runs a cake business,' rounded Sasha. 'Have you been having cosy family dinners across the road from here, without us knowing?' Anne grabbed her arm to stop her getting up too.

'What does it matter who bloody made them?'

'It matters,' said Sasha. 'You've been telling us you barely have time to visit us, but your boyfriend's family lives over the street. How often are you here?'

'Hardly ever,' said Poppy. 'He comes to my house, as it's easier for work. My studio is in a little village nearby. If I was in town, I'd tell you.' Sasha didn't look like she was convinced. Poppy threw up her hands in exasperation, picked up her bag and walked out of the café without a backward glance, even though it almost killed her.

Sasha plonked herself back down again and they all looked at each other in shock. 'You know when Chris was about to be evicted from here and he couldn't pay his lease?' asked Demi in a hushed tone. 'Poppy told him about a business grant she knew of. Do you think she helped him out too? He's like a surrogate dad to her. Plus I know she helps Gladys with food and has updated her flat. Gladys told my mum.'

'Oh crap. This is too much,' said Anne, grabbing a cream cake and stuffing it into her mouth.

CHAPTER ELEVEN

Poppy pulled into her driveway, almost running into one of the cherry trees at the side of her drive, as she wasn't paying attention. She turned off the ignition and sat silently in her car. As she watched, a few tiny petals from the blossom drifted onto the bonnet.

She thought about her awful afternoon. It had finally happened. Her friends knew everything about Dylan and her mum – and they hated her. They knew her mum had anxiety issues and that was why she lived at Green Manor, but Poppy always dodged in depth questions, or made stuff up. She'd dreaded this day, but now it was here she just felt numb. She had known they would judge her and she wouldn't fit in anymore. She'd never fitted in, if she was brutally honest. She'd always been on the outside of the group, looking in. Dating Dylan ostracized her further. Having great sex with a Taylor brother was exciting, but dreaming of anything more was stupidity.

Sasha was so confident and fierce, Anne loyal and funny. Demi was sexy and smart. Poppy was just mixed up and obsessive. She was the only one in their group without a dad, and the only one with a mum who wasn't any help either. Anne's dad had left when she was young, but they had always had an amazing relationship and she saw him often. He spent so much time with Freddie and would probably go with her to the States, as Connor had said he couldn't get time off work – which wasn't surprising considering the whole illness thing made him run a mile.

Poppy had pretended to be like them, and had done her best to mask her failings, but in the end it hadn't worked. The house of cards she'd built had come tumbling down. She was an independent woman, but she was also in love with Dylan, which made her look like she wasn't so smart after all. The lies she'd spun to protect them all had failed her. She'd tried very hard to be a good friend, but she'd let them down. Sasha was right. Poppy would have been horrified if one of them had spewed untruths like this. How could she have ever thought that she was doing them a favour, by pretending she wasn't dating someone they knew and masking her mum's illness? They had all moved on with their lives, so why shouldn't she? The problem was that her new boyfriend moved her further away from them, not closer.

She walked up to her house. Even the beautifully planted front garden, designed to make your spirits lift as you approached the house, didn't help her today. Nor did the sight of the cherry blossom on the trees she'd planted to celebrate moving into her new studio space. She paused and took a breath. Then she turned the key in the door. She didn't know if she would face an empty house, or two inquisitive men who would instantly know from her face that something had happened. They would expect her to bare her soul to them, but it just wasn't her way.

Walking into the hallway and dropping her keys in the dish, she heard laughter and music. She glanced up the stairs fleetingly and wondered if she could go and hide herself away in her own room and lick her wounds, before she faced them. But she straightened her shoulders, plastered a smile onto her face and walked towards the sunny kitchen.

Both men turned to face her. She ramped her smile up a notch, but Dylan instantly frowned and started walking her way. She was enveloped in his arms within seconds and the floodgates opened. She sobbed and sobbed. Billy seemed to sense that now was not the time for a group hug and he blended into the background and let himself out of the side door to go to his own flat.

∽

*D*ylan led her to the couch and pulled her body close to his, one strong arm still around her shoulders. He brushed her hair out of her eyes and kissed her gently. 'Want to talk about what happened? Is something wrong with your mum?' He knew she had visited Green Manor today and he hoped June was ok. He searched her face. Poppy's usual sparkle had been dulled and her skin looked pale and drawn.

'Poppy?'

'Anne saw that old article in *Starz & Homes* magazine.'

His brain whizzed at a hundred miles an hour to remember which magazine that was, then recalled the picture of Poppy and Billy the three of them had joked about. She had looked stunning in a form-fitting green dress that had made Dylan drool, but Billy shone from the page. He'd been so excited, as it was his favourite glossy celebrity read. He couldn't stop talking about it for a month. He'd joked that his old teacher, who'd always said he wouldn't amount to much, could now bite his arse.

Poppy had done her usual, hiding the magazine away, and

Dylan had not thought of it since. 'Ah. Ok. How did she react?' But he already knew the answer from her face.

She looked at him and he sighed and hugged her harder, until she squealed to be let go and mooched over to slump on the couch. He quickly went to the kitchen area, pressed a panel which started playing soothing music, and turned up the dial for sunlight in the house. The three windows in the kitchen roof slid open and let air into the room. Through the floor-to-ceiling windows that led out to the garden she could see the line of fruit trees in blossom.

He tried to hide the hurt he felt, that Poppy was adamant her friends would disapprove of him dating her. He had heard the town grapevine and of the reputation he and his brothers had, but it wasn't their fault that women liked them! His older brother, Ollie, was obsessed with work and the gym he owned, so he barely had time to breathe, let alone sleep with multiple women. Younger brother, Miles, was a tech genius. He did date, but he was building his own empire and stayed up long into the night studying. Miles wanted to learn as much as he could to expand his knowledge, so how the hell he had time to have sex, as well as work so many hours, was a mystery. Dylan felt he was the only one who had a balance. He made time for Poppy because she meant the world to him.

Picking up a bottle of rich red wine and two glasses, Dylan sat down by Poppy's side. He poured two big measures and handed her one, which she took gratefully and slugged back. She coughed and managed a watery smile.

'Sasha shouted the loudest, as expected. She said I'd lied to them all, which I have.' She looked at him and he tried to mask his *I told you so*, but she'd already seen it in his eyes. She sipped more wine. 'They probably aren't talking to me now. I'll need to make new best friends.'

Dylan tried not to laugh at her dramatics when he could

MY PERFECT EX

see her heart was breaking. He didn't understand the chip she had on her shoulder about her mum and dad, or about her relationship status. No-one cared. No-one was interested in whether she was having rampant sex or not. It was more about her own insecurity, and her need to work herself into the ground to appear professional, or have more money than she could ever spend, to know she was safe. She'd invested thousands into her own future healthcare, so as not to ever burden her mum, future partner or children. This much he understood.

Not everyone had the perfect home life, he reasoned. Then he winced, realising that, in her eyes, he had. His mum and dad were still together and living in the same house he'd grown up in. In fact, his mum had been taken ill recently. He hadn't told Poppy that he'd been to visit. She had enough on her plate without worrying about his mum, too. She loved her and would be devastated if anything happened to either of his parents. He sometimes thought she loved Fiona and Don more than him. Luckily, his mum was going to be ok. It was something that would go away with careful treatment. She did need to rest more, though, and he'd had to have a stern talk to his dad about helping her more at home. His father could be a lazy sod.

'I'm sure they'll forgive you, when you explain that you didn't want your friendship to change,' he soothed, taking her free hand and kissing it gently. She smiled, but it didn't quite reach her eyes. 'We all know that my brothers and I have got this womaniser reputation, though surely everyone's got over that by now? We aren't teenagers. We might be single… except me,' he added hastily at the sharp look she gave him, 'and I know we're still in our prime,' he joked, winking at her and raising a slight smile, 'but they need to find someone else to talk about.' He sighed and his shoulders felt heavy with the weight of worry that Poppy might not think he was worth the battle with her friends.

'Sasha was more worried about me baking the cakes for the bake sale by myself.' She pulled a face and flushed as he rolled his eyes.

He nudged her knee with his own. 'To be fair, mum did help you out there,' he laughed. She smiled then too, but her eyes were still watering. He leaned in and gently brushed the tears away with his thumb. 'You had a last minute meeting and mum was happy to bake it for you.'

'It was another lie though.' She wriggled in her seat. 'I should have admitted I had an appointment. I was too proud to confess that I hadn't made the cake. I even asked your mum to bake it a bit wonky and to keep it basic. There is no way I'd have been able to make anything near one of her creations. It must have tasted incredible for Sasha to remember it,' she held her breath and then puffed the air out all at once, clearly trying to ease the tension in her body. 'I did try to explain. They think I'm a selfish bitch who wants to keep my sex mad boyfriend and recent lavish lifestyle to myself.'

Dylan's mouth dropped open. 'Surely not? They aren't like that.' He thought of all of the times that his group of friends had hung around with hers, at school and afterwards.

'Aren't they?' she said moodily.

He sat back, stunned. 'They all know me. Do they understand how much you've done to help them all?'

Poppy sighed and sank further back into the couch, still sipping her wine. The glass was nearly empty. 'Some of it. Anne knows about the medical fund and isn't happy. I think Demi might have ideas about the other people I've helped too.'

'It's your prerogative to help them if you want to. They're your family.'

Billy stuck his head round the door and Dylan signalled that it was safe to come in. He sat on the other side of Poppy and put his arm around her shoulder. Then he took the glass from her and handed it to Dylan, who was actually glad of the interruption this time. Billy was Poppy's best friend, other than the girls, so he might be able to help. Dylan pushed aside the niggle about the bond they had. It reared its ugly head from time to time. He knew how much Poppy needed Billy in her life, and he was a pretty good friend to Dylan too. Dylan knew where Billy's loyalties lay, and he'd never tested that boundary. Billy was respectful of Dylan and Poppy's relationship… most of the time. He couldn't really complain. And at times like this, when Dylan didn't really know what to do, Billy was a godsend.

Poppy started sniffling and then rivers of tears flowed down her face again. Now Billy was signalling over her shoulder, asking what he should do. Damn, he was the one who was supposed to know. Grumpily, Dylan threw his hands up. He didn't have a clue. He'd been telling her that her lies were stupid for ages. He didn't think this was a good moment to mention that, though. He loved her and wanted the whole damn world to know about it. He wondered if she was ashamed of him sometimes, but brushed that thought aside.

Finally Dylan gently lifted her onto his lap, where she buried her face in his shirt, making it all wet. He brushed her hair out of her eyes and asked Billy to get her a box of tissues from the kitchen counter.

'Poppy,' Dylan soothed, dropping gentle kisses on her face. 'It will all be ok. Your friends love you and will understand you didn't do anything on purpose to hurt them. They know how much they mean to you. You see them every other week, however busy you are.' She sobbed and hiccoughed, rubbing her eyes and smudging her make-up. She blew her nose with a tissue and looked at him with watery eyes. He felt his heart break open a little, at this rare show of vulnerability.

Billy came back with steaming mugs of tea and broken pieces of chocolate, which finally made her smile. Dylan stared at it. *Why hadn't he thought of that?* She took the piece Dylan offered and nibbled on a corner, her shoulders still bobbing up and down with intermittent sobs between mouthfuls.

'Have you eaten anything today?' Dylan asked. He knew her mood dipped if she missed a meal.

'No… no I haven't. I saw Mum and then I got the urgent text to meet the girls. They had sandwiches, but I couldn't face one. Then Chris brought us cakes, but my stomach was tied up in knots. I could just about sip my coffee, but I was scared they'd throw theirs in my face.'

'I could make us all dinner?' offered Billy. He frowned at the look of horror on both their faces. Poppy finally smiled at his outrage. A proper smile, this time.

Billy went off to find a takeaway menu from one of the kitchen drawers, then got distracted by the building work – and the site foreman who was working late at the bottom of the garden. He wandered out to take a look at the construction work. Some of the buildings had already started going up. Poppy would feel more at home with people around, Dylan hoped. She often said she missed having neighbours. The barns that were being renovated would be a hive of activity during the day, but look calm and majestic in the evening. The apex of the roof on each top floor would be made of glass and softly illuminated at night. It would be a beautiful sight.

She snuggled into Dylan's neck and he wrapped his arms around her. His heartbeat ramped up a notch, as it always did when he was close to her. He kissed her gently on the neck, just below her ear, and felt her sigh. She had stopped crying and she lifted her face for him to drop a kiss onto her soft lips.

'You aren't in this alone. I know it probably feels like it, but I'm here for you. And so is Billy. I've known you since school and I'm one of your best friends too... I hope,' he joked. 'I know you wouldn't hurt anyone intentionally and the girls understand that too. They might just need time to come round.'

'What if they want to come round – here?' she asked, her voice wobbling.

'Here? So what? This house is beautiful and a testament to your skill. This is what you are trying to achieve for everyone, on a big or small scale. They would be proud of you, I'm sure.'

'What if they take one look at my home and think I'm going to throw my business to the wind and fill it with a hot man and babies?'

He tried not to flinch and kissed her nose. 'Would that be so terrible?' he asked. He really wanted to know. He supported her growing business, but wondered where their future slotted into her plans.

She looked horrified for a fleeting moment, then rearranged her features, a fraction too late. 'I do want a family,' she reasoned, but it didn't sit well with him. He was sure they could sort out child care between them when the time came, as his business was flexible and he could work from home, but she didn't sound convinced. 'It's taken me so long to build my business and I'm not ready to give that up yet.'

'I could be home some of the time.' Dylan didn't like the feeling of acid churning in his stomach now. She raised her eyebrows and looked out of the windows at Billy as he strolled back towards the house, as if she hadn't considered other options before. He had worked hard to build his business too, but surely they could work something out? He definitely saw a house full of kids in his future, so it was something they needed to talk about at some point. He just hadn't expected it to be today.

He got up to see what mischief Billy was causing, and where he'd got to on ordering their food. As he looked back, Poppy tried to fix a smile on her face.

Dylan only hoped he was right and she was wrong – and that her oldest friends wouldn't judge her for finding happiness, or put thoughts in her head to make her think that he wasn't the right guy for her. He grit his teeth in determination and went to find Billy.

CHAPTER TWELVE

Poppy rubbed her tired eyes and turned away from the beautifully lush green gardens at Green Manor. People were wandering in and out of the pods she'd designed. She bent down to pick up the pink blanket draped across the bed and tuck it around her mum. She couldn't help but worry. Apparently, the fever had broken now, but her mum had been incredibly unwell for the last week. Poppy had spent most of that time by her side. She'd been living back at the flat, which was completely surreal. Dylan thought she was mad, but she'd been too tired to drive up to an hour and a half back to her home each day if traffic was bad.

June moaned a bit in her sleep and Poppy picked up her hand. It wasn't so clammy and her skin was less flushed, which she hoped were good signs. The amazing staff had set up a day bed for her to snooze in, but she hadn't been able to rest. Her mum was the only family she had. June might seem like a burden, for someone looking in from the outside, but Poppy had never felt that way. When her mum was feeling well, she was the best mum in the world, showering her with kisses. The warmth of her smile could light up a room.

Poppy knew that her mum had a chemical imbalance in her brain through no fault of her own. The specialists at Green Manor eased June back into daily life, by counteracting this with incredible therapy and some medication, if required. She could cope with many things now that had been beyond her years ago. Before she'd become sick, she had even suggested a walk beyond the sanctuary garden. June had suddenly decided she wanted to know more about the outside world. To Poppy, this was a revelation. She didn't know what had caused the change, but she had been grateful. Then the fever had set in.

Poppy pressed a cold cloth to her mum's head to cool her down further, and spoke quietly to a member of staff who had poked her head round the door. After being told that the doctor had visited that morning and confirmed her mother's health was improving, Poppy took what felt like her first deep breath in days. She enjoyed the feeling of having air in her lungs, and not just fear. Poppy thanked the staff member and promised to go home and get some rest. Everyone here knew her well by now. There had even been talk about her mum being healthy enough to start visiting the flat again, with the view of getting her home permanently. This was what Poppy had dreamed of for years, but now that it was almost a reality, she was unsure and fidgety. Supposing her mum harmed herself?

She'd been assured that they wouldn't let her move home if they thought there was a risk. Poppy had had endless meetings about how it could work. When they'd discussed it recently, her mum had insisted she was fine, and that she wanted to be back in her own home sometime soon. But Poppy had seen her hand shake when she'd said this.

They couldn't keep her at the sanctuary forever, though. Others needed help more than June, now. Billy had joked about a faint suspicion he had, that they had kept her mum there longer than necessary in order to have more pods built, but she shook that idea away. Her mum had been there for years. The time had come for her to start the process of moving back home.

Poppy picked up her bag and car keys, but stopped short when she reached her car in the sanctuary car park. She must be more tired than she'd realised, as it was parked at an odd angle. Her arms ached and opening the door was an effort. She took another deep breath and rocked back on her heels. She had to get a better life balance. She couldn't tell others to stress less, if she was always overdoing things herself.

She still hadn't heard from the girls, which made her stop and catch her breath for a moment. She'd thought they might have loved her enough to forgive her, but apparently not. She'd hardly ever missed a Thursday lunch until now. Sasha always sent out a text, giving them two days' notice of the meet up and demanding their attendance on pain of death. This week she hadn't received a single message from Sasha or any of the others, just when she needed them most.

She glanced around and up at the tower block as she drove back to the flat, and parked her car behind the building. It was a free-for-all here, you just parked wherever you could. Lots of kids used the tarmacked area for skateboarding, so everyone tended to park around the edges. She'd initially winced at the thought of her pride and joy getting scratched, but it had been there for days so far and it hadn't happened yet.

She scooped her work papers into her bag and checked her laptop was inside. She was snowed under with design work and couldn't take her foot off the pedal. The project with Jared Wright was her biggest to date. She had fitted out a whole sea of single houses before, but this was one sizeable building development – right behind her own house. She wasn't just designing elements of the housing complex, as she'd originally thought. She was integral to the architectural team. This was a very big deal for her career. The barns were to be fitted with modern facilities and relaxation areas, to make a better work and life balance. She sighed and her body ached. Perhaps she should buy the unit behind her house. The commute to work would be quick, she smiled to herself. Most of her manufacturing was done by artist and crafts people, who had their own premises. Plus she'd recently bought her beautiful office on Cherry Blossom Lane. She adored that space and it felt like home too. She enjoyed working with a view across the fields of wildflowers behind the building and the little village at the end of the road bustled with shops. A few new businesses seemed to be opening in the up and coming area, so she'd bought at the right time.

She lugged the bag and laptop into the lift and slumped against the cool interior wall. She smiled at the *Tilly loves Ben* sign scrawled on the surface and tried to recall if she'd ever scrawled something similar herself. She remembered writing a diary about how in lust with Dylan she'd been and how heartbroken she felt that he barely noticed her. Look how that had turned out. She felt hopeful for Tilly and Ben.

The doors opened with a clang and a wobble and she stepped out, to see Gladys shuffling along with two shopping bags. Poppy rushed up, plonked her work down and took the shopping from her neighbour, quickly depositing it at Gladys's door and then retrieving her own bags.

The old lady opened her front door, and Poppy took the bags inside and then gratefully accepted the offer of a cup of Gladys' finest tea, which was brewed to within an inch of its life and had to be drunk with the buttery shortbread biscuits she always made. Otherwise you might be tempted to spit it straight back out again.

Gladys placed the china cup and saucer in front of her with a smile and patted Poppy on the shoulder before sitting opposite her on her little sofa that Poppy had just re-covered for her. It was now the colour of warm sand, and toned with the cool white walls with little birds dotted all over them. Gladys was an avid bird watcher and the walls made her happy, now that her eyesight wasn't quite what it had been. It was a tranquil space with lots of leafy green plants.

Poppy was pleased to see her gradual changes had improved Gladys's life, without stripping either her personality or wisdom from the room. Poppy had painted the bookcase on the back wall. It was stuffed with books, and she'd placed Gladys's bird ornaments along the top, so it looked like they were deciding which book she should read next. Poppy often brought new reads from home for Gladys. She had a penchant for racy titles with swashbuckling men and feisty damsels. It was a good job she'd finished the flat, or she'd not have had time to start it now, however much she loved Gladys like a grandma.

'I forgot to ask you last time you were here. Is that fancy car outside yours?' asked Gladys, as she handed Poppy a biscuit.

Poppy didn't pretend to play dumb. 'Yes. It is.'

Gladys's eyes shone. 'Oh, you clever girl! I know you work so hard running that business of yours. You must be doing well.' Poppy sat back in shock, as she never really discussed her work. Then she slapped herself mentally. Gladys knew Poppy better than almost anyone, even though Poppy dodged many of the questions Gladys regularly threw her way.

Poppy smiled and felt so much love for the independent

woman sitting opposite her, with her grey permed hair and sparkling blue eyes. Gladys didn't really need anyone, but she'd never made Poppy feel rebuffed. She'd very graciously let Poppy re-design her flat, probably understanding that Poppy needed to feel connected to the residents of the tower.

'I've just taken on my biggest client,' said Poppy, deciding she'd had enough of keeping things to herself. 'I've had the car for a little while now, though. I told you how I design sensory panels for people with mental health issues?' When Gladys nodded, she continued. 'Well, I also design them for everyday use, to help people stay positive and motivated. They go into housing developments, and recently some healthcare facilities have signed me up. And I've just been hired to redesign ten houses and a wholesale development with an architect, to make them breathe happiness into home and business owners' lives. The idea is to create sanctuaries at home, whatever the house size and to have some relaxation areas at work. They renew a person's energy reserves in the place where they rest and recuperate.' Poppy stopped, realising she'd been waffling.

Gladys raised her eyebrows. Then she narrowed her eyes slightly. She even stopped drinking her tea. 'That sounds like it could be a lot of fun, but also an awful amount of pressure. Is that a good idea?' Poppy felt a slither of hope fly away. Would everyone always worry that she was like her mum once they knew how bad their situation really was?

'I think so. I wouldn't do it if it didn't make me happy.'

Gladys's eyes twinkled suddenly. 'That's good, then, dear. What about the handsome stud muffin you told me about? Is he still around?'

Poppy almost spat out her tea. 'Stud muffin? Gladys!'

Gladys giggled and suddenly she seemed ageless. 'I read the term in one of those gossip magazines Sheila from down the hall leaves for me. I rather liked it and I haven't had a chance to use it until now.'

They both burst out laughing again and Poppy gave her a hug, then sat back. This woman was so precious to her. She wished her own grandmother was still around. She was never quite sure what had happened between her grandmother and her mum, it was never really spoken about. But she got the impression her grandma had hated her dad. She wasn't the only one. Poppy didn't know if he was dead or alive, but she assumed that if he'd wanted to find her, he would have done by now.

'The stud muffin…' she had to pause to catch her breath in case she giggled again, 'is very much still around.' Her life was changing so much that she decided to stop compartmentalising. Maybe the two worlds could entwine. 'His name is Dylan. I've upset Anne, Sasha and Demi, and Dylan too, by keeping them all apart. The girls are angry that I kept him a secret.'

Gladys didn't look that surprised. 'You knew?' asked Poppy.

'I know a lot of things that you don't tell me. I wouldn't push you, but you need someone to look out for you. Dylan's mum is a friend and she worries about you.' Tears sprang to Poppy's eyes and she brushed them away. 'Plus I talk to your mum on the telephone…'

'Mum knows?' gasped Poppy, her stomach suddenly full of butterflies. 'How can Mum know? She's too delicate for information like that. She'd worry about my relationship, and my business. She can't cope with change.' Poppy held her head in her hands. 'No wonder she's ill.'

This time Gladys got up and came to sit beside her, placing her arm around her and pulling her into her chest for a warm hug. Gladys smelt of talcum powder and lilacs, which made Poppy's mind flood with memories of her childhood. She accepted the embrace gratefully while tears streamed down her face. Gladys gently held her chin up. 'She's known for ages, Poppy. Her neighbours at the centre told her about your lovely new car, and they've seen Dylan drop you off occasionally. She knows you must be doing well. Although she might not want too many details, she's very proud of you. She knows you don't still live here.'

Poppy's mouth fell open in shock. 'But why hasn't she asked me about it? We talk all the time.'

Gladys patted her knee and sat back, looking at her sadly. 'Because she isn't well. She blocks things out. You know she doesn't cope with some situations, but you're her world. She's happy to know you are in a relationship that seems serious and she assumes you are living with him.'

'She thinks I've fallen on my feet?' A slight wave of anger floated into her consciousness.

Gladys smiled. 'Not at all! She'd be just as happy to know how hard you work and that you run your own business. She's so proud of the health pods you've built. You told her your boss financed them, but she's not stupid, she knows that wouldn't happen. You paid for them somehow.'

'She thinks Dylan paid for them?'

Gladys sighed. 'She thinks you saved up for them.'

Poppy's mind boggled. If her mum realised how much technology there was in each of those modest-looking pods, it would blow her mind!

'She actually saw Dylan in the car park one day and recognised him. She's so happy he's your boyfriend. She loves Dylan,' continued Gladys.

Poppy reeled back deeper into the sofa, her hands on her knees for support. Her mum had been spying on her! The thought didn't make her angry. She loved the fact her mum had cared enough to check him out. The relief that she liked

Dylan was palpable. He had broken her heart as a teenager, but she'd hidden that from her mum too. He'd visited their flat once or twice and got along well with her mum, back then. Luckily, he'd changed and had grown into a pretty amazing man, whatever the gossip said.

CHAPTER THIRTEEN

Poppy stayed at the flat for a further two days and was starting to go a bit stir crazy. She needed a proper desk to design on and she missed the view from her office. June was now sitting up in bed and eating heartily, so Poppy didn't need to be there all the time. Poppy had seen a small box of cream cakes inside her mum's bedside cabinet and had a sneaking suspicion that a certain dashing café owner might have popped by at some point, too.

Poppy had spent every night at the flat working, poring over her designs for Jared Wright, and had been on video calls with his architect, Libby, to make sure everything was exactly right for her additions to the build. The architectural plans had already been made by Libby, so Poppy coming in at this late stage was stressing everyone out. Luckily Libby admired her work and was excited to see how they could collaborate, and she was willing to bend a straight line to get things done. She was super-efficient and cool, and Poppy was learning a lot from her. Poppy had read a quote once about being the person who could walk into a room of opportunity and recommend a friend. She felt Libby was one of those people. She was secure enough in herself to share any blessings with others. Poppy wanted to be more like her.

She looked up when she heard a key in the flat's front door. It was Billy. She gave him a tired smile. He had a short beard, which was a new look for him. He was also wearing a bright red T-shirt with a designer slogan on the chest. He looked her up and down and raised his eyes to heaven. 'Did you sleep in a ditch?'

She ran her hands through her hair and realised that it was sticking out everywhere, like his, but not as a fashion statement. She pulled her aching body up to stand, leaning her hip against the wall. 'You're right. I need a shower. Can you check the document on my laptop for typos and make sure I've got the financing costs right? I'll come back glossy and wide awake, I promise.'

She got some clothes and a towel from her bedroom on the way to the shower and paused, looking at Billy. 'By the way, did you speak to anyone on your journey up here?' She wondered if the grapevine had started whispering about her private life yet.

'Oh yes. I chatted up Jason, who I met in the lift, and Molly from three doors down is aghast with you for keeping a sex god to yourself.' He stuck out his tongue and she did the same back.

She went into the little bathroom and then popped her head back out. 'How is the sex god? Have you heard from Ed at all?' she asked innocently.

Billy saw the mischievous glint in her eye and frowned. 'What did you do?'

'Nothing!' Poppy said rapidly, and quickly locked the bathroom door before Billy came and banged it down to find out if she'd meddled in his relationship. She turned on the shower and heard him retreat and go back to work. She knew he'd be furious, but she felt it was ok to tease him gently. Ed was worth fighting for.

She let the water run over her body and wash some of the stress away. Her mum was going to be fine, and might even be coming home for the odd night when she had fully recovered. Plus Ed had finally told her what had gone wrong between him and Billy. Ed had been offered a job abroad that was too good to turn down, but Billy wouldn't leave Poppy, so in the end they had tearfully parted ways. Poppy had needed to go and sit in a cool room and think for a while, when Ed told her, but she was selfishly glad Billy hadn't gone. She realised that she would have to make Billy see sense, though. Billy adored travel and he loved Ed. She knew he loved her too, but this was his chance at happiness. He had to take it.

Billy wondered what the hell Poppy had spoken to Ed about. They'd decided that the kindest way for both of them to survive was to cut all ties. It had been torture, but he was slowly coming out the other side. Now she'd gone and poked her nose in. Poppy was quite bossy and was keeping him extra busy. He loved the attention he got from her neighbours, now he was allowed to go to the flat in daylight. He hadn't been joking about the hot man in the lift or gorgeous Molly from up the hall. He'd even got a wink from a lady whom he assumed to be Gladys, when he had arrived at Poppy's door and put his key in the lock. He'd winked back and she'd thrown her head back and laughed, her grey bouffant hair bobbing gently around her face.

Stepping into the flat made him smile. Poppy had done wonders with it and he'd helped a little bit too, when she'd allowed it, as she was a tad controlling of her projects. She'd already done Gladys's place up and he was working on an invite to snoop. Poppy was quite unforthcoming with her life history, so he'd just ask her neighbour instead. It was a plan, but the flaw was that Poppy was always with him when he was at the flat.

Poppy must have added a fortune to the value of the place, but she couldn't change the rundown exterior. It didn't seem like anyone around here had free time anyway, if the chipped paint and bin bags left outside the ground floor flats were anything to go by. Perhaps the homeowners were busy saving lives, or running businesses and all the flats were like this one inside, or maybe they were even more outrageous? He'd watched a programme once where a flat owner had rammed her home with every texture and colour imaginable. It had given him a headache to watch, but he'd not been able to turn away. How she wasn't out of her mind with all of that noise from the furnishings, he didn't know – but then he grinned. He'd find a way to get Gladys on her own for a gossip.

He listened to check that Prissy Pants was still in the shower and slid the balcony door open. He knew where to find Poppy's binoculars, and leaned on the balcony to take in the view. He could see for miles from here. The block of flats backed onto a very busy road and roundabout, but beyond that were rows of nice detached Tudor houses which had little gardens backing onto a park. Poppy had told him she had spent a lot of time in that park as a kid. It was the place where she went to draw, sitting in the shade of the trees. It had been a way to get some relief from caring for her mum, while hiding what her home life had really been like from the world.

His heart broke for the scared child she'd been and for the strong, if sometimes misguided, woman she'd become. She always put on a front to others that she could cope with anything, and she probably could – in fact she already had – but he saw her softer side. She doted on her mother and was fiercely loyal to those she loved. She just had a funny way of showing it sometimes. He wondered if he was a show-off because of his own parents? He pictured his vibrant mum always telling him he was brilliant and his stern but patient dad, rolling his eyes but hugging him anyway. He decided probably not. But he grinned to himself. His mum was wonderfully bonkers and his greatest cheerleader.

He carried on scrutinising the street for a bit, and then settled on the house he was looking for. He knew Dylan's parents lived there, but he still hadn't been invited inside yet. He wondered if he would be too flamboyant for them, looking down at his trendy jeans and vibrant shirt. He had two bracelets on today, but they were designer and very chic. He heard movement in the flat behind him and quickly shoved the binoculars onto their hook. He stepped into the kitchen to make Poppy a brew.

Hearing the doorbell ring, he frowned. He'd been at the flat lots of times, but Poppy had never had a visitor. In broad daylight, too. Perhaps she did have a life outside work, after all?

CHAPTER FOURTEEN

Poppy raised an eyebrow and rubbed the towel over her freshly-washed hair. She looked over to Billy, but he shrugged. 'It's your flat!'

'It might be Gladys. No one else ever calls here.'

'Is it because you've turned into a famous entrepreneur and no one expects you to be in your old flat?' he joked.

Poppy poked her tongue out at him and opened the door, just as Anne was about to ring the buzzer again. Both stood wide-eyed in shock, though Poppy didn't know why Anne looked so surprised to see her. She was the one who had knocked on Poppy's door! 'Uh... come in.'

Poppy stood back to let Anne into the flat. Her friend's eyes were now out on stalks as she'd just spotted Billy looking sleek and sexy. Then she noticed the changes to the flat. She eyed Poppy's half-naked form, wrapped just in a towel. Poppy flushed and told them both to go into the lounge while she quickly got dressed. She was back in an instant, wearing grey joggers and a simple white T-shirt.

Poppy could see Anne gazing around in awe, before obviously remembering her manners and saying hello to Billy.

'Hi, I'm Anne,' she said, clearly trying not to drool. She held out her hand to Billy who smiled and shook it, which was unlike him, he usually flung his arms around everyone. Poppy's heart softened at his loyalty.

'Anne, this is my good friend Billy.' Anne winced and Poppy could have kicked herself for speaking without thinking. 'Billy has been helping me update Mum's flat.'

'So I can see. The last time I was here it was full of soul music posters and dead plants. It's a lot to take in.'

'Maybe you should have visited more?' said Billy nonchalantly, almost falling over as Poppy nudged him with her hip.

'Sorry, Anne,' said Poppy. 'Billy's a bit protective of me.'

Anne's cheeks flushed red. 'Because you pay him to be?'

Poppy's mouth dropped open and her eyes flashed. Billy grabbed her arm to stop her saying anything she'd regret. 'I don't need to be paid to be Poppy's friend. She's my boss, but I love her anyway,' he joked, trying hard to lighten the mood, while watching Anne's every move.

Anne hung her head and then lifted tired eyes to Poppy's. Poppy's mood immediately changed. 'Are you and Freddie ok?' She led Anne to the couch and signalled to Billy to get them all coffee.

Anne's long dark hair tumbled forward. It wasn't her usual style of soft loose curls, which put Poppy on alert. Anne obsessed constantly over having perfect hair and tried every product on the market to make it shine. 'I'm sorry for being a bitch. This whole friendship break-up has been a lot of stress. We haven't fallen out before… ever, and that's saying a lot with Sasha in the group.'

Poppy raised a faint smile, though she was still watching Anne warily.

'I heard that Sasha was a complete cow the other week,' called Billy from the kitchen.

Anne spluttered with laughter. 'Does he not have a filter?'

Poppy shook her head and laughed.

'I'm really sorry for the way things worked out,' said Anne. 'I just heard from Chris that your mum is ill. I rushed straight over, as you didn't answer your phone.'

Poppy pictured her phone in the drawer in the bathroom, rubbed her neck and sighed. 'I was in the shower.'

Anne raised her eyebrows in speculation as Billy walked back in. 'Not with him! I told you Billy likes men.'

'And the occasional hot woman,' said Billy with a wink.

'What?' said Poppy, sitting back in shock, before standing up and pacing the tiny room, which literally took four steps before she had to turn back again. She'd thought Billy was the one person, other than Dylan, that she didn't have secrets from. 'You've never told me that,' she accused.

'I'm joking, but a man does have to have some surprises in store, or he'd be a total bore,' Billy said, blanching a little at the fire in her eyes. 'I don't think Dylan would be so happy for us to be half-naked around each other if he thought I liked women too.'

Anne seemed to have brightened up, and was enjoying herself now by the look of things, even though she wasn't one to start unnecessary arguments – unlike Sasha, or even Poppy when she was backed into a corner. Poppy realised she had had to be feisty, to stop anyone sticking their nose into her life. She'd been a bit of a bulldog, hardly letting anyone into the flat to keep the secret that her mum was unwell, or absent, a lot of the time. Maybe she could now relax those boundaries, and let people help her.

'Dylan loves you, whoever you like. Why would it matter to him?' Poppy protested. She was annoyed with Billy for teasing her. Why did it have to be in front of Anne, too? She would probably relay it all to Demi and Sasha.

'He's quite protective over you, and you are a sexy minx,'

said Billy, cheekily. Poppy burst out laughing and Anne's shoulders started bobbing up and down in mirth.

'Ever the showman!' Poppy scolded, kissing his cheek.

'I didn't fancy women at all until I met you,' he said deadpan. She paused for a second and then slapped his shoulder lightly.

'You're not attracted to me, then?' she winked, theatrically pouting.

'Nope,' he confirmed. 'I go for something a bit more rugged.' Poppy pictured Ed's lithe build and immaculate attire and smothered a giggle.

'Plus you're too career-driven for me,' he continued, winking back. 'And I don't go for blondes. It's brunettes all the way for me, baby,' he waggled his eyebrows suggestively at Anne, who chuckled. Poppy envisioned Ed's dark hair and the way the curls caressed his ears and stuck her tongue out at Billy for his silliness. She took the coffee out of his hands and plonked her bottom back next to Anne.

'How is your mum?' asked Anne, serious suddenly. Poppy expected to feel sadness at the mention of her mum, but she felt happiness radiate inside her instead.

She took a deep breath. 'She's had a virus, but she's feeling much better and the scare seems to have made her see things differently at last. Honestly… growing up with Mum was a nightmare, but there were some good times too.' She lost focus for a minute while she tried to picture those good times, but even they had been dimmed by the fear that everything could change suddenly at any time.

Anne put her arm around Poppy's shoulder, and she snuggled into it, loving the familiar warmth. 'Why didn't you tell us how bad it was for you? We all thought your mum was a bit eccentric, when we were kids. We didn't know how ill she was, just that she had a very sick sister and stayed in a few different places to help with her anxiety after her sister

MY PERFECT EX

died.' Poppy winced at yet another lie, to protect her family. Her mother was an only child. 'We learned pretty early on that your aunt was a taboo subject. We'd have tried to help if we knew more.'

Poppy thought about Anne's question. It was one she had asked herself many times recently. 'I just couldn't. But something's changed for her, in the last week. I think it's the fact that an infection almost took her life, rather than her doing it on her own.' Both Billy and Anne flinched, but Poppy was done with lies. If they wanted the truth, they would get the unvarnished version. 'She's tried before and I had to watch her all the time. I made up so many lies to protect her. I'm really sorry about that,' she hung her head, bit her lip and her voice wobbled. 'I became the parent and she was the child. It's why I'm a teeny bit tyrannical at work.'

Billy sniggered at that, so she flashed him a look, making him shut up. 'It's also why I didn't tell you all about the changes in my life with my relationship with Dylan. I have to be in control and I didn't know how to blend the two worlds. Plus, you lot are always bitching about the Taylor brothers and saying how they shag everything that moves. I'm not sure how I feel about that yet, so I've been avoiding confrontations.'

Anne had the grace to blush. 'It's just gossip! Most of them are probably jealous. I haven't seen Dylan, Ollie or Miles out with anyone for ages, now I come to think about it.' Billy and Poppy exchanged glances but kept quiet for now. Anne sighed and pushed herself up to go and look out of the balcony window. 'This place looks amazing. It must have taken ages to decorate,' then she blanched and closed her eyes for a moment. 'I know I should have been here to help you organise it all.'

Poppy smiled gently and went to stand next to her, looking out at the familiar view of rooftops and roads to the park beyond. 'It pretty much all came from the internet. It's second hand or recycled, but you'd never know it. A lot of my business is about sustainability.'

'There's Dylan's mum!' Anne grabbed the binoculars and pointed to his house. Her eyes lit up. 'Do you remember how we used to spy on him when he came home from school? I can't believe you ended up with him… then again, you were pretty obsessed.'

Poppy flushed and Billy's ears were pricking up. She nudged him in the ribs as he came over to have a look at Dylan's mum too, nabbing the binoculars from Anne. 'I want to meet Dylan's mum. He hasn't let me yet! I'm determined to get into that house one day and find out all his secrets.'

Poppy snorted into her cup. Anne looked shocked for a minute before she realised he was joking. 'Billy thinks Dylan's scared of him meeting his mum. Billy is pretty hardcore in the dramatic stakes,' she laughed as he hugged her and kissed her nose. Anne's eyes went wide again. 'I'll tell you one day about how he got his job.'

'I was only joking,' Billy butted in. 'I guess Dylan's parents are probably pretty cool people by the son they raised. Plus he prefers being at your place to anywhere else. It's your own fault for building such an amazing house.'

Suddenly Anne looked thoughtful again. 'You keeping secrets from your oldest friends was never about us not liking Dylan, was it, Poppy?' she accused her friend. 'It was always about your mum. Dylan almost sounds like the perfect boyfriend, from what you told us.' There was now an edge to her voice. She took the binoculars back and hung them on their peg, before turning away and heading indoors.

Poppy looked to Billy for help, but he was useless and just shrugged and pulled a face. Poppy followed Anne. 'I thought you'd all worry constantly. I didn't want you to find out about mum and how awful it was. I'd built an illusion that she'd moved to the care home because she wanted to, not because she had to. You knew she had anxiety issues, but I never told you the truth about her mental health. I felt ashamed. You have enough to worry about with Freddie.'

Anne looked at her in confusion. 'Why would you be ashamed that your mum was ill? You needed our support and I'm used to being there for Freddie. Plus most of this happened before he was born!' Poppy gulped and her mind went blank. Billy rolled his eyes and stepped in.

'Look, Poppy is the first to admit she's made a hash of things. She, ridiculously, blames herself for her mum's health.' Anne's jaw dropped and Poppy looked uncomfortable suddenly. 'It wasn't anything about trust and she feels pretty stupid for not confiding in you all earlier.' Poppy gawped but he held up a hand to stop her saying anything. 'She's fiercely independent and didn't want your pity.'

Poppy was about to speak, but Anne interrupted furiously, eyes flashing. She leaped up and faced them both, chucking her handbag on the floor at her feet and shouting at Poppy. 'You thought we'd pity you? But Billy and Dylan won't? You were judging us.'

'No! Of course not. That's not what Billy meant at all.' Poppy wished she could grab his words back, but it was too late. She reached across and took Anne's hand, happy that her friend didn't shake her off, even though her fingers were sizzling hot. 'For the first time in my life I had built something good… besides you all.' Poppy thought for a moment. 'If I'd told you more about my work, really told you what I do and why, then you would have found out how bad it was for me with Mum. Lots of people run a mile when they hear the words, mental and health, together. I'm pretty good at handling stress, I've been doing it for most of my life, but if I as much as say I'm tired, everyone might think I'm about to do something stupid. I'm my mother's daughter, but I'm also just me. And you'd have felt I'd lied to you for years anyway.' She saw the dawning of understanding finally arrive in Billy's face.

Anne dropped her hand and faced her. Poppy tried to explain. 'I make homes to try and ensure people never have to suffer like my mum does. I've told you before that I work as an associate to big building programmes, to advise on mental health and wellbeing. It's because of mum. My sensory panels are helping people.'

Anne listened in silence, not giving anything away.

'Poppy also donates pods she's had built to care homes,' Billy added. 'To help people on their own road to recovery. She's like some crazy 'I have to save the world' entrepreneur.'

'Billy!' Poppy turned to him in shock.

He stood his ground. 'You do far too much for others and work all the hours under the sun. Plus you're a control freak who won't delegate until you're almost asleep at your desk.'

Anne raised her eyebrows. She gave Poppy one of those looks that she'd used to control them all with at school. It said, 'you've been misbehaving'. Poppy didn't know how such a group of opinionated women had stayed friends for so long without arguing – except for Demi, who was an absolute sweetheart. It was probably because the others were too scared to argue in case all hell broke loose and someone lost an arm, or something.

'Look, I work hard and I get results. It's what I'm paid to do,' Poppy protested.

Just then Billy's stomach grumbled, and it broke the tension. They all laughed.

'Anyone for a take-away? I'm starving and the cupboards in this place are bare,' he said. Poppy looked to Anne, who nodded and said she'd quickly step outside to check her mum could do some extra babysitting.

Poppy smiled her thanks at Billy and tried to quell her

unease about having a flat full of people. They had never been able to afford for friends to come round to tea or for takeaways. Her mum didn't work very often, just the odd few weeks in the café to help Chris when they were desperate and she was feeling well enough. It was why Poppy had studied so hard, attending college at night and working in the café herself whenever she could. She'd felt like a zombie those first few years and hadn't been able to make new friends. She was too exhausted to go out, and couldn't spare any money to socialise. Her leisure time was spent with her old crowd, or her mum. There was little room for anything else. Even her first couple of romances had been complete disasters. She just hadn't had time for men, until she'd met Dylan and Billy. In a way it was how she'd managed to fool her closest friends for so long about not dating anyone. They expected nothing more from her. Her dating history was dry like the desert. The thought of Dylan made her skin warm up and she caught her breath before she could analyse how much he meant to her. She knew she was strong, but with him by her side, she felt like she could move mountains.

Seeing that Billy was already on the phone to the takeaway service, and knowing he'd be getting pizza, she grinned and asked him to add extra garlic bread. She hadn't eaten since breakfast and was suddenly ravenous.

CHAPTER FIFTEEN

Poppy glanced at her watch and picked up her pace. She could feel the adrenaline flowing through her veins at the thought of her meeting with Jared Wright. They'd spoken on the phone many times now, but seeing Jared in person was always a lot of fun. He was brimming with enthusiasm, and her senses were heightened when she was with him. He had such big plans and was turning his dreams into a reality. He'd built several housing complexes and refurbished a hotel already, and he said he loved working with her. He made it seem like she was the answer to all his prayers. He'd been looking for a designer to work with for a while, he'd told her, before seeing an article about her work. He was a whirlwind of energy when he wanted something and she was happy to be swept up in it all. She was always keen to grow her business and had more clients than she could handle, really.

Jared wanted more than to be just a developer. He had a vision, like she did, of how all homes should be. They both believed the four walls surrounding any homeowner could

MY PERFECT EX

be their oasis of calm and recuperation after a long day. Achieving this didn't have to cost the earth, but it did require skill to accommodate the extra light, angles and airflow.

Stepping out of the lift and into the plush offices of JW was an experience in itself. The simple but stunning dark blue and gold logo, with its depiction of buildings within the two capital letters, caught your eye immediately. Jared hadn't designed the office building she was standing in, but he had improved it. It was now a gem. The structure had been brought to life with glass and greenery and she felt like she was stepping into the pages of an exotic interiors magazine. The rooms were glass boxes, so you could see people working away busily, but they were obviously soundproofed as she could have heard a mouse squeak. The branding of blue and gold was subtly enhanced everywhere. Suddenly a door to the offices along the front wall opened, and she could hear conversation and laughter. Her feet carried her along to the main reception where Jared's personal assistant sat, breaking off a telephone call to greet her and lead her straight to his office.

Jared stood when he saw her, a smile lighting up his face. She gulped in some air – he was so damn gorgeous – and she grinned helplessly. *How could you not, when faced with such beauty?*

Jared ran his hands through his short, dusky blond hair, making it stick out slightly as if he'd just been ravaged. Poppy hadn't had a reaction to a man other than Dylan for such a long time. She was shocked her at her body's response to her new business partner. Then again, she'd have to have been dead not to respond to Jared, especially when he came and shook her hand and then leant in to kiss her cheek and pull out a chair for her. His aftershave caught her senses, strong and spicy, and she blinked to make herself wake up.

She was not a hormonal teenager and she had a seriously hot boyfriend at home.

She leaned down and took a pad and pen from her bag, trying to look professional and not to blush too much. He was still gazing at her like she was a precious bird and she tilted her head to one side, watching him, until he coughed and snapped himself out of whatever he was thinking about. Probably the hordes of women he spent his time with. She'd read he was eternally single and enjoying it.

'How are you?' he asked, his voice making her jump. It wasn't like her to daydream, especially in front of a client, but Jared had kind of become a friend, thanks to the amount of time they spent chatting via text, email or by phone. He was a man with a lot of questions and, although she'd initially assumed he'd delegate one of his staff to deal with her, he hadn't. It was a lot of fun meeting someone who was as passionate about his dreams as she was about her own.

'Sorry! I was miles away.'

'Am I boring you already? You've literally been here for two minutes!' he laughed. She liked the sound of his voice.

She smiled and crossed her legs, feeling glad she'd worn smart black jeans and a short sleeved, fitted shirt in a soft mossy tone. It had tiny images of fern leaves dotted all over it in a slightly darker shade. She was smart but comfortable. She refused to conform to business suits. They just weren't for her, and her clients didn't seem to mind at all. 'I'm not sure you could bore anyone. I was just wondering if you'd approved my designs yet?'

Jared sat back in his hyper-modern office chair. She'd been casually eyeing it up ever since she'd got there. She wanted to jump up and go to have a closer look, and could imagine running her hands over the armrests. It really was divine. 'Is your chair made by a new designer?'

Jared laughed again and got up, gesturing that she should

sit down in his place. 'You really are too much! You're supposed to be paying attention to your client, not the chair!'

Poppy didn't need asking twice. They were both obsessed with design, and this was a beauty. They often chatted about the latest trends when they should have been working. 'It's so lovely, though,' Poppy was stoking the soft, rich blue fabric and sighing as it welcomed her body into its frame, as if they had been made for each other.

Jared propped his backside on his solid wood desk and watched her with amusement. 'I agree. I found it at a design fair and once I'd sat down in it, I couldn't leave it there. It's now my best friend.'

'It literally envelops your body and supports it, while looking incredibly modern and cool,' she sighed dreamily. 'I want one!'

'They aren't in production yet, but I'll have a word with the designer.'

He offered Poppy his hand to pull her out of the chair, which was surprisingly easy, as it was well sprung and it actually pushed her up as she moved. She looked amazed and he smiled. 'I know! Ingenious, isn't it?'

Poppy went back to her own chair but was still looking longingly at his. 'So. Back to the serious stuff. I know you like my designs, but did the architect, Libby, agree how they can work, as the build's already begun? The decision has taken a while.'

Jared settled back in his chair and linked his hands in front of him, looking at her thoughtfully. 'Your plans will work if we make a few minor changes. Libby has seen them and agreed they can only add to the overall effect of what we're trying to achieve. She's actually really excited about it. So am I.'

Poppy's eyes sparkled and she leaned forward in her chair. Her stomach felt like it was full of bees buzzing around. She only just stopped herself from jumping up and hugging him. This was what she'd dreamt of. She had worked so hard to build something that would change the way people lived with – and viewed – mental health problems. She'd dreamed of a time where every part of people's lives supported their well-being. She couldn't change the world, but she could play a small part in helping people to be happier in their own homes. Poppy hoped that with the new and improved tweaks she'd made, it might be possible. She never wanted another child to suffer the way she had.

Her daylight panels could be installed almost anywhere and the new technology for images and sounds to soothe the mind was adaptable to phones and iPads. Poppy had accepted that technology was part of people's everyday lives, even in the poorest of areas, and had designed applications to turn a screen into a sanctuary. This actually bought in another strong income stream. The big houses she was customising for Jared were the other end of the scale, with parts of the house that could move and change colour. She loved the walls that slid back to make soothing spaces to relax, and the interchangeable rooms. She had been given a very healthy budget and had been able to make the homes of her dreams. The people wealthy enough to afford to live there might well have highly stressful jobs or unhealthy lives, so the homes would become their time-out space, a place to recharge and enable them to face the world again.

Poppy's pods, like the ones she had designed for the rehabilitation centre, could be adapted for almost anywhere. They were small, and although not cheap, were affordable if people with more modest means wanted to install one in a garden. The application she'd designed with a team of creators meant that anyone could have a slice of paradise on their phones or devices, for a tiny fee. It had meant years of research and development and had eaten a lot of her savings, but a scaled up version could now be installed into Jared's houses. She knew it worked – the panel in her own home rarely failed to soothe her tired mind. Jared had loved the idea and immediately offered to invest, but she was managing on her own right now. This was her baby. When he used the technology in his homes, her company's value would skyrocket. That in itself made her nervous. Jared was paying for the privilege of having her panels installed in the properties, but she owned the design outright. She was very comfortably off now, but then she would become uberwealthy. The online application developers had negotiated a percentage for their work and she'd felt that was fair, but taking on a partner in her panels for homes was different. It could make things easier – or it could make them worse. Jared had a wealth of knowledge and contacts and she didn't want to alienate him. She was still debating what to do.

'So,' said Jared, recapturing her attention. 'Libby asked us to meet her later for a drink to finalise the plans. She's got a manic day at the site and said it would be easier this evening, plus she'll probably need a drink after telling her staff about our ideas. I'm not sure they will be happy, at this stage, but we will make the alterations.'

Poppy smiled at him, admiring his chiselled jaw and clean-shaven chin, but then realised he was looking very serious. She couldn't help but worry that it was too late to make changes in the structure. She'd suggested moving walls to make room for indoor gardens, and incorporating the screens they would need for technology and light. She knew Libby had been given a real headache. 'You're free to meet up with Libby tonight?' asked Jared. It was more of a statement than a question.

Poppy winced. She'd already promised to meet Dylan that evening. She'd been so busy with her mum, then trying to make it up to Anne, and worrying about Sasha and Demi, that the rest of her time had been taken up with work. As a result, she knew Dylan was feeling left out and unappreciated. He had a lot more spare time than her as he worked his own hours – and there didn't seem to be that many of them, as his business was more established.

'Uh… of course I can meet you both for a drink. I think we all need one after taking on a project like this. I hope the results will be worth the stress. I think I'm getting frown lines with the worry,' she joked, noticing that the sky was darkening already.

Jared smiled at her in satisfaction and sank back into his chair. 'You are as beautiful as ever, but I'm not surprised that you're tired. You've been just as determined as me to make this work.' He crossed his legs and studied her as she blushed. She couldn't think of a witty retort, but he carried on. 'The exhaustion will be worth it when everyone wants to buy our homes. They are going to revolutionise the way people live. We are going to make a happier society.'

'For people who can afford it,' she sighed, wishing the bees in her stomach that always appeared when she was near him, would buzz off. Jared leaned forward and studied her.

'We are running a business. But I've seen what you've done with the pods at Green Manor,' said Jared.

Poppy gasped. 'How do you know about that?'

Jared smiled. 'I always check out the work of anyone I do business with. Those pods are part of your history.' When she seemed about to protest, he held his hands up. 'I wouldn't be in business if I didn't check references. The owner at Green Manor was more than happy to chat to me about your work and show me the pods. I have to be thorough.'

'Then you'll know about my mum.' Her voice had an underlying edge that he didn't miss.

'I do,' was all he said.

'Does that change your view of me?' she asked pointedly.

'Why would it?' he seemed confused for a moment. 'Your mother obviously inspired your work, and it is incredible. I won't ask anything else about your past unless you want to tell me. Will your projects there interfere with your input for me?'

'Nothing comes before my work,' she said, her skin glowing hot and her back sweating suddenly.

Jared stood up and came round the desk to take her hand and help her up. It seemed that the meeting was over for now. 'Then we have nothing to worry about.' He didn't let go of her hand and she looked at it in a daze. Her skin was warm there, too. Finally he let her go, almost regretfully. 'I'd like to chat to you about the pods too. Perhaps we can incorporate them into a site that people with smaller homes can visit?'

The bees were back in her stomach. Her mouth dropped open in shock. Why hadn't she thought of that? He was talking out loud as if he was sifting through his thoughts. 'I was thinking kind of like a brain spa. Somewhere people who are tired or in need of help could go to, to rest and recuperate for a few hours.' Poppy's heartbeat ramped up. This was a brilliant idea. She suddenly envisaged one in every town and she wanted to jump around and hug him, but she held herself in check. Her hands trembled at the memory that he'd poked around in her past. *Welcome to the world of big business.* Wasn't this what she'd always aspired to?

Jared's personal assistant poked his head around the door after knocking softly. She told Jared his next appointment had arrived. Poppy wanted to stay and talk for hours, and huffed under her breath. He glanced her way and laughed. It was as if he could see into her mind. The thought disturbed and excited her at the same time. 'Drinks with Libby, later tonight. We can chat about everything then,' he soothed as he walked her to the door, his hand resting on the small of her back.

Poppy rearranged her features into a picture of professional charm and he laughed at that too, then escorted her all the way to the reception, thanking her for her time and leaving her feeling bereft as he greeted his next client.

CHAPTER SIXTEEN

Poppy sat in her car in the pub car park and tried to calm herself down. She'd been back in her little office in Cherry Blossom Lane all afternoon, but was still going over and over the idea of sites in towns to help communities. She knew it would take years of research and development, but it was something to work towards. She wasn't sure how she felt about discussing it with Libby, as the pods were very close to her heart, but she guessed that, with the way her business was growing and the fact that her two lives were meshing, she'd have to face opening up about them soon enough. There was a huge gym complex just across the road from her office that looked like it was being developed. She wondered if the pods would integrate well on sites like that too.

She looked up at the façade of the pub Libby had chosen to meet at. It was modern, with little fuss and discreet lighting. Flowers bloomed from tubs below every windowsill. It was picture-perfect. Poppy took a moment to enjoy the view and store it in her memory banks. She thought back to the times she'd sat on her mum's balcony and stared at the bustling world outside and wished she could be a part of it. Now here she was, a successful business owner, about to sit down with her contemporaries and discuss the deal of her life. She could almost pinch herself, and she would have – if Dylan hadn't just tried to kill her mood by being a total grump.

She thought back to their phone conversation a few minutes ago. It was unlike him to get angry about anything, but he'd tried to draw the line at her going out again and not spending time with him. She'd explained she had little choice, but he'd not wanted to listen. If he'd got involved in the project and met Jared, like she'd suggested, they could have all been working together. Dylan was a master craftsman and Jared appreciated skills like his, but Dylan hadn't been interested. Now he was complaining at being left out. He was behaving like a petulant child.

She grabbed her keys and bag and stepped out of the car into the warm night air. She breathed in the scent of lavender and tried to calm her nerves. Dylan would have to understand that she was juggling her mum, her friendships, him and her workload at the moment. If he didn't like it… that thought stopped her in her tracks and made her gulp in some air. Without Dylan she'd be lost. He was her rock. She could kick herself for not taking more care of their relationship. She vowed to rectify that later and to surprise him by stopping at his flat on the way home.

Pushing open the pub door and blinking to adjust to the lighting, after the inky darkness of the evening, she took in the sleek bar and people chatting happily beside it. A few others were sat at round tables, and a couple glanced her way and then continued their conversation. The interior of the pub was much like the outside, modern with traditional twists. There was a lot of natural wood, but it was teamed with metal fixtures and fittings. Everything sparkled and fresh flowers burst out of vases dotted around. The scent of the blooms filled the air in a sweet mixture with the hops from the beer pumps that were lined up on the bar.

Walking into a place alone had never bothered Poppy. From an early age, she'd had to develop the confidence to go into shops and buy food, pretending her mum was busy outside. She'd also had to attend appointments on her own, or lie to school teachers. She'd hated that part, as they had all been pretty kind to her. She'd wondered if they'd suspected what was going on from time to time. But she was clean and presentable, after working out how to launder her own clothes. She then mastered the decrepit iron, learning the hard way how to not to burn herself. Her mum had been horrified and cried for hours when she'd seen the mark on her arm. She'd even stepped up and appeared at a doctor's appointment and even one parents' evening after that, but the downward spiral always began again after a good spell like that one.

Poppy closed her eyes for a second and breathed in enticing scents from the kitchen as she walked into the conservatory at the back, where Jared had told her to meet them. Now was not the time to be seen to be crying. It was supposed to be one of the best times of her life. She wished Dylan was more on board with it, and didn't feel threatened by her work schedule. He wasn't driven to succeed like her and Jared. He just enjoyed his job and that was all he needed.

She turned as she heard someone call her name and smiled. Jared was sitting in a corner booth with a bottle of red wine and three glasses in front of him. Her stomach grumbled when she saw he'd ordered a selection of snacks for them to nibble on. She'd forgotten lunch again. He got up as she approached and she swung herself into the seat next to him. He offered her a glass of wine and she sipped it gratefully, eyeing up the food. 'Are you expecting a party tonight?'

Jared looked at the platters and laughed. 'I've been in back-to-back meetings since ours. I assumed you'd be busy and forget to eat too, so I ordered plenty.' Her skin fizzed at the idea that he might have been thinking about her. 'Libby's probably exhausted too. She never rests when the schedule is tight.' The warm glow of excitement dimmed a little and Poppy smirked to herself at her own self-importance. Jared was kind to all his employees. It was one of the reasons she'd wanted to work with him. His reputation as a rising star with ethics went before him.

Jared's phone buzzed as they began to talk about their project whilst tucking into the food. They had decided not to wait for Libby as she'd already sent a text to say she was running late. He glanced at the screen and sighed. 'Libby's not coming after all. Sorry about that, Poppy. It looks like you've got me to yourself tonight. Is that a problem?' His eyes were still sparkling and the one glass of wine she was allowing herself before driving home had warmed the mood up considerably.

'What? No. Of course not. I'd love to have seen what Libby thinks about the plans, but I know we've added to her workload. It's a good job she likes us both or she'd be giving us what for,' she joked.

Jared grinned and it was impossible not to feel a bit lightheaded in the face of such masculine beauty and charisma. 'We might as well polish off the food and talk about anything we missed from the meeting today. Unless you need to rush off?'

Poppy thought of Dylan, sitting at home and probably sulking about the amount of attention she was currently giving Jared, and shook her head. 'Nope. I'm free. Explain to me again about how we could build a community pod centre – or two hundred,' she laughed.

Two hours later, Poppy looked at her watch and realised how late it was. She'd already decided to leave her car at the pub overnight, as she had consumed enough wine to make her head fizz. She hadn't laughed so much in ages and had finally confided more to Jared about her mum and why she'd built her business in the first place. It hadn't been as hard as she'd thought to tell a stranger, even though Jared was more like a friend now, and he already knew the bare bones anyway. They would be working together on this project for months. While their heads were bent together, devouring the delicious food, they had come up with a few plans for potential future projects. The way they both envisaged their businesses progressing seemed to ebb and flow together. There were lots of places where they could interlink to benefit their mutual growth.

When she'd explained why she was driven to succeed, he'd sat back and listened without interrupting and seemed to find her story fascinating. He'd taken her hand at one point when she'd thought she might cry, and she hadn't grabbed it back. Now they were talking about her old school friends and the guys Jared grew up with, including his boisterous bunch of brothers. She didn't want the night to end. When he offered to share a cab back it seemed like the most natural thing in the world to agree, although she had no idea what direction he lived in. He knew where her place was, though. He'd previously asked to come and see how her technology worked. Her best example was her own home, so he'd popped by once or twice already after a site visit next door.

She settled herself into the cab and made sure she didn't slide along the seat and touch legs with him. His eyes were sparkling and she could see small laughter lines on his face. She filed away moments from their evening together to savour later. Who wouldn't enjoy working with a red-hot property developer? Then her equilibrium came crashing down as she remembered that she didn't have anyone other than Billy to share her news with. He'd already said he thought Jared was 'smoking', but Dylan definitely wouldn't appreciate that thought, and her girlfriends were still annoyed with her. She wished now that she'd told them everything long ago, so they could help her celebrate her successes. In the early days of her business, she'd just bought a cheap bottle of plonk and had a glass on her own. Now she had Dylan and Billy – and Dylan usually spoilt her rotten with flowers and kisses.

The car pulled up outside her house and she saw the door open as she got out. She frowned and wished Billy wouldn't take quite so many liberties, then saw Dylan step outside. She didn't think that midnight was the best time to be introducing Jared and Dylan to each other. She said a hasty thank you to Jared, who bid her a good week and settled back into the car seat, already glancing at his phone as she shut the door. Dylan looked pointedly at the cab as it drove off.

'Hi! What are you doing here? Jared dropped me home. I decided to leave the car at the pub and ask Billy to take me over there to pick it up in the morning,' she looked at her watch. 'Oh – today. It's after midnight!' She leant in for a kiss, but Dylan didn't look happy and stepped back inside without a word. She rushed after him, the wine making her thoughts fuzzy. What was his problem?

'Didn't your new friend want to say hello?' he finally asked, turning round. She could see little worry lines around his eyes and for the first time thought he might have had bad news or something.

'Is everything ok?' It was unlike Dylan to sound jealous.

'I came round to surprise my girlfriend as I've been in a bad mood lately, then I find her in a taxi with another guy.'

Poppy laughed nervously and took his hand. He didn't shrug her away. 'I told you I was out with Libby and Jared. Libby got called away, so we ate a meal and talked shop for a couple of hours. If I'd have known you were here, I'd have cut the meeting short.'

He raised his eyebrows at her. 'Meeting? Come off it, Poppy! It sounds like you had a dinner date and drank some wine.'

The hairs on the back of Poppy's neck rose. She wasn't a child. 'I drank wine and ate a meal with a client. What's your problem?'

Dylan sighed and rubbed his temples. 'I don't honestly know. I've barely seen you lately and when you do have a spare minute, you're still *working*.' He laid the emphasis on the last word and she had to bite her tongue. Then her own shoulders slumped and she went to link her arms around his waist and place her cheek on his solid chest. He was immoveable for a moment, then gave in and hugged her back, his hands sliding towards her backside.

'I know I've been busy,' she leant back and looked into his handsome face. 'This contract is a big deal for me and my business. I've never been handed anything in my life and I'm doing this because someone believes in me.' She stopped him when he was about to speak, by slipping her hands around his back and into his jeans to touch his warm skin. He gasped and bent down to capture her lips in a soft kiss.

'I believe in you,' he said huskily. She sighed and her body moulded into his, her hands sliding up his back and finding taut muscles.

'I know you do.' She reached up on tiptoes and kissed him back. This time with passion, to show him how much she'd missed him lately. His eyes were dark pools of anger and lust.

'I'm sorry if I haven't been there for you and I'll try harder to cut back on work where I can.'

He started groaned and nibbling in the sensitive place behind her ear and her blood began to heat up. When he swung her into his arms and carried her to her bedroom, all thoughts of Jared and his exciting ideas were forgotten.

CHAPTER SEVENTEEN

Poppy pushed open the café door, thinking her heart might jump out of her throat. She was now talking to Anne quite regularly, but she hadn't seen Demi or Sasha since their argument. She'd tried to reach out to them, but it had taken Anne calling a crisis meeting to get everyone together. Demi would always side with Sasha over anything, however sweet she was. She and Poppy had never really fought before, so their relationship had not been tested until now.

She looked over at her three friends defiantly. She was fed up with being in the doghouse. They could either accept she'd lied, and get over it, or never speak to her again. Demi nervously smiled her way but Sasha met Poppy's glance with her own fire. Anne just smiled jovially, as if this happened every day of the week. She signalled to Chris to bring the drinks over. Poppy dodged round some chairs and said hello to a couple of regulars, who had obviously heard everything over the grapevine as they barely replied. Poppy sighed and grabbed two coffees from Chris, sitting down and handing one to Anne. Sasha noted the move and reached out for her own order.

'So,' said Anne, over-brightly. 'Let's try and be grownups and talk this thing through. The fighting has gone on long enough and quite honestly, my son behaves better than you lot.'

'It's her fault for lying to us for half of her life!' snarled Sasha.

Poppy looked round the table at them all. 'Look, I know I've been an idiot and I'm sorry. I didn't mean to keep the other side of my life from you, but I didn't think you'd approve.' She rubbed her tired eyes. Her mum's health was getting better, but June still wouldn't hear of coming home just yet. It was driving Poppy nuts. She would talk about it and then make up an excuse not to do it. Work was so busy, and then there was Dylan… she was exhausted.

Anne gave Sasha a warning glare and took Poppy's hand. She rubbed some warmth into it. 'How is your mum?'

Poppy looked around warily, but then her shoulders slumped and the fight left her. It was too tiring to try and keep up a pretence that everything was fine. Everyone probably thought she led a charmed life, but that was about to change. If they wanted the truth, they could have it all. 'She's not great. She sees the care home as her real home. She doesn't have any responsibilities and refuses to come back to the flat, even though she gets my hopes up by saying she will all the time. She still hasn't even seen it, though I've slogged my guts out making it beautiful for her. She could even move in with me. But she just stays put.'

'You told her about your hot new boyfriend, yet' Sasha sniped, then yelped as Anne kicked her under the table.

Poppy bit her lip and clashed eyes with her friends. 'She knows I'm dating Dylan, but she never asks me about it. Deep chats make her anxious. She keeps everything surface

MY PERFECT EX

level.' Poppy hung her head. 'It's my fault she's like that, anyway.'

'What? Don't be daft,' said Anne. 'How can it be your fault?'

'She didn't have mental health issues until I was born. She was fine before that.'

'How do you know that?' asked Sasha, her tone softening slightly.

Poppy frowned and started fiddling with a napkin on the table. 'Uh... I don't know. It's just something that's always gone unsaid. Dad left and she had to bring me up on her own. It was a huge responsibility and it must have been too much for her.'

'So her choice of having a baby, one she clearly loved and still loves with all her heart, was the reason she needed help from those strangers that we used to see turn up at your flat?' said Sasha.

'Sasha!' It was Demi this time. Poppy and Anne looked on aghast.

Sasha had the grace to blush. 'You know what I mean,' she sulked. 'Your mum dotes on you. None of us even knew you had a problem. We just thought you were broke and couldn't afford to have us round for tea and that maybe your mum had weird friends, as they seemed a bit shifty. Now we know they were being discreet. Your mum was happy when we did pop round – and you hid the situation well.'

'I think what you mean is that Poppy was scared of being taken away from her mum, and became the parent, Sasha!' said Anne, a warning tone in her voice.

Sasha's mouth formed a thin line and Poppy could see she and Demi were thinking back, recalling all the moments when Poppy might have been shielding her mother. Demi's eyes dropped to the table and a tear slid from her eye. 'I'm sorry that you felt you had to hide it from us, Poppy. We might have been able to help you.' She pushed her chair back and went to go and give Poppy a hug from behind. She rested her cheek on Poppy's head and Poppy sank into her embrace, tears springing to her own eyes. She'd had to be strong for so long, it was weird for another person to be offering support. She raised her head to see Sasha's eyes glistening too. Then Sasha kicked her under the table and Poppy yelped and sat up, almost braining Demi, who jumped back.

'That's for not trusting us with your secret.'

Poppy leaned forward and rubbed her sore leg. 'Ow.'

'You deserved it. Now, drink your coffee and eat something. You look scrawny.' Sasha signalled to Chris to bring over a plate of sandwiches. Then she took Poppy's hand and pulled her closer for a hug. Poppy hesitated for a second, then let herself slide sideways until she was almost sitting on Sasha's lap! Anne smiled in satisfaction and Demi pushed her hair from her face and grinned her sweet smile, before grabbing the first sandwich as the plate was put in front of them. She handed it to Poppy.

Poppy took the peace offering and finally managed to draw some air into her lungs and sit back in her own chair. 'I'm working on a big project and haven't had much time to eat,' she admitted, cramming the bread, cheese and crisp lettuce into her mouth and sighing in bliss.

'Hasn't Dylan been stuffing you?' asked Sasha drolly. They all burst out laughing, making Poppy's skin tinge red. She wiped her mouth and giggled too. 'I've got no complaints there.' They all sniggered and wanted to know more.

'Look, it's about time you met up with him again, seeing as we are all from this area.'

'I often see Dylan visiting his mum and stop to say hello,' said Sasha, and Poppy held her breath. 'He's never mentioned you, which I now find very strange if he's your boyfriend.

How long have you been dating officially?' Sasha arched an eyebrow and Poppy knew she meant business.

'Like I told you before, we've been seeing each other for around six months, although we've never talked about it being official. It just feels that way.' Poppy wondered is Sasha was trying to catch her out in more lies, but she was done with that.

'So you might just be his bit on the side?'

'Sasha!' It was Demi's turn to be indignant. 'I'm sure it's not like that, if they're dating.'

'She just said it wasn't official,' protested Sasha. 'Have you ever been to his house?'

'Which one?' said Poppy defiantly. 'He's got a flat, and still visits his parents' home often. 'I've met his mum.'

'Here in town?'

Poppy paused. 'Occasionally, yes.'

'So you've been in town and not told us that, too?' Sasha's face was taking on that puce hue again.

'Yes. I'm sorry. Dylan used to have such a reputation. You were always warning me away from him. He wanted to tell you. I asked him not to and it was a point of contention.'

'But you were still drawn to him like a magnet,' said Sasha scornfully.

'I thought you liked Dylan,' said Poppy, through gritted teeth.

'I do. He's a playboy, though. He's always had loads of girlfriends.'

Poppy gave her a furious stare and Sasha finally looked away. 'This is why I didn't tell you,' said Poppy, as she slammed her coffee mug back on the table and made them all jump.

'Look,' said Anne, 'let's all calm down and stop being complete cows.' She looked pointedly at Sasha who frowned and bit into a sandwich. 'Poppy is sorry she lied to us for so long and we are starting to understand her reasons. We might not like them, but she felt they were valid at the time.'

Sasha was still staring at Poppy. Poppy's shoulders drooped in exhaustion. She was fed up with arguing. She nibbled at the edge of a tuna sandwich and then placed it on her plate, taking a big glug of now-cool coffee and wishing her brain wasn't so full of stress these days. Thinking about it, most of her life had been like that. She tried not to glance at her watch. She knew she should really be in her office, sourcing materials for the interactive panels she was having made for Jared. Although Dylan had been mad at her for working so hard, he was smiling more and things were almost back on track. She needed to try harder to let him know how important he was to her, and how sorry she was for neglecting him.

'Why don't you all come round to my place for dinner? I'll cook something nice and you can properly meet Billy and Dylan… again.'

'We don't like any of that fancy food, where there's barely anything on the plate,' said Sasha, but Poppy's spirits lifted, as this meant she was coming. Anne tutted, but asked, 'How long does it take to get there?' Poppy knew she didn't like to be too far from Freddie.

'It's about an hour's drive in good traffic. Bring Freddie, he can play in the garden and eat with us. If he gets tired, you can both sleep in the spare room.' Sasha opened her mouth to speak, but a stern glance from Anne stopped her and she picked up her coffee and then grimaced when the cool liquid hit her mouth. Poppy grinned and got up to order them all another round of coffees and hot chocolates, earning a swift hug from Chris and a free cream cake.

'What's that for?' she asked.

'For being brave and facing your fears at last.' He winked and turned to go back into the kitchen. Poppy wasn't as shocked as she thought she'd be. Chris was the eyes and ears of the community and she'd been a fool to think she could keep anything from him. He'd looked out for her for years. She loved him even more now. She blew a kiss to his retreating back and waited for the cries of fury when she returned to the table with only one cake. She stuffed the whole thing into her mouth quickly and almost went cross-eyed in sugary bliss.

CHAPTER EIGHTEEN

Poppy stepped out onto the patio area directly behind her house and took in the stunning view. She'd carefully planted the whole garden so that there were spaces to stretch, relax, excite and calm. She wandered over the big expanse of lawn that led to the back brick wall and ran her hand over the petals of the climbing roses, filing the air with their scent. There was a sweetheart bench and an arbour with more roses trailing lazily over it. Her heart always soared at the sight of it after a long day at work.

She was starting to feel the pressure of such a big project, as she still had other clients to keep happy, but she was full of exhilaration too. Her new office space on Cherry Blossom Lane went a long way to helping her focus, as it was a pleasure to walk in to every day and she loved drawing up plans on her desk, with the huge windows open to the fields beyond. Jared was inspiring and dedicated and his team of builders was working steadily on the plot of land behind her house. The warehouses had been renovated and ten executive homes were going up, a fair way towards being done. The shells were complete and the insides were being put in place gradually. The noise often reached her, but it was worth it. She hadn't liked not having neighbours close by, as she was used to seeing people around. She'd bought her plot long before the area had become trendy, and hers had been the biggest house around. Gradually new-build places were going up and it was becoming more sought-after. Jared had spotted the trend not long before he contacted her, and had bought up much of the farmland that was left.

She'd been surprised when he'd first got in touch, as she'd only worked on individual homes and projects to that point, but now she knew him better, she realised that he was usually ahead of the game. He had a knack of seeing potential. She couldn't wait to see the houses with her work inside. She'd also love seeing happy faces coming in and out of the buildings, if her designs did their job. She would have to stop herself from popping around too often after they were built to see the transformation, or the new residents might think she was obsessed. Not a good first impression to make on your new neighbours. She didn't even mind the dust and chatter from the workers. It was nice, after having lived alone for so long, apart from Billy of course. He was noisier than a horde of people. She'd heard from Jared that one of the industrial units had been snapped up already, by a popular local ceramicist. Perhaps it would become the hub of a creative community that she herself could be part of.

She bit her lip and headed for the small water feature she'd had made to the right of her garden. She'd built a low bench that was planted with ivy at each end. She watched the colourful fish dart about in the pond and listened to the sound of the fountain splashing, easing her tired mind. She hoped Dylan would come round that evening, and that Billy would stay in his flat. She and Dylan needed quality time together. Although she knew Dylan was never that busy, he was being stubborn and making her wait to see him. He was still communicating with her, but there was an underlying message she didn't understand. Something was definitely wrong.

She smiled when Dylan walked into the garden. She'd given him a key ages ago, but he rarely used it nowadays, which made her heart hurt. She got up as he approached and she could see how tired he looked. His hair was messier than usual and he was frowning, which also seemed to happen a lot these days. She reached out for his hand and pulled his body towards hers. She sighed at the contact and rested her head on his chest. She was a tall woman, but he still towered over her. She linked her hands behind him and slipped her fingers under his shirt, loving the feel of the warm skin on his back. Dylan froze for a second, but she felt it, dropped her hands and looked up at him. He was gazing at the structures behind the wall. 'I didn't realise you would be able to see so much from here. Don't you find it obtrusive, after having privacy?'

She stepped back from him, but scooped his hand into hers and kissed it. 'I like it. It can get lonely here sometimes and I enjoy having neighbours. You can only really see the top floor of the main warehouse when you're upstairs in my house. Otherwise they are so far away you just see the rooftops. The workspaces are gorgeous and although the houses don't have big gardens, they are going to be beautifully landscaped, like this one. It's all part of the Poppy Marlowe Mood scheme.'

Dylan looked at their entwined hands and pulled her closer, to tuck her under his arm. Her heart was beating fiercely and she wasn't quite sure how to behave. It was crushing. He was the love of her life and she felt like she was losing him. 'Do you want to take a look? I'm allowed on site and I'd like to show you.'

He didn't pause this time. 'I'd love to.' He dropped his arm and reached for her hand. She grinned up at him, before pushing up onto her tiptoes to plant a kiss on his lips. He growled and pulled her to him and plundered her mouth until she thought she might faint in sheer bliss. She was pliable in his arms and he had to support her when he pulled away. 'I've missed you,' he said huskily.

'Me too,' she smiled with swollen lips and sparkling eyes. 'So much. Can we not fight again? I hate it.'

'Me too,' he grinned, giving her another swift kiss and sweeping his palm around to cup her backside. They walked amiably to the side gate and around to the building plot. They were given hard hats by the foreman and she pulled Dylan along excitedly as she pointed out feature after feature of how the houses and office spaces would work with busy lifestyles, or even more quiet ones. The houses would almost breathe new life and vigour into anyone living there. Dylan smiled at her enthusiasm and he seemed to finally understand how much work the project demanded.

'I guess I should have taken more notice of the dedication you have to have, to be involved in a project like this. I've worked on enough sites of my own to know the drill, but I thought you were just supplying your usual sensory panel designs.'

Poppy pouted. *Just!* 'I told you I was their mental health advisor. I've designed panels, lighting, moved walls, integrated my technology and had consultations with the garden landscaper. The homes have indoor gardens to bring light and oxygen into the houses. These will be a JW build, in conjunction with Poppy Marlowe homes. My brand is on them.'

At the mention of Jared's firm Dylan asked a question. 'Why did Jared choose this particular plot? Surely there are lots more, in busier locations?' Before she could answer, he continued his train of thought. 'Why did he keep the barns? Aren't they a bit industrial?'

Poppy wanted to stamp her foot, and could feel her hackles rising. 'Not all businesses want a busy location. Some need a peaceful environment to shine. We're hoping those units are bought by artisans, like you. People who thrive with beautiful scenery to gaze at and who like to be part of a community.' Her breath hissed from her mouth. This man drove her nuts! 'The whole point of a wellbeing house or office, is it's in a quieter location. Here you have views of the hills beyond. Every point of the house reflects mental health. It's built to ease the mind, not fill it with noise and distraction.' She sighed and closed her eyes for a moment. 'It's why I built on my own plot and the reason that I bought my offices in Cherry Blossom Lane,' she said, looking up at him. 'If I'd had the money, I'd have bought more land. Jared saw the possibility too. It's why I suggested you work with him. You could have been a major contractor in the build if you'd pitched to him. Your work is already so well respected in the building trade.'

'I have enough work of my own, Poppy,' he frowned. 'I don't need handouts from your friend Jared.' Dylan moved away from her and went to speak to one of the builders that he'd worked with before. They shook hands and started talking.

Poppy wanted to storm off. Why couldn't he see potential, like Jared had? She'd literally handed the contract to him, but he'd thought it beneath him to even try. A deal like this could have set him up for life and made contacts that would otherwise take years to find. Jared was on his way up and Poppy was by his side. She wasn't going to miss a golden opportunity like this for a grumpy man with ego issues.

CHAPTER NINETEEN

'Why are you so jittery?' asked Dylan, wrapping his arms around her and kissing her. 'They won't bite,' he joked about the impending visit from her old school friends.

They'd talked long into the night the evening before and made up with hot and steamy sex, but she still couldn't quite relax. Was she supposed to be happy, that her boyfriend had forgiven her for working too hard on a business she had built from the ground up?

She tried to push the catty thoughts away, but her claws were still out. Dylan hadn't complained when she'd trailed her nails across his back last night – but he'd better watch out. She was walking on a tightrope and could fall either way. She plastered on a smile and held back from stamping on his toes for now.

Billy walked in with a bottle of red wine and started uncorking it. 'Sasha will want gin, and Demi only drinks sparkles. I brought some prosecco for her earlier today,' Poppy said, fiddling with the napkins she'd ironed board-straight. She placed them on the table. Dylan and Billy exchanged glances.

'I'm sure they'll be happy with whatever you give them,' soothed Dylan. Both Billy and Poppy shook their heads at his stupidity this time. Billy hadn't met Sasha, but he'd heard enough about her. Dylan should know better. Dylan actually knew them all well, even if he hadn't seen much of them in recent years. He saw them all through rose-tinted glasses and had forgotten how feisty they could all be when they were together.

Poppy jumped as the doorbell chimed. She wiped her sweaty palms on her apron, yanked it over her head and threw it on a hook behind the larder door, before rushing to greet them.

She stood for a moment and took a deep breath, her hand on the handle, then put on a bright smile. Opening the door to the expectant faces of her three best friends, and gorgeous little Freddie, she couldn't help but unfurl a real smile. She really did love this lot. She welcomed them in and they all stood gazing around in awe at her opulent home.

'Wow, Poppy!' said Anne with something Poppy couldn't identify in her voice. Freddie bowled in and hugged Poppy's legs and she bent down to hug him back. This was what she needed. Love just emanated from her effortlessly when Freddie was around. She wondered how she could love someone who wasn't her own child so much, but she did. She knew lots of people found this, it wasn't unusual, but her only experience was with Freddie. He was her world. His mum was too. It made Poppy choke up a bit and a tear sprang to her eye which she quickly dashed away before anyone saw.

She'd been an idiot to keep them away. Of course they wouldn't disparage her relationship. They actually seemed really happy for her. She could have kicked herself for wasting so much time. She picked Freddie up with a theatrical 'Ooof...' and carried the giggling boy over her shoulder into the kitchen. The whole party trailed behind her, glancing round and taking in every detail.

'It's beautiful, Poppy,' said Sasha and Poppy grinned and pulled her into a hug until Freddie squealed he was being squashed, and she put him down. She pointed out the garden, which he ran off to through the open sliding windows. The welcoming scent of roses was already wafting into the room.

The women followed Poppy and chatted animatedly, until they saw Dylan and Billy sitting on the couch in the lounge. Everyone fell silent. Dylan hoisted himself up with a big grin on his face and walked over to pull the women into a fast hug, which made them blush and slap his arm for keeping his big news from them. They were all girly and giggly, especially Anne and Demi, while Sasha stayed a little behind, but she was smiling too. Poppy's shoulders relaxed and she called for Billy to join them. She introduced everyone to her assistant, while he joked about being her actual boyfriend.

Poppy offered them all a glass of wine and Billy took the bottle from her shaking hand and scooted her outside, so that her friends could admire the garden. They were all laughing at something Dylan was saying. 'It's ok,' said Billy, kissing the top of her head. 'Dylan is charming them all and they love you and the house. Do you want me to do the cooking, so that you can relax?'

'No!' said Poppy forcefully and then regretted it instantly. 'You need to schmooze them as if they were our most precious clients. Get them drunk and they might forget what an idiot I've been.'

'Who's driving?'

'Anne. I invited them to stay, but she's the designated driver. She won't drink even one glass with Freddie in the car, so I've bought loads of fizzy non-alcoholic stuff for her.

Get the others as pissed as you can.' She watched Sasha throw her head back and laugh at something Dylan said, and finally felt the rest of the tension leave her body. 'I can do this,' she chanted under her breath.

Sasha looked her way as Poppy joined them and pulled her into her arms for a hug, surprising everyone. 'No wonder you love it here. It's stunning, Poppy. Did you really design all this on your own? You're so clever!'

Poppy's eyes sparkled at Dylan, who grinned her way. 'I designed elements of it. It's a Poppy Marlowe Mood Home,' she explained. 'Every aspect of the house is supposed to breathe life back into a weary mind and support your mental health.' She held her breath for the questions about her mum.

'So it's like a house that makes your day better,' said Freddie innocently and they all laughed.

'That's exactly it, Freddie!' She scooped him up and he wound his thin arms around her neck and snuggled in. 'The house is designed with lighting to make you feel better, sounds to soothe a tired mind and scents to uplift your spirits.'

'Couldn't you just have a shag?' asked Sasha and then she shoved her hand over her mouth when Freddie bust into giggles, as Poppy placed his feet back on solid ground.

'Sasha!' admonished Anne, but she was trying not to laugh too.

Poppy smiled, but it didn't quite reach her eyes. Dylan slipped his hand into hers and gave it a squeeze and she took a deep breath and held her head high. 'I guess that could work too.'

Billy called them all to the outdoor table, in the centre of which sat a fat vase with delicate fragrant roses draping out of it, in hues of wine red and lipstick pink. He placed the drinks in the centre and began handing out glasses until everyone, including Freddie, had a glass. 'To Poppy and her incredible creations.' Everyone raised their glasses and drank before Freddie announced he was starving. Dylan asked him to help fire up the barbeque. Freddie squealed in delight and ran around in circles, making them all laugh. As Billy went to find the salads Poppy had prepared earlier, they all sat around the table.

'Well, this is a bit different from Chris' café,' said Demi. 'No wonder you love it here.'

'I adore Chris, and the café too, but I had to follow my dreams,' said Poppy.

'Well, it looks like it's worked out for you. This place is amazing,' said Sasha, taking in the double doors and the veranda upstairs, leading off the master suite.

'Thanks, Sasha. That means a lot.' Poppy raised her glass to her friend, but noticed that Sasha's attention had already turned to Billy, Freddie and Dylan, who were busy burning the sausages.

'Would you like a tour of the house while they decimate our lunch?' Poppy asked. The girls all jumped up in excitement, then waited while Anne put a hat on Freddie's head and rubbed in a little sun cream. He wriggled away from her and shushed her for disturbing men's talk. Anne chuckled. 'I think Freddie and I might move in, and I haven't even seen the rest of the place yet,' she joked.

'If you're moving in, then I'm coming with you,' said Demi, and Sasha readily agreed.

'You are all welcome to stay over whenever you like,' said Poppy, realising that she meant it. She slipped her arm around Demi's waist as they climbed the stairs. Before she could tell them about anything, they had all rushed to different doors and were pushing them open and exclaiming about how beautiful her house was and how clever she was. They wanted to try out all the gadgets and hear about each design.

Poppy's heart swelled with pride as she explained her work and what it could mean for future generations. She noticed even Sasha picking things up and examining them carefully. It made her wish she'd invited them round earlier. They hadn't put her relationship down or said that she was wasting her time with her dreams, or her new man. They'd congratulated her, and finally seemed to understand her a whole lot better.

Perhaps her life would have been easier all this time if she hadn't carried her burdens alone. She had dreaded her secret about her mother's ill health coming out, but if her friends had confided in their own families, perhaps one of their parents would have stepped in and offered help, not social services. She'd been too scared to think straight. She thought back to the frightened child she'd been for so long and finally decided to let her go. The memory was not a good one and she'd carried the fear around for too long.

Poppy was a strong and independent woman now, and she could rely on herself before anyone else, but she was learning that it was ok to ask for help or support when she needed it. Her friends would be there for her. They'd proven that. Even if the journey had been a bit bumpy. She could rely on them, she hoped.

CHAPTER TWENTY

A few weeks had passed since the lunch date, and Poppy's schedule was becoming crowded. She adored her work though, so each new meeting left her fizzing with excitement. She sometimes sat in her beautiful office, looking out across the fields beyond and wondered how she'd got so lucky. Billy came in with boxes of her notes, all neatly filed, and handed her a USB stick with everything she needed for her next meeting with Jared.

Jared had popped into the house a few times now, while visiting the construction site, and had met Dylan. The houses were shaping up fast as he had so many contractors working on them. He'd invited Dylan for a tour, not realising he'd already had a look. Jared asked about Dylan's own work, and Dylan dodged the questions as much as possible. He was still happy roaming through life at his own pace, which made Poppy clench her jaw. He was quite content with living at his flat, working when he needed to and visiting his mates and parents. She sometimes caught herself wishing he was more driven, like Jared.

Poppy blew Billy a kiss when he announced he was going

out to get coffee. Then he added that he might stick his head into Verity's shop to see if he could pick Poppy up some clothes, as she was looking messy. She stuck her tongue out at him. 'Give Verity my love. I promise I'll be a better friend as soon as this project is finished.'

'She'll probably say 'Poppy who?'' he joked, sticking his tongue out at her too and then grinning.

'You're such a child,' she sniggered.

'You started it. You're so unprofessional.'

Poppy laughed. 'Have you heard from Ed lately?' she called after his retreating back. But Billy pretended not to hear. She sighed and rubbed her eyes. She'd spoken to Ed a few times herself and, although he was enjoying himself abroad, he talked endlessly about Billy. She had told him to call, and wondered if he had. Billy had been cleaning obsessively lately, which was out of character. She needed to take some time off and check on everyone in her life. Looking at her watch, she made a swift decision. She typed out a text to tell Billy she was going out and then another to Anne, to say that she could make lunch after all. She'd missed the last two, so felt galvanised by her decision today.

Billy's reply said *What the hell?* but Anne's response had loads of smiley faces and kisses, and made her move faster. If Billy got back first he'd rip into her. They had so much to do before their part in the building project was complete. It would only be a few more weeks, though, and then she could step back and sign off everything at their end.

Word had got out about her collaboration with Jared and her phone rang incessantly, until she'd handed all calls to Billy and let him sort them out. They desperately needed another staff member and it was top of their list to organise soon. She grabbed the bag at her feet, noticing for the first time that it was looking a bit worn out. Billy was right. She needed to shape up if she was going to compete for clients with the big boys and girls – if she wasn't careful she would burn herself out. She stopped for a moment to stare at the stunning view across the fields behind her desk. It never failed to restore her spirits. She thought of her mum and how June had mentioned visiting the flat again, before finally pouring her heart out. She said it was all she'd dreamt of for years, but now the moment was almost here, she was scared. That was one of what seemed like many boulders weighing down Poppy's shoulders.

She needed to shrug those mental rocks off, and stand tall. 'I'm a strong woman, I can do this,' she chanted over and over – before bowling headfirst into Billy, who was holding two takeaway cups of coffee.

She yelped and he jumped back, holding the cups up high. He was wearing a beautifully tailored waistcoat and a dark shirt which made him swoon-worthily handsome. His trouser choice, skinny jeans that looked like they had splashes of paint all over the ankles, were typical Billy.

'What are you doing?' he demanded. 'Have you gone mad…?' he trailed off and winced. 'Sorry.'

She rolled her eyes and stood facing him. 'You can mention the words 'mental' and 'mad' around me, you know.' This came out a little harshly and she suddenly wanted to kick something, preferably Billy. 'My brain's tired. I need a rest and the girls are having lunch together today. I've already let them down twice.'

'The girls understand… kind of.' Billy was still looking at her warily and knew her well enough to put some distance between them. 'Plus you *are* mad for taking time off now, but I agree you need it. The bags under your eyes are so big that they look like they're full of shopping,' he joked.

'They don't really understand about my not turning up,' Poppy said, exhaustion clear in her voice. 'They say they do, but I can hear the undertones in their conversation. They feel I've let them down again.'

'I'm coming with you,' said Billy, handing her the coffee.

Poppy smiled at last and took a sip of the peace offering coffee, eyes going wide at the amount of caramel he'd added. 'You needed some sugar, for energy.'

He also handed her a bag of wonky fruit and she placed it on her desk. They always joked about saving the wonky fruit and vegetables that no one else wanted, in this world where everyone searched for perfection.

'I'd love you to come with me, but one of us needs to be here, and you've got to reorganise our diary to fit in two new meetings with Jared,' Poppy said.

'What? How?' Billy ran his spare hand through his hair and succeeded in making it stand on end.

'Look,' she placated. 'I know you're exhausted too. How about I promote you and we also make headway into putting together an advert for that new staff member?'

Billy's eyes narrowed. 'Promote me to what? I already do everything you don't do.'

'I don't know. Come up with a title you'd like and I'll think about it.' When he was about to speak, Poppy interrupted him, glancing at her watch again and pushing past him. 'Except I'm not calling you my mentor, or inspirational muse. I've already told you that!' She laughed and headed for the door, trying to shake off her guilt at the thought that he needed a rest too.

As she reached her car, she paused and sent him a text, promising to pay for him to visit Ed after the project was finished. She smiled at his immediate response, that he'd take the holiday but Ed could go and stuff himself. No joy with them making up anytime soon, then. Billy was clearly still licking his wounds.

Driving towards her old home actually gave Poppy space

to think and clear her head. She'd invite Dylan over for a meal and she'd take the time to cook it. She was going to try to stop being irritated and irritable around him. He deserved better than that. She had managed to carve out some time for him recently – they'd had an amazing weekend together, spending most of it in bed. He had joked, though, that she only wanted him for sex. Not that he was exactly complaining.

She'd promised the project would end soon and she'd take some time off then, but her client list was building. Although the new projects coming up were smaller than this one, she was still buzzing with the excitement of being in demand. She was a hot topic and she couldn't believe how much she was enjoying it, for once. She didn't want to hide behind Billy anymore and she secretly wondered if she was turning into a bit of a diva. She had enjoyed the most recent photoshoot she had done for a magazine with Jared. The staff on set had catered to their every whim throughout, but she noticed a lot of the assistants were drooling at Jared and slipping him their phone numbers.

He had so much excitable energy, and it helped Poppy stop fretting and have fun. In the end they'd chosen a photo of the two of them on a striking blue sofa, leaning over plans for the houses and laughing together. Poppy hadn't realised that his arm was actually behind her and it kind of looked like they were a couple, but they both knew that wasn't the case and she was excited to be photographed with him. He was a hot property and now so was she.

However tiring this project was, she couldn't fault the way it had been run, and she was so grateful for her part in it. If it meant she could build community pods to help others like her mum, then she would feel all of her dreams had come true. She smirked. She knew herself well enough to realise she'd have fresh dreams by then, but she was still proud of achieving so much at her age.

She'd like to rub that in her dad's face, if she ever saw him again. Who was the failure now? He might want to know her if he saw her in a flashy magazine – but in reality he would probably never recognise her as the child he'd abandoned so long ago. She could try to find her dad, she supposed, but what would be the point?

She frowned at her train of thought. She never, ever thought about her father. She'd blocked him out a long time ago, so why was he suddenly in her mind now? 'I must be more tired than I realised,' she mumbled to herself, as she pulled into a parking space behind the flats and waved at Gladys, who was sitting on a bench at the side of the car park. Poppy ran as fast as her aching bones would carry her, gave Gladys a quick hug, then explained that she'd call her later as she was meeting the girls for lunch.

'You aren't eating enough,' said Gladys, looking at Poppy's skinny frame. 'Go and have a proper lunch – and I don't mean drain a cup of coffee in ten minutes and then leave,' she scolded. Poppy promised she'd eat, and rushed away, slinging her bag over her shoulder and weaving her way between the parked cars to the café.

Chris waved as she entered the café and she breathed in the familiar scents of coffee and cake. She was happy to see she was the first one there, for once. They must all be running later than she was, which was unusual, especially for Anne who was anally retentive about punctuality. She was always telling them off and they didn't usually dare be more than a few minutes behind schedule.

Poppy's hair had been softly highlighted recently and she ran her fingers through it and smiled. She eyed a free table and threw her bag on a seat before walking over to Chris and enjoying a warm hug from him and a kiss on the top of her head. She hugged him back and kissed his leathery cheek, noticing he'd recently shaved and that he was wearing aftershave that smelt spicy and warming.

'Chris!' she stepped back and grinned at him. 'Have you got yourself a lady friend? You look and smell amazing,' she teased, prodding him in the shoulder, and taking in the crisply ironed T-shirt he was wearing instead of his usual attire of his favourite scruffy apron. The apron had seen better days, but it had been a gift from Poppy and her mum when Poppy was a teenager. Chris flushed bright red and shushed her towards the table, batting her away with his hands as if the air would carry her and her questions to a distant shore.

She took a step back and her eyes sparkled. 'Ok. I won't ask if you aren't ready to tell yet, but I will be wanting answers, young man.'

She waggled her finger at him and he looked at his feet before raising his head and smiling shyly at her, promising to tell her later. She sat at the table while he started making her coffee order, even though she hadn't actually told him it yet. She wondered what would happen if she asked for something crazy, like an Americano coffee with cinnamon. He'd probably nod his head and make the same thing he'd been giving her for years. She loved that man so much. Chris didn't say a lot, but he was her rock. She'd spent hours and hours in the café, doing her homework after school, and he'd always made sure she was fed and watered without comment. She'd repaid him recently, though. She'd bought a food van for him that Terry, Chris's delivery guy and kitchen hand, used for his rounds. She'd got it from Demi's dad's garage. It was shiny and drove like a dream, apparently. Chris hadn't wanted to accept it from her, but she'd implored him to understand how much what he'd done for her as a child meant. It had been the fine line between survival and the destruction of her family.

Gladys and Chris had become her surrogate parental figures and between them, they'd shielded her secret, and protected her.

CHAPTER TWENTY-ONE

Sasha burst through the café door with a flurry of noise – and big hair. Poppy smothered a laugh. 'Wow, that's a... new look,' she said. Sasha's locks were huge, frizzy and fierce, like she'd been swept into a tornado which, when Poppy thought about it, quite suited her snarky personality.

Sasha waved to Chris, then she did a double-take. 'Is Chris going on a date, or meeting the tax man?' she whispered as she sat down.

Poppy burst out laughing. 'That's what I asked. He's not sharing, though.' Changing the subject before Sasha demanded answers from their host, she pointed to Sasha's hair. 'Seriously. Is that a fashion trend I don't know about?'

Sasha grinned. 'I've got a new job.'

'Exciting!' Poppy clapped her hands in glee and kissed Sasha's cheek. 'You do look like you've just stepped out of a wind tunnel, though,' teased Poppy.

Sasha pulled a face as Demi opened the door and looked around for them. Sasha ignored Demi's open-mouthed look and pushed a chair out for her as Chris placed their coffees and hot chocolates on the table. Even he raised an eyebrow at Sasha's new hairdo, though he didn't comment.

'She's got a new job,' Poppy told Demi, leaning in and kissing her cheek too. Demi always looked beautiful and perfectly made up, the subtle tones and highlighters she used contrasting all the more with Sasha.

'Wha…'

'Don't,' Sasha held her hand up to stop the conversation as Poppy giggled into her mug of froth. 'I'm a model.'

Demi almost choked on her hot chocolate and Sasha happily whacked her back to help her cough it up, making her eyes water.

'Um… a model for what, exactly?' Poppy really was curious now. Sasha was stunning and curvaceous, with her Italian heritage and piercing green eyes, but she'd never once talked about modelling and she currently looked as though she had been dragged through a hedge backwards.

Sasha took a fortifying sip of her drink. 'There's a new hot guy at the gym and his little sister wants to be a stylist. She's quite good, or so he said. He told me I looked beautiful, and said his sister needed models to fill her portfolio.'

'And you fell for that?' Poppy and Demi laughed so hard that Sasha bunched her fists. 'Seriously though, do you need to borrow a hairbrush?' Demi asked.

Sasha rooted round in her bag, but Poppy was ahead of her and opened her palm to offer a scrunchie, which Sasha promptly tamed her hair with. They all sighed in relief. 'Is it that bad? The stylist girl only had a tiny mirror and I had to rush here as I was running late.'

Demi bit her lip, but only succeeded in making herself look more pouty. Poppy just grimaced.

'The kid needed a break.' Sasha shrugged.

'A break from her career ideas,' Demi giggled.

Sasha finally stood up and checked herself out in the

mirror that always hung behind the heaving food counter. Her shoulders drooped. Her make-up was dark and moody and her hair was already escaping the hairband. Without a word, Demi reached into her own bag and handed Sasha a make-up wipe. Poppy tried not to say anything else, but it was so tempting.

'The lesson here is not to do favours for hot men, to get a date,' grinned Demi, moving swiftly away before she got a slap. Seeing Sasha's face, Demi burst out laughing, making a few people turn their way as, for such a gorgeous girl, she had quite a high-pitched laugh at times. 'You didn't even get the date, did you?'

'I haven't seen him yet,' grumbled Sasha.

'Good job, maybe,' smirked Demi. 'Where's Anne, by the way? She shouts at us if we're ever late.'

Anne had just got back from America with Freddie and they were all dying to hear about how the treatment had gone. At that moment, she walked in and saw them. Anne noted Sasha's big hair, but didn't comment. She hugged them all. Chris put a plate of sandwiches in front of them that Terry had just made in the kitchen and they all grabbed one and sighed in bliss. Terry was the master of a good sandwich, and Chris baked cakes that made your mouth water just by looking at them. It was what kept the locals coming back and meant the café always busy. Simple, tasty food, honestly prepared.

Everyone looked expectantly at Anne and she caved quite quickly. 'Sorry I'm late.' Anne's dark hair was swept off her face with a sparkly clip, which was unlike her, and she was wearing mascara. Her face was slightly tanned and she was wearing a simple summer dress.

Poppy touched her arm, looking at Anne's luminous face. She seemed younger and brighter somehow. 'Was the trip a success?'

Anne's eyes shone and she smiled, taking Demi's hand. 'It was!' She was fidgety and she blew a kiss to Chris, who started setting out more cups for coffee. 'Not only does America have the sexiest doctors on the planet, but they've set up a new care plan for Freddie.'

She took the steaming coffee from Chris and he patted her shoulder happily. He'd obviously already heard the news. Poppy had been updated daily at first, but by the second week, the calls had dwindled and she'd worried incessantly. A text a few days ago to say things were progressing had meant she could relax a bit. 'He's been accepted onto the treatment trials and they are really happy with him.'

Poppy got up and hugged Anne. 'That's great news! Why didn't you call us?'

'I wanted to tell you in person. I thought they'd say no, as we don't live there, but Freddie's condition is quite rare and they are happy for us to continue the programme from home now they've seen him. He passed all their tests, he didn't complain once, and we even managed to sneak in a short visit to Disneyland! The charity money paid for it all,' she looked pointedly at Poppy who suddenly found a speck of dust on the table incredibly interesting. 'It's been a whirlwind,' continued Anne, 'and not the one Sasha's obviously been through.' She eyed her friend, then ducked as Sasha threw a sugar sachet at her head.

'That's incredible,' said Demi.

'It's thanks to all of you, and your hard work for the charity. They think Freddie could live for years on this medication. He could almost live a normal life, whatever that is. He could become an adult and have his own family, if they keep discovering new ways to treat his condition.' Tears were forming in all of their eyes. 'Even Connor's been round to visit.' They all raised their eyebrows but said nothing about Connor. It was a difficult subject to broach as Anne always took whatever they said about his involvement in Freddie's life the wrong way.

'Let's celebrate!' said Sasha loudly, and she pulled a hip flask out of her bag and sloshed a nip of vodka into their drinks.

Poppy eyed the hip flask and frowned, but picked up her drink and sipped it anyway. No one else had commented, so perhaps it was usual for Sasha to have drink stashed in her handbag these days.

'So they really can help Freddie?' Poppy felt like she'd been holding her breath for ages, and was finally able to let it out. She pictured his sunny face and bright dark eyes and smiled.

Anne squeezed her hand. 'They can. He's been taking the medication for two weeks and already I can see positive change. The doctor I spoke to said they might bring the service to the UK, one day. We can visit our usual doctor in between trips. The trials for this drug have been incredible so far.'

'You're taking a chance, though,' said Sasha, suddenly sombre. Poppy knew she adored her godson too.

Anne's face fell and her eyes glistened. She slugged back her alcoholic coffee. 'It's the only choice I have. There's nothing as advanced here. Freddie gets exhausted so easily at the moment, but this could be life-changing. The kids I saw in the states were living their lives to the full. I want that for my son.'

'We know you do.' Poppy reached her arm around Anne's shoulders. 'Now, tell us more about these hot doctors, and where we can get one?'

They all smiled, but Sasha's eyes narrowed. 'You don't need another man, with all the sexy totty in your house. Can we move in?'

Poppy's smile slipped from her face, but she tried to bring it back. It didn't quite meet her eyes. 'You'd soon get bored.'

'Billy's gorgeous,' said Anne, steering the conversation away from Sasha and Dylan, which was dangerous territory. 'Shame he's not interested in women,' she giggled and flicked her hair. 'So he probably fancies Dylan and not Poppy,' she cackled, slapping the table in mirth and making them all jump.

'He doesn't fancy either of us,' defended Poppy. 'We're his friends. I don't drool after every man I meet.'

'You fancy Dylan, and he was our friend for years before you hooked up with him,' pointed out Demi.

'I don't think Poppy's thoughts about Dylan have ever been that friendly,' joked Anne. 'She always wanted to rip his clothes off with her teeth, even when we were teenagers. She just never got her chance.'

Poppy spluttered on her coffee, but did giggle this time, until she caught Anne raising an eyebrow at Sasha, who stuck her tongue out at her.

'I'm not sure you're the best match ever, but he'd make the perfect ex. It would be like a taste of forbidden fruit. Delicious but deadly. He's great as a friend, but not a partner.' Sasha screwed up her nose and threw the comment onto the table and left everyone mute for a second – before Poppy exploded.

'What? Why the hell not? He's kind, fit, supportive and sexy as hell.'

Sasha took her hand to placate her. The other women were looking shiftily into their coffees as if this was something they had discussed without her. 'You are an amazing woman whose business is going to make her famous, we now know.' Sasha warmed to her theme while Poppy fumed inside. 'But Dylan's a bit of a laid-back guy where work is concerned, to be honest,' she continued, her words like daggers in Poppy's side. 'He's always seemed more like me, someone who works to make money to survive and party. He doesn't want to build an empire or a pension fit for the queen and her mum.'

Sasha looked into Poppy's eyes and refused to back down. 'We all love Dylan, but is he really the right man for a go-getter like you? He'll drain you dry and become a layabout, while you're out working all day. He'll probably end up staying home with the kids and become eye candy for the school mums.'

'What's wrong with that? Loads of men stay with their kids, or work from home!' Poppy's hackles rose. It was mainly because Sasha had hit a nerve, but also because they were slagging off the love of her life. She pictured Dylan's sparkling eyes and sleek muscles for a split second. Her fists bunched in her lap and her eyes were spitting fire. She took a deep breath and tried to calm down. The girls were only looking out for her. She frowned and saw they were anxiously glancing at each other, except for Sasha, who was smiling smugly.

'Dylan's an entrepreneur who works at his own pace. He's the boss, so he can pick and choose jobs. He's very motivated, and he's not a sponger!' Poppy protested.

'That's not what Sasha meant at all,' defended Anne. 'What she means is that Dylan seems quite at home in your place, but we worry what he's actually contributed to it? Who pays when you go out, for instance?'

Poppy frowned. She never thought about who paid for what. It didn't matter. 'I have to fight him to pay for anything. He's a gentleman, but I'm independent. We share things. Anyway, that's none of your business. I don't ask you how you pay for your home or if Allan pays for Demi when they go out. Sasha has so many boyfriends that she's probably forgotten who pays for what!'

'Poppy!' Sasha face was now an angry red and Demi's face was flushed too.

'It's true. I've got a solid relationship and you all want to pick holes in it. It's why I didn't tell you in the first place. No one is ever good enough for you. You all expect a man to pay for everything, have a glittering career while you have yours, give you multiple orgasms every day and still have the energy to treat you like a princess.' Her thoughts flitted to Jared for a moment, but she knew that was dangerous territory. 'That man doesn't exist!' She took a deep breath and saw Chris glancing over at them with a worried expression on his face. He hated for them to argue and was always telling Poppy to keep her friends close, as they were the only family she had – other than her mum, him and Gladys.

'I'm a modern woman and I can take care of myself. I've been doing it since I was a kid! I don't need a man to pay my way.'

'That's not what I meant,' said Sasha fiercely. 'I don't have multiple boyfriends…' she tutted when they all looked dubious and stared them all out calmly. 'What I meant, before you attacked my personality, was that Dylan's not as career-driven as you, Poppy. You need someone with goals and ambitions. Like you have yourself.' She thought for a moment. 'Plus it's unlike you to be bitchy – and that means you're not happy.'

Poppy's shoulders slumped. Chris bustled over with fresh drinks. She'd be peeing every ten minutes at this rate! She sipped the coffee and it took the edge off her raw nerves. It seemed like they might be there for a while, hashing this out. 'I'm sorry for upsetting you. I know you only have a moderate amount of boyfriends,' she joked, winking at Sasha who grinned. 'I guess I got a bit defensive. I want you all to be happy for me. I love Dylan. I always have.'

'That doesn't mean he's the right choice for you, though.

He's lovely, don't get me wrong, and he's very fit, but you need a go-getter,' Sasha was like a dog with a bone. 'Not someone to pay your way, but someone who's as ambitious as you.' Jared's face appeared in Poppy's mind again and her skin warmed up, her cheeks going rosy.

'Look, we all love Dylan,' said Demi. 'He's part of our lives too. We love the fact that he's a chilled-out dude who enjoys his job. We want you to be happy… but he's always been a bit of a player. We're just trying to protect your heart.'

Poppy felt tears spring to her eyes. She had known this would happen. Once her friends realised her profile was growing, they'd expect her to date someone like her. Dylan might not be as career-driven as she was, but he was kind and loving and gorgeous. But now her old doubts came right back and sat firmly in the forefront of her mind, when she'd been avoiding them for months.

Dylan and Poppy were poles apart when it came to ambition and she couldn't deny her growing irritation about his lack of drive. She thought about Jared and then closed her eyes and sighed. Maybe they were right.

CHAPTER TWENTY-TWO

Dylan walked into the kitchen and came up behind Poppy as she was preparing dinner, slipping his hands around her waist, hugging her and kissing her neck. She leaned into him and smiled, before abandoning the cooking and pressing her lips to his, linking her arms behind him and then running her hands over his delectable derriere.

'I've not seen you all week,' she said. 'Have you got a new work contract?'

He wandered over to grab a beer from the fridge and stood looking at her. 'No. I'm still working on the same contracts. My friend Jim asked me to go and look at his site. We spent a few days drinking beer and talking about our businesses. It was a lot of fun.'

Poppy rooted around in her mind for some cautious optimism. She wished she could take some holiday. She was determined to snaffle a few days after the project with Jared was over, although they had now started speaking in earnest about new ideas. She chatted to him almost daily at the moment, and she enjoyed the banter and camaraderie. 'That sounds nice,' she commented. 'Is Jim a possible future work contact?'

Dylan threw up his hands and stalked off to look out of the garden windows. 'Not everything has to be about work, Poppy. Jim's a good friend. You know that. We like spending time together. We relaxed and had fun. *Fun…* you remember what that word means?'

When her face crumpled slightly, he walked back and took her hand. The casserole she'd just made was now simmering in the oven and the kitchen was full of scents that made her stomach growl.

'Have you been missing meals again? You're looking thin,' he said.

Poppy's mouth dropped open. Dylan never said anything bad about the way she looked before. She bit her lip to stop herself from saying she'd been working such long hours. That would just rile him. She gritted her teeth and sniffed. Her eyes were watering. When had everything suddenly become so hard?

'I've been out walking across the hills a lot lately to focus my mind on which direction I want my business to go in next. Maybe I've toned up.'

Dylan scoffed, as they both knew her muscles had always been hard and sleek. She flushed at her lie and wondered why the first thing out of her mouth was an untruth these days. She rolled her neck and fiddled with her earrings, finally taking both out and dropping them into a tiny hand-painted dish on her kitchen counter that matched her favourite one by the front door. Her stomach grumbled again – the air was thick with the scent of roast vegetables and stock. She grabbed an apple from the pretty fruit bowl she'd discovered in an artist's market. It was painted with waves splashing around the sides and there were glimpses of sand. It had made her feel like it had been washed up by the sea and she'd not been able to take her eyes off it. She had artistic splashes of vibrance all over her house, sitting alongside streamlined surfaces and minimal design. Billy often commented on what a contradiction she was, but she just liked simple things that were made well.

She poured herself a glass of chilled white wine from the wine fridge under the counter and sighed as the crisp liquid hit her parched throat. Dylan was moving around the kitchen and making her nervous. He usually slumped down onto the couch and pulled her with him for a cuddle and a searing kiss. 'You ok?' she asked, holding her breath for a moment.

He looked up, but his smile didn't meet his eyes. 'I've barely seen you lately, but you have time to walk in the hills?'

She could have kicked herself for being stupid and saying that. 'I was joking! I just look out of the window and imagine I'm strolling in the fields. If I'd been out there, I'd have called you to join me.' She walked over and took his beer from him, placing both of their drinks on a side table by the window.

'You're too busy to see me now.'

She took his hands and led him to the couch, sitting on his lap and winding her arms around his neck. 'I'm never too busy for you. But I'm dealing with the biggest project of my life, I'm having friendship issues and Mum is recovering from an infection – and she finally wants to come home. It's a lot to deal with.'

Dylan's eyes bored into hers. He was ignoring her pleading and sitting ramrod straight. 'What issues with friends? I thought that was all sorted out.'

Poppy winced. She hadn't told him about the lunch this week, and the way the girls had beaten her down by criticising her life choices, just as she'd known they would. They'd always thought Dylan was a heartbreaker and had warned her off him from an early age, but she thought they'd

MY PERFECT EX

got over that. She'd hoped they would see he had changed, but they were blinkered to his good qualities, it seemed. 'I'm a grown-up and can make my own decisions, but they think some of my choices are wrong,' she said gently, kissing his nose.

His eyebrows shot up and he looked genuinely astounded. 'They still don't like you dating me?'

She unlinked her arms from his neck. She was starting to wish she'd kept her big mouth shut. 'Of course they do! They love you. But they've always meddled in our relationship. It's why we never got together when we were younger.'

'What? I didn't know that.' He got up, dropping her from his lap with a thud, walked away and then turned to face her. 'I thought we were all friends?'

'I know. We *are* friends. It's just that they think you've had a lot of girlfriends and you'll break my heart,' her lip wobbled. She didn't want to cry, but she was fed up with arguing. Dylan ran his hands through his hair distractedly and stormed into the garden before turning and coming back. He looked sexy as hell when he was mad. Her heart skipped a beat and her skin grew hot.

'I dated while we were in school and college. I dated a lot. It's not my fault that girls liked me. I certainly didn't sleep around. For a start, my mum would have killed me!' Poppy smiled sadly but pictured his mum's face when she was cross and could see his point. Dylan's mum had needed to be strong, with three boisterous boys in the house, and often gaggles of excitable girls who wanted to date them all.

'Anne kept me updated about the endless girls you slept with after we left school, so I kept well away after that.'

'What? I did date women, but they were never the person I was really interested in.' He waggled his eyebrows at her. 'Practically everyone in town knew that,' he rolled his eyes at her blatant confusion. 'It was pretty obvious by the way I always brought your name into conversations and asked anyone who would listen about your new business. Gladys told me to 'man up' and ask you out,' he laughed. Poppy's mouth dropped open in horror.

'You can't be serious? Why would Anne and Sasha lie?'

'To keep us apart. The same as they're trying to do now, I guess. You were living somewhere exciting and forging new relationships. Maybe they wanted that for you,' he shrugged. 'Perhaps they thought you'd escaped from small town life and my dastardly clutches.' She could hear the underlying hurt in his words.

Poppy felt tears threaten to spill out, but she refused to let them fall. 'What the hell? They both knew how much I liked you back then.'

Dylan wandered over, his features softening now. 'Back then? How much did you like me?' She swatted his hands away as they were reaching for her backside and she couldn't think straight when he was near.

'A lot. You were all I could think about and the girls knew that.'

Dylan slipped his arms round her waist and pulled her core into contact with his. She tried to lean away as she was so riled up, but her body knew its mate, and had other ideas. Her hands were already creeping up into his hair and her face was inches from his before she realised what she was doing. By then it was too late and their lips met and the world ignited around them. She always felt like this with him.

She groaned and moved her neck to one side so he could kiss his way down while his hands picked her up and placed her on the kitchen counter. Her legs wound around him and she gasped for air. There were too many clothes on them both and Dylan immediately started lifting her top over her head while she reached out for the buttons on his jeans. His mouth came back to hers as they discarded the rest of their clothes and his body slammed into hers as if their lives depended on it. Her body flamed with lust and she called out his name as their slick skin glided together. Their hands reached out to touch each other and she cried in ecstasy as they moved fluidly together until fireworks exploded in her brain.

He carried her to the couch and covered them with a blanket. She awoke, hours later, to find his mouth exploring her body and his hands creating magic of their own. She smiled dozily at him and then gave in to the sensations and trailed her hands around him to have an adventure of their own.

'I hate fighting, but making up is almost worth it,' she murmured, kissing her way up his chest until he caught her hands in his own. His dark eyes gazed into hers and she couldn't help but smile at his mussed-up hair. He looked like he'd just stepped out of a sexy magazine shoot.

'I hate fighting too.' He kissed her, then rolled over and sat up, rubbing his neck where he'd dozed off at a funny angle. He grinned at her wolfishly and his eyes sparkled. 'But I have always liked this part.' He drew the blanket back from her flushed skin and she yelped and grabbed it, even though he'd seen every inch of her many times before. Suddenly she had a flash of courage and she let the blanket fall, so his eyes could feast on her aroused body. His eyes grew big and he pulled her back into his arms, trailing his fingers down her spine, before she giggled and had to push him away.

'I forgot about dinner!' She glanced around and couldn't see her clothes, then she remembered that they'd stripped off in the kitchen and eventually moved into the living room, him picking her up in his arms and carrying her there, her legs still wrapped around him. She pictured the pile of clothes and then heard Billy come into the kitchen, singing off-key. Poppy gasped and hid her face in Dylan's chest, giggling. Billy's tune stopped short when he obviously found the pile of clothes. She could hear him quickly opening cupboards and finding food.

'I turned the oven off,' said Dylan, reaching for a throw from a neat pile by the couch and draping it around himself, before heading for the shower. 'Want to join me?' he asked. She looked longingly at his tanned skin and taut muscles and her mouth went dry, but she shook her head and grabbed another fleecy blanket to wind around her body before padding back into the kitchen to find Billy.

Their other clothes had been placed in a neat pile on the kitchen counter. 'Looks like a hurricane went through here?' Billy said, scooping some casserole onto his plate and shoving it into the microwave, while eyeing her attire.

Poppy ignored his remark. 'Help yourself to dinner.' She said pointedly.

'Well, it didn't look like you two were eating it. Otherwise occupied?' he raised an eyebrow and she grinned and stuck her tongue out. She grabbed a plate and helped herself, leaving plenty for her man. She was ravenous. She quickly pulled on Dylan's T-shirt, which hung down to mid-thigh, and folded the blanket, placing it beside the pile of clothes.

Billy handed her his plate and plonked hers in the microwave instead as Dylan walked in, clad only in a towel and drying his hair with another. Both Poppy and Billy stood in awe. He really was enough to make anyone drool. No wonder Sasha fancied him. Poppy's smile slipped and she remembered what the fight had been about. Who did she believe, though? Had they slept together or not? Anne didn't usually lie to her, but Poppy knew how much Sasha had fancied Dylan and his brothers. She still took every opportunity to 'bump into' him whenever he was visiting his mum. She'd said as much at lunch a few weeks previously. She was always visiting Dylan's brother Ollie at the gym he owned locally too.

Billy was frowning at her, so she smiled and started eating her food. He then sighed dramatically and held his own plate out to Dylan, preparing to fill a third. 'You two worked up an appetite?' he joked. Dylan grinned as he took the casserole, almost losing his towel as he did so.

Poppy threw Dylan's jeans at his head and he caught them with his spare hand, this time really dropping the towel. He turned away to slip them on. Both Billy and Poppy kept staring until Poppy clipped Billy's ear and he stopped. 'I don't even like beefcakes...' muttered Billy. 'I like my men long and lean.'

'You mean skinny and stacked.' Poppy laughed and pictured Ed's sweet face and cute spectacles and then turned to look at Dylan's wide back. He worked outdoors a lot, with his hands, so he'd sculpted muscle onto his body naturally.

It was pitch black outside now. She told the boys she was going to find them a movie to watch, like they'd used to do before her working life became too crazy.

She pictured Sasha and her long talons clawing along Dylan's smooth skin. No, she had to shut the door firmly on that picture. But she would speak to Anne and find out what the hell had been going on.

CHAPTER TWENTY-THREE

It had been a week since the argument and make-up session with Dylan. Poppy hadn't seen him for more than a kiss and a coffee since. She held up some seriously sparkly earrings to her earlobes and decided they were a bit too flashy. She was attending the opening event for the housing and industrial development. They were inviting prospective buyers along to see what they'd created, and would demonstrate how people could live in their homes, or balance work and play. She was fired up with excitement and looked at her watch. She needed to get a move on, or the car would turn up and she wouldn't be ready. Jared was picking her up en route to the glitzy hotel where the event was being hosted. He'd explained the evening could open doors for both of them, so she needed to be ready for any questions thrown at them by potential investors.

If all the plots sold, Jared would be very happy and Poppy would have fulfilled many of her dreams. Poppy Marlowe Mood Homes would be real at last, available to the public and not just in a small way, like her pods. They'd been pieces of a development, but this was on a different scale. Her brand was attached to the outcome and she needed it to be a success.

She picked up the midnight blue silk sheath with a shimmering gold under layer that she was going to wear, just as Billy walked in. His jaw dropped. He hadn't seen her look seriously sexy very often. The dark pool of fabric she was slithering into looked like moonlight glistening on the surface of a pool. She couldn't wear more than a wisp of underwear beneath it. He took everything in, but didn't stare, he just came over and helped her.

'Do you feel up to talking to me about Ed yet?' she asked. She hoped he could hear the hurt in her voice. They'd always confided everything to each other before this.

'Not really,' he said.

She smoothed the dress over her hips and he straightened the hem, stepping back and whistling. Then he met her eyes in the mirror and looked downcast. 'I was so happy with Ed. I though he was my soul mate. I didn't think he'd leave.' His shoulders sagged and his lip wobbled. She reached up and pulled him into a hug, but he didn't stay there for long, commenting about creasing her dress.

'How many people have you loved?' she couldn't help asking.

He grinned, and she thought he was going to say hundreds. 'Only two. They have to be pretty special,' he teased, and winked at her to show she was one of them.

She threw a pillow from the bed at his head. 'I know you love me, you idiot. I love you too. You know that's not what I meant.' Poppy walked over to stand next to him and slipped her hand round his waist to pull their bodies into contact. She laid her head on his shoulder. 'I'm here if you ever do want to talk about it. I'm sorry I interfered and asked Ed to contact you. Did he?'

Billy sighed and moved to look at her. 'You need some

seriously sparkly earrings to offset that pool of deep silk.' He reached out for the flashy earrings she'd tried earlier and insisted she put them on, along with a dazzling crystal bangle she'd bought from Verity's shop. It had layers of beads which shone and reflected light as she moved. 'You really are stunning.'

She accepted the question dodge. Perhaps he'd talk about what had happened with Ed another time. She could call Ed herself, but she had interfered enough. It was up to Billy if he wanted to forgive Ed for leaving. Maybe it was just too raw right now.

The bedroom door was ajar and the window was open, letting the cool breeze drift through the house. She heard a car pull onto the driveaway. She glanced at her gold watch and gasped in horror. 'I haven't sorted out a clutch bag yet, or decided on shoes!'

Billy simply walked into her wardrobe, returning seconds later with towering midnight blue heels with a tiny glittering motif on the side and a matching bag with a silver clasp. He sneaked over to the window and peeked out, before rushing back and scooping a selection of makeup from her vanity unit into the bag, and then adding a condom from the drawer, for good measure.

'Billy!' she burst out laughing at the salacious look on his face.

'I've just seen Jared get out of the car and he's looking delicious,' he grinned. 'If you don't want him, save him for me!' he pointed towards the condom packet.

'You're a nightmare!' she grabbed the purse and chucked the condom at him. 'Don't judge everyone by your own slutty standards,' she giggled. 'Dylan would kill you if he heard you say that.'

'Dylan hasn't been around much lately though, has he?' That raised eyebrow was back.

She grabbed a tonal silver silk shawl and draped it over her shoulder. 'Stop trying to ruin my night. Is this your way of telling me to pay Dylan more attention?' But Billy had already turned to the window and was waving to Jared, letting him know she was on her way down. Jared stood beside the car talking to someone on his phone. He signalled that he'd seen Billy and carried on chatting.

'I support you whatever you decide.' Billy turned to look at her and brushed her golden hair from her shoulder so it hung in soft waves down her back. 'But from an outsider's point of view, and from the way Jared looks like he wants to eat you alive every time we have a meeting with him, I'd say you have two suitors in the picture.'

Poppy's mouth fell open and he cheerfully lifted her chin to close it. 'For a smart woman, you are so dumb. My vote is for Dylan, of course, but I can see how different you are.'

She didn't know what Billy was talking about. Jared had met Dylan. And he'd never said anything to suggest he was interested in her that way. Billy was such a drama queen.

'Opposites attract,' she snapped, rushing down the hall and turning to shut the front door in Billy's face as he followed her. She ran over to the car and smiled sweetly at Jared, her heart racing. He took her hands and twirled her round, making her dress swish in the evening breeze.

'Wow!' he said. 'You look incredible.' He kissed her hand and she blushed.

Jared's hand slipped to her back and she felt a frisson of heat flare where his fingers touched her bare skin. She grew hot and feverish and almost fumbled with the open car door. She stepped into the car and he got in next to her, telling his driver to take them to the party. Poppy gulped in some air and smiled at Jared, but he had changed suddenly from a business partner she had half-fancied from afar, to a red hot male who might privately reciprocate her lustful imaginings.

∽

As the evening progressed, Jared didn't leave her side. He escorted her from group to group, introducing her and her company and helping her gain vital contacts. Everyone adored their concept. She was handed so many fresh glasses of wine that her head began to spin. She had completely lost count of how many she'd nervously sipped, until her confidence finally began to grow and she threw herself into enjoying her moment. Now she was laughing and holding court everywhere she went. Jared often whispered into her ear about how well she was doing and the hairs on the nape of her neck were permanently on red alert. His hand was once again resting on the small of her back as he guided her around. By the time most of their guests had left and they'd flopped gratefully into plush seats by the hotel bar, she was on cloud nine about how well it had gone.

'That was amazing,' he laughed. '*You* were amazing! You had them all eating out of the palm of your hand. You're going to have to employ more staff. I bet your phone rings off the hook on Monday.'

Poppy smiled and her cheeks grew warm. Her eyes were sparkling and she couldn't remember when she'd enjoyed herself more. Dylan would never take her to an event like this – and now she'd been to one, she wanted more. Jared signalled to the waiter for a bottle of wine and she held up her hand and asked for water.

'Just one more glass, so we can toast our latest development,' Jared said.

Poppy giggled and leaned her head back on the velvet couch, making his pupils dilate as he glanced at the milky expanse of her throat. He gently pulled her back up, brushing her hair away from her collarbone and making her senses reel. She couldn't think straight when he was so close.

'How are things with you and Dylan?'

Suddenly the mood had changed and she groggily tried to focus. It had been a long day and she just wanted to curl up somewhere warm to sleep. She somehow knew this was a better plan than slipping onto his lap for warmth. That would be playing with fire – but her friends would be happy at last. Jared was holding her hand and staring at her so intently. She shook her head slightly to clear it.

'Um, they have been better.' She tried to shake off the disloyal feeling that was creeping into her veins. She couldn't tell anyone else, as they all either loved Dylan, or didn't think he was good enough for her. Her wine-fuddled brain decided that Jared was her friend now, so she could tell him. 'We barely ever used to argue, but that's changed recently.'

Jared was stroking her hand now and she frowned in confusion. It kept distracting her. Mm, it felt so good. 'What's changed?' he asked.

'I have, I guess. I've always been career-driven and hardworking, but a project of this size has taken all my time.' When he started to speak, she put her hand to his mouth to stop him, then her eyes went wide as he lifted her hand away and kissed the palm. 'Uh… I think Dylan feels neglected and that's my fault.'

Jared still had hold of her hand, but sounded cross now. 'It's not your fault that you've got dreams and ambitions. That's to be applauded. We work well together and we'd both be crazy to miss that opportunity.' He looked into her eyes and she could feel herself blushing again. She placed her hands in her lap, but was wide-eyed at how passionately he spoke about their dreams. They seemed to be interweaving, tying the two of them together. 'He should understand that and support you.'

Poppy hung her head. 'I know. That's what frustrates me. He's not ambitious at all. He's happy to work a nine-to-five job – sometimes nine-to-three. I'd be out there looking for more business in my free time.'

'That's what separates the two of you. You need someone as driven to succeed as you are. Someone who'll lift you up, and not tear you down. I always go after what I want.'

Jared's eyes blazed into hers and she realised he was serious. He'd pushed up the sleeves of his formal shirt and his suit jacket had been discarded on the chair arm. He looked relaxed – yet about to pounce! An undercurrent of tension – or was it lust? – filled her bones. She hadn't looked at another man this way since dating Dylan, but Jared was hard to ignore. He was masculine and sexy, with his slicked-back thick blond hair and sparkling, intelligent eyes.

Poppy licked her lips. 'My friends think he's lazy too,' she gasped and covered her mouth. 'I shouldn't have said that,' she said, but she was smothering a giggle.

Jared threw back his head and laughed. 'I think I'd like your friends. When can I meet them?'

Poppy smiled. 'They'd adore you – but they'd eat you alive.'

'Sounds exciting!' he joked. Poppy didn't quite like the sudden lump that had lodged in her throat, at the thought of Jared with one of her friends.

'Not as exciting as you think. They're pretty outspoken and bossy, although to be honest, that's what I love about them' she looked him up and down slowly, not sure where her bravado was coming from. 'Looking like you do, they'd assume you're a player.' Jared roared with laughter and stood up, pulling her with him.

'I do like to get ahead of the game from time to time. Are we getting a car home, or do you want to stay the night here?'

Suddenly you could have heard a pin drop and she felt

like all of the air had just whooshed out of her lungs. She locked eyes with him, as he waited for her answer.

CHAPTER TWENTY-FOUR

Poppy's head was still banging and she was wearing sunglasses. Even the soft lights indoors hurt her eyes. It was mid-afternoon and the sun was blazing down so much that the grass outside looked parched. She pressed a switch and her sprinkler system started up. She was in pain and her stomach felt like she was standing on the deck of a boat on the high seas. She recalled some of the previous evening, before she'd had the last bottle of wine, but the rest was hazy. She flinched when she heard Billy come in and switch on the coffee machine.

'Dirty stop-out,' he said, holding up a coffee cup. She winced and nodded, moving her sunglasses to the top of her head. 'What time did you get back this morning? I didn't know you were staying out. I was worried about you.'

He wandered over and handed her a steaming mug of coffee. She breathed in the scent and sighed. He pulled a packet of painkillers out of his pocket and slapped them into her other hand, before leading her to sit down at the beautifully crafted table and chair set that Dylan had made her, which made her stomach lurch again.

'Spill,' he demanded, looking at her crossly. 'I know I joked about the condom, but I hope you bloody well used one.' He seemed upset and agitated.

She took his hand and he stared at it. 'You ok?' she asked hoarsely. He shook her off.

'Ed called. He wants me to join him, now he's settled and missing me,' he said sarcastically. She winced again at his harsh tone, but was glad it was directed away from her for a moment. 'And don't think I am letting you off the hook,' Billy went on. 'Tell me all about last night. I want every detail and if you've done what I think you've done, I love you, but I hate you as well. Dylan deserves better.'

Her eyes blazed into his before she pushed her sunglasses back onto her face. 'I don't need to be scolded like a child, by my assistant,' she barked at him and he jolted in surprise. She never usually shouted at him, but her temper was frayed.

She closed her eyes and rubbed her temples, throwing the glasses onto the table. 'I stayed in my own room at the hotel because I was exhausted. I celebrated the best night of my working life alone – so I don't need censure from my friends.'

Billy hung his head. 'Sorry. I didn't mean to be snarky, but Ed riled me and actually, I was hurt that you didn't invite me to the party.'

Poppy took a deep breath and let it out slowly, counting to five in her mind. 'I didn't organise the party. It was Jared's night and I was just along for the ride.' When he raised one eyebrow at her, she rolled her eyes, then threw her hands up. 'I did not ride Jared! Although it seems that he does want me to,' she waited to see his shocked face.

'Well, we all know that. It's as plain as day.'

Poppy's mouth formed a big O as Billy pulled something out of his back pocket and slapped it onto the table. Poppy frowned and opened out a national newspaper. It was turned to the celebrity gossip pages and her face stared back out at her. Jared was laughing about something she'd said and his arm was around her waist. Her dress looked like it was made from molten gold in the camera flashlight. It clung to her body as she was smiling up at him. 'Oh shit.'

'Yep.'

'Has Dylan seen this?'

'What do you think? Have you heard from him today? I bet his friends will have loved telling him about his girlfriend's big night and asking why he wasn't the dude draped all over you.'

'Bloody hell.'

'Yep.' He pushed her coffee back towards her but she ignored it, picking up her phone. There were several text messages from Dylan.

'Dylan could have come, but he hates schmoozing… his word,' she said, when Billy raised an enquiring eyebrow.

'It was your big night, though!' Billy was obviously shocked. His loyalty to Dylan was fierce, but he was even more protective of Poppy. He was almost like a lioness with a cub. Even when he was telling her off, he was always on her side. And she was the same with Billy, in turn – even when he was annoying the hell out of her. She now knew this friendship was the reason why he hadn't gone with Ed. She hated thinking she'd ruined Billy's beautiful relationship while he was picking up the pieces of hers.

'That's the reason I stayed out. I was annoyed with Dylan. He'd asked me to stay at his after the party, but he couldn't be bothered to come with me. Jared was there for me. He knew how important last night was. Why didn't Dylan?'

'Jared kind of had to be there. It was his gig,' Billy pointed out. Poppy slapped his arm and he yelped. 'That, and the fact that he's in lust with you of course.' Poppy stayed silent. 'See! Even you admit it now.'

'He asked me to stay at the hotel with him last night.'

'And you turned him down? You're a stronger human than me.'

Poppy rubbed her eyes and winced. Her headache seemed to be getting worse. 'I was so pissed off with Dylan that I was tempted, but I'd never do that to him, however annoyed I am that he's broken my heart and trampled all over it with his big feet.'

Billy shuffled his chair over, which was a mighty feat as they were made of solid wood, and pulled her into a hug, which wasn't that comfortable. He let her go, pushing her coffee closer to her again. 'Drink up. You're probably dehydrated.'

Poppy smiled at last. 'I'm not sure coffee hydrates you, Billy,' but she took a sip anyway and the caffeine seeped into her bones.

They both turned when they heard a noise and Dylan walked in, with a face like thunder, the newspaper in his hand. He took in the sight of them and then saw the newspaper was already on the table. He threw his copy on top.

'I see everyone has a copy of the photo of my girlfriend draped all over another man.'

'It's just a photo, Dylan. It doesn't mean anything,' Poppy said, pushing her chair back and reaching for Dylan, but he shook her off.

'It means something to me. You didn't come to my place last night. Where did you sleep?' he demanded to know.

Poppy had never seen him this angry and looked to Billy for help, but he just shrugged helplessly and mumbled something about getting them all fresh coffee, rapidly backing away and running for the kitchen.

'If you'd come with me, to the most important business event of my life, then I wouldn't have been papped with

Jared!' she seethed, refusing to back down when she'd done nothing wrong. This was so unfair.

Dylan moved closer to her and she refused to step back but glared at him. 'Where did you stay last night?' he asked again.

'At the hotel,' was all she said, eyes spitting fire.

Dylan's mouth creased into a thin line and he ran his hand through his dark hair, ruffling it up and making him look even more sexy, in his jeans and white T-shirt. She hated it when he was angry, but how dare he speak to her that way? Dylan took one more look at her and then turned away in disgust, just as Billy arrived back with three mugs of steaming coffee.

Billy called after Dylan as he stalked past and out of the front door, but Dylan ignored him. Billy placed the tray down. 'You told him nothing happened, right?'

Tears sprung from Poppy's eyes and she dashed them away. 'He didn't give me the chance. Judge and jury, without any evidence.'

Billy pulled her into his arms while tears formed rivers on her face. His shirt was soaked when she finally came up for air. 'Sorry,' she patted him down. The sun was shining, so he whipped the shirt off over his head and she laughed manically. 'Dylan will think I'm sleeping with you, next.'

'Look, the topic of Jared has come up,' sighed Billy, pulling out a chair for her again and sitting next to her. 'Dylan knows I still love Ed, and he asked what I'd do if anyone else was in the picture.'

Poppy took in a huge breath and held it before letting it go. She didn't want to talk about her and Dylan anymore. Or her and Jared. 'Tell me about Ed. You've been so closed off about it.'

'He broke my heart,' said Billy as if it was that simple. 'It was too painful to talk about,' he looked at Poppy. She nodded sympathetically, and thought of Dylan's angry face just now. Maybe she should have run after him, but he'd made her so mad with his assumptions.

'I kind of understand why Ed left now,' said Billy. 'It was a choice between his career and mine. He was acting as if his was more important, and I should just uproot my life for him and start again. No thought was given to how hard that might be for me.' Poppy took his hand and squeezed it. 'Ed thought of my career as frivolous and his actions proved that.'

'Can't you work through it? Maybe he was exited about his new opportunity and forgot about you for a minute.'

Billy hung his head and played with the edge of the table, running his fingers along the smooth wood. 'I'm not sure. It's a bit like Dylan not supporting you. Dylan knows how hard you work. I can't believe he didn't go with you to the party. I assumed he wasn't invited... like me.'

Poppy bit her lip. 'I'm sorry. I should have asked Jared to invite you, but I thought I needed to stand on my own for once and start facing up to the fact I'm the head of the company. It seems stupid to keep hiding behind you.' She sipped her coffee thoughtfully. 'It didn't occur to me you'd want to come. It was full of business talk with investors. I got a bit sloshed to calm my nerves, to be honest,' she sighed. 'I assumed it would be deadly dull for you, but I could have asked instead of making that decision for you. Sorry.' Her bottom lip wobbled and he leaned in and kissed her cheek.

'It's ok. You're probably right and I'd have been bored in seconds. You were just looking out for me. I can see that. I was being overly dramatic and you don't need a chaperone.'

'I'm sorry about sticking my oar in with you and Ed, too. He's missing you and I miss him, but it's up to you to contact him.'

Billy raised a smile. 'We are in such a mess! Both of us

were happily loved-up not so long ago.' A tear slipped out of Poppy's eye and Billy caught it with his finger and pulled her up for a proper cuddle. 'Come on, let's go and find somewhere decadent for lunch. We can drink off your hangover.'

Poppy raised a watery smile and slipped her hand into his. 'I really love you, you know,' she said, lifting her face up to his. She knew she looked hideous, with smudged mascara and messed up hair. He bent down and kissed the top of her head. 'I love you too. Now let's go and stuff our faces and drink to forget the tosspots who think they rule our lives.'

Poppy's eyebrows shot up. Billy had never said a bad word about Dylan before, but his jaw was set. Who needed a boyfriend, when you had a friend like Billy?

CHAPTER TWENTY-FIVE

Jared stared out of the window of his penthouse flat and crossed his arms over his naked chest. He'd just got back from the hotel, body aching from lack of sleep, and had changed into a pair of casual trousers while he tried to sit and read the papers that were delivered each day.

Now he thought back to the night before and could have kicked himself for playing his cards too soon. He was like a moth to a flame, with Poppy. It frustrated the hell out of him. He couldn't seem to get enough of her.

He scheduled meetings when they didn't need them and when he knew she was exhausted already from the extra work this project had brought with it. He tried to stay away, but it was impossible. He felt pride swell in his chest at the beautiful development he'd made at the site. Poppy's additions, even at the late stage when they'd been made, had changed everything. The houses and barns now had extra appeal and a unique selling point to help them stand out. It was a dream combination, as far as his public relations company was concerned. They were loving promoting the unique health benefits that went with the new properties.

Jared felt galvanised by the project, like Poppy, but before knowing her, his decisions had always been primarily based on business values, not personal ones. It *had* made sense to involve her, even though it had been a headache in planning. The houses were now built and the exteriors were starting to take shape. But the interiors were the parts that cemented the dream. These properties really would change people's lives once they were finished. It was ground-breaking work. This was the development he was most proud of, and he wanted Poppy by his side.

He thought back to when he'd read about her in a magazine he'd been leafing through. She'd come across as shy and slightly reclusive. In articles he'd sourced afterwards, it had appeared that her assistant, Billy, was the driving force behind any marketing achievements. He had been the spokesperson for the company. Now that he knew Billy, he could see why. Involving Billy was actually a savvy business move. Billy looked the part and he was a born salesman. He enjoyed the limelight.

Jared had no idea why Poppy had felt the need to hide, but wondered if it had anything to do with her mum. Reading that original article had convinced him to set up an initial meeting. Her designs were inventive and she'd caught a trend before it had got established. She'd set herself up as the designer everyone wanted to know, without even realising it. Her unavailability was addictive, and people were now doing their best to seek her out.

From his research, he knew they could scale up her ideas. When she'd shown him her own home, he'd been speechless for a while, which didn't happen often. The place was ingenious!

She hadn't thought of building houses for other people, as

she was so focussed on designing pods and panels that could be fitted by anyone. Seeing her vision at her own home had changed everything, though.

Poppy had been pleasingly business like when he'd arranged a meeting and he'd enjoyed seeing her plans. When she'd invited him to her home, he'd fleetingly wondered if she was coming on to him, and had, if he was brutally honest with himself, been quite disappointed when she'd just wanted to show him her designs in action.

He hadn't been able to keep her out of his mind since. Unluckily, she was already in a relationship.

Jared finally smiled. His stomach was growling. He decided to make himself an omelette. He'd missed out on breakfast at the hotel, as Poppy had already left. Now he was really hungry.

His mistake had been inviting Poppy to his hotel room, when he knew she had a boyfriend. But when she'd leaned on his arm, her perfume had enslaved his senses. Then she'd told him how lonely she was. From that moment he'd been lost. Her lips were plump and rosy and her skin had glistened in the sultry bar lighting. Jared cursed the memory, and almost scorched his hand on the omelette pan. It was obvious that Dylan neglected her. He hadn't shown up for her big night. She'd shed a few tears after everyone had gone. Jared had only meant to ask her up for a nightcap. One look into his eyes, though, and she must have been able to see the longing. It had scared her away.

She had been tempted, he realised, but she'd said she was tired and needed to get home. He'd finally persuaded her to stay in her own room and get some sleep as it was so late, but in the morning, she was gone, which was another punch to his ego.

He stirred the egg mixture in his pan. Then he threw in some chopped herbs. A couple of minutes later he slid the omelette on to a plate, with a couple of pieces of bread. He took his feast to the table, overlooking the river that wound through the town. He wondered what Poppy was looking at right now.

Jared sighed at the first mouthful of omelette. The chili flakes he'd scattered over the top had just the right amount of heat. He really was hungry. Not just for food – but it would have to do for now.

He finished the last bite of toast and got up, muscles tensing as he made a decision and picked up his phone. He was tired of playing second fiddle to a carpenter who didn't know what he had when it was already curled up in his hand. If Dylan didn't look after the precious gift he'd been given, then Jared would have no qualms in taking Poppy from him.

CHAPTER TWENTY-SIX

Poppy nearly jumped out of her skin when the doorbell rang. She and Billy had been stretching out in the garden and still hadn't gotten round to deciding where to go for lunch. Billy jumped up and went to answer the door. Poppy smiled after him. 'It is your day off, you know. You're not my assistant on the weekends.'

Billy turned and grinned at her. 'You might scare people away looking like that.'

Poppy rubbed her tear-stained face and pushed herself to get up and go and wash in the kitchen, in case Dylan had decided to come back. He hadn't answered her texts since leaving and her stomach was churning. Surely he was the one in the wrong, not showing up for her big night – even though she'd expressly told him he had an invite? Her stomach turned over again. Perhaps she had been wrong to arrive with Jared, but what else was she supposed to do? Go alone? He was her client, for goodness sake! Dylan had never been jealous of clients before. At least a couple of them were gorgeous and had big businesses. She splashed more water on her face. Ok, none of them looked like Jared, or were as successful, but still…

A huge bouquet of flowers walked into the room on legs, until Billy oof-ed and plonked it down on the kitchen counter. Poppy's heart skipped a beat. Dylan wasn't one for showy displays of affection, but he must have realised how much he'd hurt her. 'The delivery guy was so sexy, I almost invited him in.'

'Billy!' she laughed, feeling much better now. 'You're incorrigible!'

Poppy pushed her nose into the flowers and breathed in the heavenly scent. It seemed to fill up the whole kitchen and her heart swelled. Billy handed her the card, hopping from foot to foot like an excited child. She grinned and tore the envelope open, revealing a pretty blue and white picture.

Her eyes went wide when she read the message and her heartbeat ramped up a notch. She handed it silently to Billy and walked to look out onto her garden. The sound of the waterfall on the back wall soothed her tired mind, but she didn't know how to feel.

Jared's handwriting was strong and looped. She'd seen it many times now. He'd actually taken the time to go into a flower shop and write the card himself. He had congratulated her on her success at the party and then had mentioned that he'd missed her the next morning. He'd signed off with his initial and a kiss.

Billy came and hugged her and she rested her head on his chest, listening to his heartbeat. Her bottom lip wobbled. How had she got herself into such a mess? The flowers were simply stunning, but her bones felt like mush and all she wanted to do was cry. This should have been her happiest day, but here she was, sniffling into her best friend's chest. She pressed her face into his arms.

She wasn't sure when, exactly, but Billy *had* become her

best friend. She found she was increasingly wary of Demi, Sasha and Anne these days. She paused for a second. Perhaps not Anne, so much. Anne didn't tell her off all the time for her life choices, and try to foist different men onto her, in order to nab her boyfriend. Poppy was sure that Sasha still had the hots for Dylan and that was the real reason she'd said he wasn't good enough for her. Poppy wasn't stupid. She could sense these things. It had almost caused them to fall out in school, but Anne and Demi had been there to make sure it hadn't happened. It had also meant that she and Dylan hadn't happened then, either. This time she was determined not to let Sasha get in the way.

Billy tilted her head up and kissed her nose, keeping her tucked under his arm. 'Come on. I'm treating you to that celebratory meal, and we're inviting Verity. She's been asking where the hell you've been, as you haven't bought any clothes from her shop in ages. The place I'm thinking of for food is just down the road from the Cherry Blossom Lane. You need new friends for the glamorous life you're starting. The old ones are dragging you down.' He brushed the tears from her eyes and gave her a final squeeze before sending her up for a quick shower and wandering over to the flowers to set them in a vase. He picked up the dainty card and turned it over to look at the scrawled text with a frown.

Placing it back on the counter, he went to slide the kitchen doors back into place, and grabbed the morning paper to take another look at the gorgeous photo that had caused so much trouble for his feisty friend.

CHAPTER TWENTY-SEVEN

Dylan kicked the car door shut and balanced the bag of groceries under one arm, while he searched in his pocket for the keys to his flat. Usually the sight of the building made him happy. He liked being here almost as much as he loved Poppy's house. He knew it should be the other way round, but her place was designed to sing to the soul and it did that every time he stepped into it. She'd created her home to make you feel relaxed and welcome.

The one thing missing from his flat was Poppy. She was what felt like home. He admired all that she'd achieved, but it was her dynamism and energy that made everything around her shine. It was what Dylan saw in her – but he knew that others did too, now. He felt selfish wanting to keep her to himself, when the whole world was demanding her attention. She was too talented to stay hidden for long, however hard she'd tried to mask her skills.

His stomach turned over at the thought that he couldn't control what would happen next. He'd tried to be supportive. He had been! But he also realised that she wanted more from him than he could give. It caused endless rows. He wasn't made like her. His business meant the world to him, but didn't crave dizzy heights of fame. He was driven enough to be able to pay his way comfortably, have creative control and Poppy by his side. It seemed he wasn't enough for her, though. The niggling doubts that he wasn't ambitious enough for her were now jumping around and shouting in his mind. She wanted a go-getter like Jared, even though Dylan had been running his very successful business for years and could afford to slow down a little bit, now. His lip curled into a snarl and his fists bunched. He felt adrenaline punch through his veins and he stomped indoors and dumped the groceries on the kitchen counter, spilling them everywhere.

He looked around his own domain. There were sleek wooden surfaces and floor to ceiling windows, with great views over the park. He felt at home here. He was near enough to be able to check in on his parents and have beers with his brothers. They were a raucous bunch, but there was a lot of love. They all adored Poppy, too. Oliver was always teasing her about her job, which she took with good humour. Miles was a computer geek who was obsessed with cars. He was in awe of what Poppy had achieved and was determined that his own business would grow at the same speed. He worked hard at college and was forging his way in the world. Dylan had a sneaking suspicion that Miles had a crush on Poppy's friend Demi, but she was unavailable, so was out of bounds. Not that men like Jared seemed to care about those unwritten rules, grumbled Dylan, kicking a metal bin and enjoying the satisfying crack as it hit the wall.

Miles always spoke to Poppy about the tech she used in her projects. She'd even asked his advice from time to time and Dylan had to admit he'd felt left out.

Dylan started opening and shutting his beautifully crafted

kitchen doors and putting things away. Well, chucking them in haphazardly and ignoring the mess.

Things with Poppy had seemed so simple a few weeks ago, but now they were complicated. Perhaps she did need to be with someone who was uber-rich and could help her fulfil her dreams? He shook his head to get rid of that idea as he pictured Poppy's fiery eyes. That woman would get where she wanted to be on her own. She didn't need help from anyone. So why didn't she appreciate the toil it had taken Dylan to be able to sit back and relax for a while?

He turned the coffee machine on and sighed. He could have kicked himself for not joining Poppy on her big night, but the evening had been a nightmare for him. He'd made stupid choices and was paying for them now. Poppy had sent him numerous texts since he'd seen her, but in truth his own guilt was spurring his anger.

Instead of escorting her to her big event, like she'd asked him to, he'd wanted to surprise her by being there when she arrived. It was such an important night for her and she deserved to know how special she was. He'd asked her back to his flat after the event to throw her off the scent, but had actually booked a suite at the hotel, and filled it with roses and champagne.

The phone call that had come in from Anne while he was on his way to the party had prevented him from attending and changed everything. The photos the next day had confirmed what he'd heard on the town grapevine that morning, and struck a knife into his heart. Poppy hadn't even denied she'd stayed at the hotel. He'd only missed one night! A pretty important night, he admitted, but that had been out of his control.

Dylan went and stood looking out of the window onto the bustling scene in the park below. Kids were kicking a football around and some parents strolled along with their toddler and a yappy dog. He sighed and gritted his teeth. He'd asked Poppy to her face if she'd stayed with Jared. Instead of denying it, like he'd hoped and prayed she would, she'd turned a shade of green and looked away.

His insides churned and his veins filled with liquid fire. Poppy had made her choice. Now Dylan felt he'd never really stood a chance. If high-powered was what she wanted, then that's what he'd give her, but when she came back begging for forgiveness, he'd turn her away. She wasn't the only one with other options. Maybe he'd been blind to his own for too long.

He grabbed a coffee, opened the windows, and stood on the balcony overlooking the park. He sipped the bitter liquid, wincing. He'd forgotten to add any milk. He didn't enjoy frothy drinks like Poppy did, but black coffee wasn't for him either. He wondered if Jared drank his coffee straight. He tossed the coffee into a nearby plant pot, then wished he hadn't. It was one Poppy had nurtured to make the little oasis on his small outdoor area. He cursed and went in to pick up his phone. It was about time he stepped back into the world of the living.

If Poppy could play the field, then so could he.

CHAPTER TWENTY-EIGHT

Anne pushed her chair away and pulled Poppy into a hug. Poppy carried on sobbing quietly into her hands, her shoulders bobbing up and down. The three other girls' eyes darted back and forth between themselves, trying to work out what to do. No one knew how to handle this. They were all shocked to see Poppy's emotions in plain sight. She was a tough cookie and usually brushed things off. Anne knew she had a heart of gold, but Poppy had always seemed quite distant. Up until now.

Sasha and Demi looked on, concern on their faces. Both reached across to pat Poppy's back. 'Don't cry, Poppy,' said Demi, signalling to a very worried-looking Chris to bring emergency coffee and cake, which he did at double speed. Poppy never cried in public and had barely shed a tear in front of them, the whole time they had known her. She was the one you went to when *you* needed to cry.

They only ever knew she was upset by her wobbly bottom lip. She took all the pain inside and dealt with her problems on her own. Anne had sometimes even wondered if Poppy felt anything at all, for anyone other than her mum and the people round the table, so these silent tears were quite a shock. Anne had never seen her friend cry over a man.

She handed Poppy the coffee. Poppy rubbed her puffy eyes and sipped it gratefully. Anne sighed in relief. Poppy was the workaholic, Sasha was the bossy, annoying one, Demi was the raving beauty who had men's slavish devotion but didn't seem to notice and Anne was the nurturer who worried about them all endlessly. She was concerned about Poppy working too hard, Sasha becoming a spinster, Demi never reaching her potential as she spent her life in a daydream, and herself being left on the shelf with a sick child. With just one hiccup recently, which had been swiftly rectified, Freddie was getting better and better. Anne felt her usual burst of anger that they hadn't been able to find the same medication nearer home, then she felt the punch of guilt that Poppy had been the one to raise most of the money to help them.

She pushed a plate of cake towards Poppy, who shook her head. Chris hovered around nervously, but Anne motioned that she had the situation covered. Then she turned to Poppy. 'Tell us again what happened.'

Poppy lifted her face and Sasha leaned in and brushed away some tears from her friend's watery eyes, then squeezed her hand. 'If Dylan is behaving like a dick, I can break his legs for you?' She flexed muscles honed from her many hours at the gym, and Poppy raised a weak smile.

'He saw a photo of me and Jared at my work party. It was in the paper,' she looked around the table. Sasha winced and Anne and Demi looked shiftily away.

'Um... We've all seen the photo. It didn't look great,' said Sasha, brutally. 'I mean, you looked stunning, but Jared was eating you alive with his eyes and his arm was wrapped round you. You both looked like you'd just had sex – or were about to!' She pulled a face to soften her words, but the question was left unsaid. *Were they having sex?* Poppy flushed but stayed silent.

'Plus, Jared's a total babe, so most men would be jealous,' chirped in Demi, then winced as Anne shot a pained look her way.

Poppy sniffed and held her hands round her coffee mug, trying to raise a smile for Chris so he wouldn't keep popping back to check on them every two minutes. 'He's not been answering my texts.'

'Jared?' asked Demi in confusion and Sasha nudged her in the ribs. 'What?'

Poppy drew in a shaky breath. Anne glanced at her watch and tried to cover it with picking up her bag, but Sasha saw her and frowned. 'You have somewhere else to be?'

All eyes turned to Anne. She could have kicked Sasha. She did have somewhere else to be, for once, but Sasha definitely wouldn't think that anything in Anne's life could be more important right now. They would all understand completely if she told them she was supposed to be calling the clinic to check on Freddie's latest blood results, but she'd already rung and done that earlier and everything was fine. She'd feel awful if she used that for an excuse and they found out. Damn, what did she do now?

Anne was gradually shredding the napkin in her lap. She pushed the detritus on the floor, silently apologising to Chris for when he had to sweep up. Anne knew that Sasha also had a secret and she wanted to investigate it more, but Poppy turning up out of the blue had scuppered that plan. She did feel awful for Poppy, but she was pretty sure that Jared was the ideal man for her. Poppy just needed to get Dylan out of her system and see what was right in front of her. A red-hot male, who could help her fulfil her every dream. The girl was mad if she couldn't see she was with the wrong man.

Anne stopped wriggling and sighed. She'd have to think of ways of distracting Poppy so that she could recover from the breakdown of her relationship. Anne knew that she and the other girls were right: Dylan was not the man for Poppy. They were better off as friends and Poppy would realise that soon enough. He was too laid back and didn't appreciate her. She needed someone as driven and ambitious as she was. Not a local boy made good. He would never reach for the stars, like Poppy did. He had achieved a lot, but was intrinsically set in his ways. He visited his mum each week on the same day, for goodness sake! Anne had always told Poppy that her crush on him was a waste of time. He wasn't that interested. She looked under her lashes at Sasha and quickly reapplied her lip gloss while she bided her time. Poppy wasn't the only one who had been lying to them for years.

CHAPTER TWENTY-NINE

Poppy stood staring out of her bedroom window, in the direction of the houses built beyond her garden wall. She had spent the last few weeks immersing herself in new work projects and was spending far too much time at her studio on Cherry Blossom Lane.

She'd been so inundated with requests that she had decided to hire a receptionist, so that Billy could be freed up to assist her in the more detailed planning of each job. He now ordered stock, spoke to suppliers – and charmed everyone. He sat at a desk next to hers, his chest thrust out like a peacock, a satisfied smile on his face. He was still watching her like a hawk, though, ever since Dylan had told Poppy that they needed some time apart. Poppy was now planning to move Billy's desk to the room next door to get some peace and quiet. Plus he was suddenly ridiculously tidy and she couldn't put a sheet of paper down before it was whisked away and filed.

She'd felt like Dylan had trampled on her heart at first – and still did, if she was brutally honest with herself. She'd fallen apart in the first two weeks, but now she felt stronger.

But it was as if she'd never meant anything to him in the first place. She had thought they were unbreakable. It showed how wrong she could be. She should never have tried to blend the two sides of her life. Her friends had insisted he was wrong for her and the cracks had begun to show the minute there had been external pressure.

Dylan had never been jealous before, but then suddenly he didn't want her to work with Jared. That had been impossible and unfair. They'd had a huge row, after he'd seen the newspaper photograph. Several small articles followed, and that didn't help. Especially as one or two had found out about her mother. One reporter had even called Green Manor and asked to speak to June. Luckily staff had fielded the call. She felt like her insides had been wrung out. It was her worst nightmare and her nerves were shredded. Every time she had met with Dylan, they'd shouted at each other.

Now Poppy had to attend an industry event for local developers and innovators, when all she wanted to do was curl up and cry. She was busy at work, which had been both a blessing and pure torture.

In the first few days, she'd wanted to run after Dylan and plead for him to reconsider, but her pride wouldn't let her. She'd have given up almost anything for him, but she'd put blood, sweat and tears into building her brand and this was the pivotal moment of her career. His price was too high. She'd never have asked him to walk away from his own business.

Dylan had more staff than she did, but he could sit in his office, his arm hooked over the back of his chair, chatting to suppliers and putting his feet up. He had loads of free time. She'd often asked him his secret, but he'd always shrugged and laughed it off, saying she was the go-getter, not him. His business ran itself. She wished hers did at the moment. Now everyone knew her name. People had seen the newspapers linking her and Jared as the building industry's new golden couple. Overnight, her life had become much more complicated.

The girls had comforted Poppy over Dylan. Anne had said it would blow over, and she should enjoy every minute of her time in the limelight, but it just wasn't Poppy's thing. Anne had even booked nights out where loads of gorgeous men seemed to hang around, but Poppy couldn't even think about other men right now. Her heart was splintered into shards and she didn't know how she would ever recover from the pain.

Poppy much preferred sitting in her little office in Cherry Blossom Lane, with its views across the hills and the blossom trees, to nights out. Before, she'd been able to choose her clients without any furore. Now everyone knew her name and the demands on her time and expertise were exhausting. People were turning up unannounced at her studio and she was worried that the lane was starting to look like a car park. She could finally see why Dylan kept some big contracts at bay. He was the master and did as he pleased. She had new respect for his methods, which had seemed so alien before. He had skills that were in demand, but he delegated and was secure in his own worth. He didn't need to please anyone but himself. Her friends were wrong about him. He *was* ambitious enough for her. He was everything she'd ever dreamt of, and she'd blown it. Now she'd heard he was working himself into the ground and that felt like it was aimed at her, too. For someone who didn't care about her, he was certainly making sure she noticed him. Suddenly he was already contracted to practically every big project she landed. It seemed he had contacts everywhere. She had just been blind to it.

She'd listened to people bending her ear and believed their voices above her own. She'd known Sasha had a thing for Dylan and she should have expected her to try and ruin things, but instead, she'd been burnt. Poppy had poured her heart out to Sasha and the girls, but in the end, they were still telling her Jared should be her man. Why didn't they fight for what she loved? Why didn't they support her choices? *Was it because they wanted them for themselves?*

Her blood boiled when she thought about Dylan, too. He had preferred to believe gossip, even though she had told him there was nothing going on between her and Jared. During one argument, he'd shouted at her that he had been planning to surprise her and turn up at her launch night. If that was actually true, then where had he been? He said he'd booked a room at the hotel, and filled it with flowers and gifts. When she'd asked him why he hadn't shown up, he hadn't been able to answer. He'd just said it was complicated, hung his head and then stormed out in exasperation.

It was too late for Dylan to realise he'd made a mistake by not supporting her, and to try to rectify that after the event. She had to put on her big girl pants and pretend it didn't hurt like hell. She sniffed and refused to cry again. She picked up her dress and slipped it over her head. She wasn't in the mood for fuss, but she'd be damned if she didn't put on a good front. She was going to appear like she hadn't a care in the world. Her dress was silver and embellished with thousands of beads which shone as she moved. It dipped almost indecently low at the back. Normally she'd worry that the swell of her breasts showed from the way the bodice of the dress was sculpted, but tonight she straightened her shoulders and stood proudly. She knew Dylan would be at the party and hoped he felt her loss like a knife to the heart. She'd heard through the grapevine that he'd swooped in and landed several big contracts lately, one of which was from the meeting he'd had with his friend Jim a few weeks back. So much for a relaxed chat and not much else, the lying toad.

At the time he'd been noncommittal about taking more work on, but now he must be under pressure to meet the demands of his huge client list. She couldn't understand why she'd tried for so long to help his business prosper, while he had turned her down every time, and now suddenly he was doing it on his own. Her face burned with humiliation. He seemed to want to show her how little he'd ever needed her advice and how powerful he could be, if he so chose.

She didn't want to go to the party, but she couldn't let Billy down, after not getting Jared to invite him last time. Billy had persuaded her to wear the silver 'knock them dead' dress to let Dylan see what he was missing. It didn't seem like he was missing her at all, though, if she was honest, and a lone tear escaped from her eye. She quickly brushed it away with the back of her hand. She'd cried rivers over the past weeks and, as she looked at herself in the mirror, she decided her days of trying to second-guess a man were over. She could be happy on her own. Men were more trouble than they were worth.

Her fair hair fell in glossy waves around her shoulders and she slipped long sparkling earrings into her lobes and sent up a prayer of thanks that Billy had marched her into a beauty salon in the village and told them to give her the works. She'd been primped, pampered and plucked to within an inch of her life – but now she looked sophisticated, glamorous and fierce! She had fire in her eyes and she forced her posture into an even more confident stance and held her chin up. She would look everyone straight in the eye tonight, including Dylan.

She grabbed her beaded purse just as Billy walked in. He whistled at her and made her do a twirl, kissing her on the lips and telling her how stunning she looked, which was just what her dented ego needed to hear. Dylan hadn't thought she was worth fighting for, but she'd make him regret that, when he saw her on Billy's arm tonight.

'You look so handsome,' she said, making Billy do a twirl too. She pressed her lips to his cheek and he batted her away, blushing for once. He really did look sensational in his blue suit and deeper toned tie, with a pressed white shirt and a patterned waistcoat. His blond hair had been cut and he was freshly shaved. He smelt divine. She finally took in a calming breath. She was with an incredible man who loved her unconditionally and, at the moment, he was the one constant in her life.

She hugged him and he grinned. 'What was that for?'

'For being my best friend and for always being at my side.'

'I always will be. We make a great team.'

Poppy smiled. Whoever ended up with this man would be so lucky. He tucked her arm under his and led her to the taxi that was taking them to the function suite at a nearby hotel.

'It's not quite the limo that picked you up last time,' he joked as they settled in and gave the taxi driver the address. Poppy straightened her dress and smiled at Billy. 'It's perfect, because this time, you're with me.' She squeezed his hand. He could obviously tell, by the way she was shaking, that she needed support. He scooted over and slipped his arm around her. She snuggled in with a sigh and wished that she and Billy could fall in love together. Then her life would be so much easier.

CHAPTER THIRTY

Poppy quickly reapplied her lipstick as they pulled up outside the hotel. It was a huge modern building, a past project of Jared's. She admired the design and breathed in the scent of vibrant flowers spilling out of huge urns standing like sentries along the front wall. Billy slipped his hand into hers and she sent him what felt like her first genuine smile of the evening. She knew he was almost as nervous at seeing Dylan as she was. Billy had told Dylan in no uncertain terms that he should be supporting Poppy, not behaving like a child. Poppy had never expected him to take sides, but Dylan's behaviour was irrational. She knew Billy was hurting and missing Dylan's friendship, too.

Flashbulbs went off as they approached the red carpet that was laid out for guests. She saw the 'I love the limelight' switch go on in Billy's brain. She was happy to see him enjoy it, but he didn't let go of her hand. She sighed. That photo of them together, looking like a couple, might be another front page tomorrow. People seeing it would probably think she was a complete strumpet, with loads of fit men on the go. Then she kicked herself for being ridiculous. She was

MY PERFECT EX

tougher than this. So what if she had hordes of gorgeous companions? Lucky her!

She'd survived without a man in her life for so long, at the beginning of her career. And she'd achieved her dreams without a man's help. She'd show them that she didn't need anybody. She let go of Billy's hand and chatted to the photographers. She smiled and won them over, then found herself telling them about her company. She graciously let them take some close-ups. Then she beckoned Billy over to join her. She introduced him as her Account Director, which sent them into another frenzy. Billy stood open-mouthed until she nudged him. Then he grinned and kissed her cheek, excitement fizzing in his eyes.

After a few more minutes they rushed into the foyer of the hotel and found themselves a corner behind a massive plant where they could giggle like school kids. 'What was that all about?' Billy asked, when they had calmed down. 'For a second I thought you wanted to hog the limelight yourself? And now you've made me a director?'

'Well, I did promise you a title change at work, didn't I? We've been too busy to do anything about it, but I hadn't forgotten. And I've been thinking that you might like to learn more about my design process. I've got more work than I can handle right now. Although I don't want a partner, I think you have some great ideas and it's something we could work towards. You deserve a shareholding too.'

Billy clearly didn't know what to say, for once. Then he swept her off her feet into a hug, just as Jared poked his head around the huge plant they were standing behind. He looked jaw-droppingly handsome in his dinner suit and crisp white shirt. His aftershave made Poppy's senses spin, it was so bold and sexy.

'Am I disturbing something?' There was an edge to his voice, but Poppy chose to ignore it. She leaned in to kiss his cheek and he guided her out towards the other guests. 'I saw you arrive. The flashbulbs gave you away.' Billy followed them, with a huge smile on his face. Poppy felt a warm glow fill her body at his open show of happiness. It was time he took more of an active role at work and it would ease up her own schedule. She trusted him. She gave Jared a megawatt smile and his step faltered.

'You are the hot topic right now,' he grinned. 'I hope you can still find time for me in your diary? We have lots more projects to create together. I've also been looking into where we could site some of the health pods we talked about.'

They heard some journalists walk past discussing their last project. Jared's eyes crinkled at the corners. 'Maybe we should even build our own pod in a field where no one can find us?' he said cheekily. Poppy threw back her head and laughed. She loved that they could play like this again and adored talking about business with Jared. After what she'd been through, she could finally enjoy some flirty banter.

Jared had been nothing but courteous since the day after the last party, when she'd rung him to say thank you for the flowers. They'd met many times since then, but it had been business not pleasure and they had fallen back into their usual easy camaraderie. She had other things on her mind and he seemed to understand she'd needed space to mourn her relationship with Dylan. Tonight, though, Jared was back on form and a frisson of excitement filled her veins.

They walked into the huge function room, with glamorous people milling around and chatting. Some were crowded around the long bar at the back of the room. For a moment, she had a strong urge to get drunk and forget everything else for one night – but she needed to be on her best behaviour for their clients.

The room itself was a showcase of different natural products and she glanced around taking it all in, her heart beating at such beauty. The walls had hammered steel panels running across the centre, sparkling thanks to the huge bespoke modern chandeliers that were hung from the ceiling at intervals. The tables had been set without cloths, as the woodwork was too beautiful to be covered up. Poppy couldn't help gasping as she recognised Dylan's signature style as they walked past. Each table was arranged with scented candles and bowls overflowing with blooms, filling the air with the scent of wild flowers. Crystal glasses sat alongside handmade plates and silverware. She ran her hand along the plush velvet chairs. The combination of textures was breathtaking. Jared paused with her and enjoyed her response to the room. 'It's beautiful,' she praised. Even Billy was stunned.

Jared inclined his head. 'Thank you. This was a labour of love. It hasn't been open for very long, but it's already one of our best hotel projects.'

Billy had also noticed Dylan's work and was frowning. Neither of them had known that Jared and Dylan had worked together in the past. They had met a few times when Jared had been visiting the building site behind Poppy's house and dropped in to say hello. But why wouldn't they have mentioned a collaboration?

Then Billy started frantically trying to signal to Poppy with his eyes. She turned and the breath was sucked out of her. Standing at the bar and chatting to someone on his left was Dylan. His hair was slicked back and he was wearing a dark suit with an open-necked shirt. He looked devastatingly handsome. Poppy's heart felt like it was going to jump out of her chest. The person on his right spoke, and his hand slipped around her waist. Her long dark hair hung in curls down her back and her dress was sleek and sexy, but a touch too tight. *How could Sasha do this to her?* Poppy thought.

Poppy's world was now spinning on its axis. Billy was stunned too, still rooted to the spot. Then the woman turned at the same time as Dylan did, and they both saw her. Poppy gasped.

Jared noticed something was wrong immediately and his hand wound its way around her own waist to offer support. Then he spotted Dylan and the woman standing with him. Her hand was now proprietorially on his arm. Jared pulled Poppy closer to his side, his eyes glittering with anger.

'I'm sorry you had to see that, Poppy,' he said, looking round for a way out.

Dylan dropped his hand immediately and looked pointedly at Jared's. Poppy pushed Jared away and rushed outside, with Billy guiding her through a throng of people that suddenly felt so oppressive. Billy stayed with her until they stepped through the floor-to-ceiling doors leading out into the hotel gardens. They found a private space beside a wall, half hidden by ivy.

'How could she?' Poppy demanded to know. She didn't cry – the rage boiling up inside her was almost too much to bear and at this point it would have turned her tears into steam.

'I don't understand,' said Billy, leading her to a nearby seating area and pulling out a chair for her. She took it gratefully, glad to sit down before her legs buckled under her. 'Why is Dylan here with Anne? And what's with the touchy feely stuff?'

Poppy pinched her arm so she wouldn't weep at this double betrayal, but a small sob escaped her lips. Billy took her hand in his.

'I'm confused. I thought you said *Sasha* had always liked him?' he frowned and his eyes darted around the other guests in the distance, as if they would have the answers.

'She does.' Poppy thought for a moment and then made a low sound of someone in pain. 'Or I suppose that's what Anne wanted me to think. Ever since school, Anne has warned me off Dylan. She said it was because Sasha had slept with him. She said Dylan used women and discarded them. That's not the Dylan I know, but I believed Anne. She was my best friend. Why would I not?'

'Because she's after your man?'

Poppy looked up at Billy and he smiled politely at a couple of people wandering past, shielding her with his body before he turned back to her. 'Do you think both of them liked him, and that's why they didn't want you together?'

Poppy handed her phone to Billy and he nodded and quickly dialled Sasha's number. He spoke quietly to her, before holding the phone away while she screamed down the line. He winced and hung up. 'Nope. Sasha's never slept with Dylan and she made a sick noise at the very mention of it.' He could obviously see Poppy's doubt. 'She demanded to speak to you, but I said it would have to wait. She yelled right in my ear when I told her what was going on here.' He rubbed his earlobe and Poppy raised her first half-smile before it slid away again. Her eyes glistened with unshed tears.

Poppy thought of Freddie, and how hard his long illness had been on Anne, then her heart iced over when she pictured Dylan's hand on Anne's waist. It seemed such a familiar gesture somehow. The thought made her feel sick.

As if she had manifested him, Dylan appeared, a pinched, unhappy expression on his face. Billy stood in front of him, but Poppy put a restraining hand on his arm. 'It's ok, Billy.' He gave her a curt nod, almost snarling at Dylan, and stalked away to get them both what she hoped was a bloody big drink. Stuff the clients.

Dylan ran his hands through his hair and walked over to where she was standing. Poppy faced the man she loved, her heart breaking into a million pieces. 'Anne? My best friend?' she ground out, wishing she had something to throw in his smug face.

Dylan's eyes glittered and he took his jacket off and hung it over the nearest chair, his muscles bunching in his white shirt. She averted her gaze for a moment while she gathered her strength. It was so hard being near him and not touching him. She supposed that was Anne's prerogative right now. The thought made her stomach turn over, but her resolve hardened.

'I guess even though your friends thought I wasn't good enough for you, they were happy to snare me for themselves,' he said.

Poppy's eyes lit with fire and he almost stepped back, but stood his ground. She needed more air. Her hands bunched into fists and she'd never wanted to punch someone more, in her whole life. She didn't care that he was twice her size. 'So this is to prove what? A point? That Anne and the others wanted you the whole time? You could have just told me that!'

'You seemed to have moved on with Jared, so I can do what I like.'

She grit her teeth and snarled. 'Nothing has happened with Jared. He likes me. That's not my fault. So get over it!' she raged, not caring who was glancing their way. 'It seems you and Jared have worked alongside each other, judging by the look of your work in the hotel here. Why are you suddenly enemies? Why didn't you tell me you knew each other so well?'

'We didn't, really. As far as I was concerned, this was an order from the hotel. I didn't know the tables would be part of Jared's design scheme. I worked with an interior designer who was outsourced, like you were for the housing project. But, nevertheless, the way you spoke about Jared – I didn't like it,' he admitted finally.

'So you were jealous? But that didn't give you the right to sleep with my best friend!' She pushed her hands against his chest and made him move back so she could breathe. Her head was spinning. 'Is that why you didn't turn up at my launch? You were too busy shagging Anne as a way to make me pay? You could have just cut me loose and I'd have got drunk and slept with Jared. At least then both of us could have had a good time.'

Dylan cursed and took a step closer to her. 'Poppy. I made a mistake.' The heat from their bodies ignited. He took her hand and felt her pulse, but after a second she shook him loose.

'Don't you dare touch me. You lost that right the minute you slept with Anne.'

'She called me on your launch night and told me Freddie was unwell. She didn't want to worry you during your big event.' Poppy caught her breath. Her face started to flush and she steeled herself for the agony of having to face Anne, wherever she might be at that precise moment. The woman would pay for her treachery.

'But she was happy to call my boyfriend and not her other best friends, like Sasha and Demi?'

'She said everyone else was busy and it was urgent.'

'Of course it was! She told me when I met her the other week that she'd mixed up Freddie's medication, and freaked out, but that it was quickly sorted out, after a call to the doctor,' Poppy snarled. 'She even mentioned how lucky she was that she hadn't had to make an emergency visit, as the surgery was still open. They shut at six. My event started at eight. She didn't tell me that you were being her knight in shining armour, though. What did she ask you to do?'

Dylan hung his head and wouldn't meet her eye. 'She said she might need me to take Freddie into hospital, but in the end it wasn't necessary. She was in such state. It took hours to calm her down. After that, it was too late to join you.'

'I'm guessing that was her plan,' said Poppy, staring

around but not really seeing anything. Everyone else was just a blur. 'When we were kids, she told me to steer clear of you because you'd slept with Sasha.'

'What? I've never slept with Sasha.' Dylan's skin flushed.

'I know that now, but it's what she wanted me to believe, to keep us apart. It worked for years.'

'You were too busy with work to be bothered about what I was doing,' he ground out.

'That's not true, Dylan.' She was so tired that she wanted to drop to the ground and sleep for years. He'd just ripped her heart out and stamped on it. She looked into his eyes, and saw hurt there too. 'To be fair, you were just lazy.' She wanted him to feel her pain.

He took a step back and straightened his shoulders, making the fabric pull taut across his back. She tried to focus, but she could feel her eyes dilating. She hated her body's response to him now.

He reached out a hand to her but she just stared at it, so he dropped it to his side again. 'I work hard and want to relax in the evening. You build these amazing houses to help people wind down and enjoy life, but you are the antithesis of that. You don't know how to slow down. You have no work-life balance. You're a workaholic!' he said, noticing Billy hovering. Dylan gave him a warning look and Billy backed off. 'I didn't feel the need to work every hour as you do, my business is different. Clients approach me through word of mouth.'

He kicked a stray pebble on the paved floor and she could almost touch his frustration, the air was so thick with emotion. 'I started working harder, to please you, but that meant none of us were home. My work is artisan and in high demand. I could work every single hour of every day, but I chose not to, so I could see you!' he ground out.

Poppy could feel her relationship slipping away through

her fingers, but was at a loss about how to save it. He'd overstepped the mark with Anne – and there was no coming back from it.

His eyes implored her. 'You were the one that evaded me at school. Now you've got away twice. I admit I dated Sasha once, but she's been in love with Ollie for years and admitted she only went out with me that time to make my brother jealous. I wanted the same reaction from you, but you were always a closed book.' He turned and watched a couple clink glasses and toast the success of the evening. 'Why do you think Sasha keeps men at arm's length and spends all of her free time in the gym Oliver owns?'

Poppy paused in her fury for a second, and then remembered all the times Sasha had bumped into Dylan outside his house. She must have been hoping Oliver was visiting his mum, not Dylan. Poor Sasha! It all made sense now.

'Why wouldn't she have told me?'

'Because she knew that both you and Anne had a crush on me. When she came round to your house that first time, she confided in me that she had finally given up Oliver. She didn't tell you because she was embarrassed that he never noticed her. He's an idiot.'

Poppy's face flamed red. 'It seems that we've all been lying to each other for years. Anne always told me that you were a player who dated loads of girls. She said you'd break my heart – and she was right. I thought we were just having some space from each other, but it seems that you've moved on.' She tried to walk past him but he caught her arm.

'It seems to me that *you're* the one who has moved on,' Dylan fumed, but her look froze him and he dropped her arm.

Anne had joined Billy and glanced their way before heading towards them.

'I swear if she comes near me, I'll hurt her,' hissed Poppy under her breath.

Dylan turned and saw Anne, panic filling his face as if he knew his time was running out. 'Look, I'll admit this wasn't one of my brightest ideas. I was tormented from seeing you with Jared. Nothing's going on with me and Anne.' He implored her to believe him. Poppy stared down her nose at him like he was something on her shoe and then she looked directly at Anne. Anne's step faltered and she stopped.

Poppy walked up to her, back straight and voice calm. 'Don't think that I don't know exactly what you did here.' Anne's face flushed, but she stood her ground with bravado, tossing her hair over her shoulders. Poppy then moved her face closer to Anne's, and Anne finally flinched.

'I've heard Sasha's side and talked to Dylan. I feel like I know you better than I ever did before,' Poppy said. Anne's eyelids lowered for a second, but then she stared back at Poppy defiantly.

'Thank you for trying to ruin my life,' Poppy added, before moving past her, close enough for Anne to have to step back or get bumped in the shoulder.

'I fell in love with him first,' hissed Anne. 'Then you waltzed in and tried to take him away. All that spying on him you used to do from your mum's balcony was pathetic. He was never yours to keep.'

Poppy felt like she been hit the stomach, but refused to show it. She turned back briefly. 'You made sure of that, didn't you? How could you treat me this way?' The woman before her was a stranger now. 'I thought we were best friends.'

Poppy could have wailed and raged at the world, but she gripped her clutch bag as if her life depended on it and held herself together as Dylan and Billy looked on. Dylan tried to intercept her, but Billy put out a restraining hand on his chest.

'Best friends don't lie to each other for years,' said Anne cruelly. 'You never needed or confided in any of us. You always had loads of boys drooling after you, while we got overlooked. You don't want Dylan really, or you'd have tried harder – like I did. Go and find Jared, for goodness sake!'

Poppy's face blanched. She couldn't pinpoint when Anne had turned into a complete stranger. 'You were happy to take my money and let me finance your son's medical care, while you were trying to steal my boyfriend.'

Anne's face flamed scarlet. 'Oh don't be so bloody dramatic! What else was I going to do? I didn't know you'd funded most of it yourself until recently and by then it was too late. Freddie had started the treatment.'

Poppy felt like she had fire in her veins. 'I wouldn't begrudge Freddie anything. It's just a shame about the ethics of his mother. Don't ever contact me again.' Poppy signalled to Billy to follow her. Dylan was silenced with one look and understood not to come too. Jared came outside, looking around for them, and took a moment to grasp what was happening from people's body language. He placed a palm on Poppy's back and started to guide her inside, handing her a flute of champagne.

'You ok?' he asked with a worried frown, shooting Dylan a warning look which was returned with force.

Poppy gave Jared her brightest smile and gulped down some of the wine, trying hard not to choke on the tiny bubbles, her eyes smarting in pain. 'I'm fine,' she answered. 'Just moving on from the past and beginning my future.'

As they were sheltered from the view of most of the guests now, who were busily finding their seats and filling the room with laughter, she leant in and kissed Jared full on the mouth, making him gasp in surprise. Dylan chose that exact moment to come back inside with Anne.

From the triumphant look on Anne's face and the thunderous one on Dylan's, she knew her arrow had hit its target. But Poppy no longer cared what Anne thought about a single thing in her life. She took Jared's hand in hers and drew him back into the party and onto the dance floor. She quickly checked that Billy was ok. He was now talking to an old client, his eyes still darting between her and Dylan every so often. Dylan stood at the bar watching her every move, Anne seemingly forgotten and sitting morosely by his side on a bar stool, head bowed. Poppy took strength from the adrenalin flowing around her body. She was nobody's fool. She smiled up at Jared, who still had his arm curved protectively around her, and set about seducing her sexy business partner into her bed.

CHAPTER THIRTY-ONE

*P*oppy's head was pounding again. She dragged herself out of bed and into the shower, letting the water run in rivulets down her body, soothing her tired mind and washing the stain of last night from her skin. She hated the silence of the empty house and decided to go over to Billy's flat above her garage and snuggle up with him all day. Pulling on some comfy jogging bottoms and an un-ironed T-shirt, she padded across the back garden and let herself in – barrelling straight into Sasha.

'What the hell?' Poppy jumped back. 'What are you doing here...?'

Sasha grinned, just as Billy walked into the little kitchen area.

Poppy rolled her eyes. 'I might have known – you two have been plotting.'

'Busted,' said Billy. 'Sasha turned up here looking for you late last night, after we rang her from the party, remember? I didn't think it was a good time to bother you, as you'd only just calmed down.' He looked at Poppy's puffy skin and crumpled clothes and pulled a face.

She tugged at the hem of her T-shirt and rubbed her tired eyes. 'I know I look a mess,' she said.

Sasha glanced round for coffee or hot chocolate. She was a creature of habit. 'Second cupboard on the left,' sighed Poppy, feeling like her bones were made of lead.

Poppy leaned against the kitchen counter. Her whole world had tilted on its axis the previous evening. Billy nudged Sasha over to her. She pulled Poppy into a hug and linked her arms around her waist, keeping her close.

'Billy told me what happened. I just can't believe it! I'm so confused.'

'Go and sit on the couch and I'll bring coffee,' soothed Billy. 'And chocolate,' he added after seeing Sasha's pout. Poppy let herself be led away.

'Wait a minute,' Poppy said to Sasha. 'Dylan told me you'd been in love with Oliver for years.'

Sasha winced and hung her head. 'Well, it's true, I did lust after him for years. Why do you think I never date anyone for long, and I'm always at that stupid gym?'

Poppy's brow creased in concentration. 'Why didn't you ever tell me?'

'Because you and Anne were so besotted with Dylan and I thought you'd find it creepy that I was equally daft over his older brother. You'd both definitely have told me to back off.'

'I wouldn't. Why would I?'

'Anne said you were really precious about the whole family and would think I was trying to get in there first.'

'What the hell is wrong with that woman?' stormed Poppy, jumping up and pacing the room. 'She told me you'd slept with Dylan,' she raged. 'So I stayed away and didn't step on your toes for years until I decided you weren't interested anymore, Sasha. Now I know it's because she wanted him for herself. There's been so much wasted time. It was the real reason I didn't tell you we were dating. I thought you might have moved on, but was still unsure and didn't want to upset you. Too bad I didn't know I was worrying about the wrong brother.'

'I hadn't moved on from Oliver. Well, not until last night.'

Poppy sat back in shock. 'What changed?'

'I came to see you, and ended up here chatting to Billy. We talked about why I can't seem to let Oliver go and it's made me realise I need to change' Sasha hid her face and then looked at Poppy through her fingers. 'Do you think I'm an idiot?'

'What? No! Why on earth would I think that? I love you and want you to be happy. Oliver or no Oliver. He's stupid if he can't see what's in front of him. Seems that runs in the family,' she said snarkily.

'Billy and I were both stressed last night and I haven't had a man sit and talk to me about my life and my worries in years. I'm tired of waiting for Oliver to realise I'm the girl of his dreams.'

'He's an idiot,' seethed Poppy.

'So's Dylan!' Sasha said protectively. 'I'm so sorry for what you've gone through. Anne said Dylan was lazy and treated you really badly, by not supporting your new business. It's why Demi and I backed her up when she said Jared was the man for you. Is he?'

Poppy rubbed her sore stomach as Billy came in with two mugs of steaming coffee and a frothy hot chocolate for Sasha. 'I honestly don't know. I've spent so long crying over Dylan, but I haven't yet given him the chance to explain properly. He said Anne set him up and nothing was going on between them, but the way he was holding her waist as we walked in spoke volumes. It was so familiar.' Poppy felt tears sting her eyes and sniffed. 'Billy stopped me doing anything drastic last night. If it had been down to me, I might have done something stupid like sleeping with Jared, but that wouldn't have been fair on either of us. I know Jared likes me and I'm confused. I spent all night watching Dylan but pretending I couldn't care less about him.'

'Oh, Poppy!' said Sasha, sipping her drink and yelping as it was still scorching hot. She blew on it to cool it down and frowned, mumbling at the mess they were all in.

'I wanted to scratch Dylan's eyes out by the end of the night,' Poppy continued. 'Anne left after an hour. Dylan must have called a cab for her, but she didn't seem to want to go. He had to escort her out and she was grabbing his arm. He shook her off but still made sure she was safely in the cab. Ever the gentleman,' she said sarcastically. 'You were great, Billy, reporting back to me – like an dazzlingly gorgeous bodyguard,' she tried to laugh but just smiled sadly at him.

'I had to physically drag you home, Poppy,' said Billy. 'I'm pretty sure you would have screamed the place down if you'd actually spoken to Dylan again. I was worried you'd jump on Jared! Not that he'd have complained. He didn't want you to leave either.'

'You're a fine one to talk!' Poppy teased Billy. 'I saw you chatting up Fred from that architectural practice we worked with last year,' she smiled at Sasha, who pretended to be aghast at the scandal. 'In between your bodyguard duties, of course,' Poppy jabbed him in the ribs.

'We're just friends,' he grinned, with a smug smile. 'I've had my eye on Fred for a while, though. The owner of the firm might be a good match for you, Sasha. He's upfront and loaded,' he winked at Sasha, and she actually full-on blushed, meaning she'd already seen his picture somehow. Sasha never went soppy over a man!

Poppy wasn't quite sure how she felt about this development, but she was too tired to care right now. Jared had been the perfect gentleman all night and had stuck by her side, never letting anyone monopolise her for too long. She'd had to use every inch of her willpower to stay and not run straight home crying, but she refused to let Dylan or Anne know how much they had hurt her. Dylan had tried to approach her a couple of times but she had never been alone.

Jared had explained that he'd bought the consignment of bespoke furniture on the recommendation of his interior design team. He hadn't even known it was made by Dylan, until he'd arrived to make sure everything was set up correctly. Apparently Dylan was well regarded in the industry as an expert in furniture design. When she'd pointed out it must have taken a gargantuan amount of work to meet the deadline, he'd shrugged and said Dylan had expanded his team. That was news to her.

It killed Poppy to think that Dylan had only started to take on more work after they had split up. Before that, he'd not been interested at all in progressing in the industry. Maybe she'd been holding him back, somehow? She shook her head to try and clear it and a tear slipped out of her eye. Billy put an arm around her. She snuggled under his arm, then felt a bit awkward suddenly, as she wasn't properly dressed yet and Sasha was watching them. It had never been an issue before, they'd seen each other naked loads of times, but having another person there made her wince and move away from him, making him frown. She didn't want Sasha to start getting ideas about her friendship with Billy. Poppy had had enough tension to last a lifetime right now.

'Uh... I need to go back indoors and get dressed. I've got a presentation to work on for the group that owns Green Manor. You know, the facility Mum is at.'

Billy turned round in surprise as he went to make more coffee and chocolate. 'More new clients?'

'No, old ones. They want more of the pods I donated to them, but they are willing to pay for them now. They can see how they benefit their patients and want them for all their centres.'

Billy's eyebrows rose and his mouth dropped open. 'Wow. From memory from when you built the first ones, they have several sites across the UK.' Then he frowned. 'Do we have enough hours in the day to take on more work?'

'We do – if you do decide to step up as account director, and Sasha stops messing about and joins us, to run our schedule.' She looked at Sasha, who had her mouth hanging open in shock.

'What?' Sasha stared at Poppy and Billy. 'Is this because of Anne? Are you trying to get me onside? I'm not a charity case. You can't be serious!'

Billy moved a step back in shock at the ferocity of Sasha's words and Poppy almost growled at her lack of faith in herself. Then Billy burst out laughing, and Poppy couldn't help but follow suit. Sasha looked so outraged it was downright comical. 'What is it with you two?' fumed Sasha.

'You are not a charity case, Sasha,' said Poppy. 'You just need to find a job that actually interests you, and not one that just has fit men working there.'

'Oi!' said Billy.

Poppy smiled. 'Other than Billy, obviously.'

'I don't only take jobs to have a hot boss,' Sasha grumbled, but she wouldn't meet their eyes and she stopped protesting. It looked like she was going to consider the idea. Billy laughed and shook his head. 'Does this mean I can move in here with Billy?' Sasha winked at him suddenly, seeming brighter.

'You can move into one of my spare rooms if you want,' said Poppy, liking the idea of building her own little community, but not one hundred percent sure that Sasha wouldn't drive her mad within hours by bossing her around.

'You're a bit too straight-laced for me, but this flat is

amazing and I wouldn't even make a mess,' she batted her eyelashes at Billy. Billy snorted and turned to get the coffee. Poppy threw her hands up in exasperation.

'Are you really offering me a job?' asked Sasha, suddenly looking shy and glancing at Billy for his reaction to the news. Would he be put out about her getting between him and Poppy all of a sudden?

'Don't mind me! I'm not going to stop you getting a job now you've used my home and settled in,' Billy joked. 'You were just after a new flatmate the whole time.'

'You enjoyed having me here!' Sasha's face was red now. 'I wish you fancied women. Do you want a girlfriend?' she joked back.

It was Billy's turn to look uncomfortable and Poppy watched him carefully. 'Even delicious Fred couldn't stop me thinking about Ed. Might be fun to have you staying here for a while, but not all of the time! I might decide to invite someone back.' He waggled his eyebrows suggestively at Sasha and she laughed. Poppy pulled a sick face at their camaraderie, but secretly she was thrilled they were getting on so well. She loved them both.

'Concentrate, you two! I was not expecting to hold a board meeting at…' she glanced at her watch and looked up. 'Well, stupid o'clock on a weekend, when we should all be in bed. But you'll soon learn that we don't conform to regular office hours, or rules you might be used to in the other million places you've worked in, Sash.'

Sasha ignored the jibe and seemed to be mulling over the idea of changing jobs.

'Come on, you told me you hated your latest boss,' cajoled Poppy. 'Plus we now know that you were staying local for Ollie and all that's about to change. Let him see you working in a red hot company with sexy bosses,' she nodded at Billy, who was grinning from ear to ear at being called a boss.

'Show him you don't need to be around him to be happy. It's time we all moved on from that loathsome family!'

Sasha flinched. Poppy hadn't quite realised how much she'd raised her voice. 'Think about it,' Poppy added a bit more quietly, and then she left them to it.

CHAPTER THIRTY-TWO

Dylan rubbed his hands through his hair and tried to quell the anger that burned inside him. He was working twelve-hour days and it numbed his brain to most other things. New orders arrived daily and he had decided to bring in a team of artisans that he sometimes worked with. At this rate he'd need bigger warehouse space.

It was actually a lot of fun having them around, they were raucous and creative, but extra work meant more time behind his beautifully crafted oak desk and less time living his life. Ok, he was making a lot of money, but he'd been doing that before. He'd always had enough contracts to live very comfortably, without the headache of juggling staff rotas and shipping consignments all over the world. But word had got out about the hotels he'd supplied furniture to, and he now needed a secretary, fast. He fleetingly thought of Sasha, but she'd probably bite his head off after the way he'd treated Poppy and Anne.

All he'd ever wanted, since he was a teenager, was to have Poppy by his side. But it had never quite worked out, for some reason. Now he understood that reason was Anne. He hadn't realised she was obsessed by him, but maybe he should have guessed it was a possibility. He'd known Sasha had mooned for years over his thick-skulled big brother, Ollie. He'd assumed that Anne had often popped up when he was with his brother because she was keeping an eye on Sasha. Now he knew differently.

Oliver was too stupid to notice Sasha. He'd always had someone by his side, but not one of those girls was a patch on feisty Sasha. Sasha's attempts to be subtle hadn't worked when she popped by, or bumped into him and then grilled him on his brother's whereabouts. Dylan had known what was going on and tried to steer her away. Ollie just wasn't interested. The idiot. But now Dylan realised he was pretty thick himself, for not seeing Anne's obsessive interest, either.

Dylan sighed and rolled his neck to ease some tension. He found himself stomping around and growling at people when he thought of Poppy, and was working to prove her wrong. Anne had told him Poppy thought he was lazy and not good enough for her. Now he knew what Anne had been up to. She'd succeeded in jamming a wedge between them, by slithering around whispering untruths. Poppy might have been frustrated by his laid-back ways, but he knew she was proud of him really. She'd changed lately, though. If a man like Jared was what she wanted, well then, Dylan would show her he could be successful too.

He pictured Jared's hand slipping around her waist. His fists clenched and his muscles reacted. He had wanted to punch Jared's smug face, but one look from Billy told him that would have been the wrong thing to do. It would have sent Poppy further into Jared's web and he might never have been able to get her back. Dylan wasn't about to sit around and have another man take the love of his life. He would prove to Poppy that he was worthy of her… as soon as he had a minute to clear his head and streamline his ever-growing business.

Dylan could have kicked himself for starting all this off by missing her opening night, but Anne had been crying on the phone. His instincts had kicked in. He'd assumed that Poppy would be proud of him for helping her friend and that she'd throw her arms around him and understand that he had been planning to surprise her. But no, she'd had fire in her eyes and she'd not accepted his reasoning, even though it was all to help her beloved Freddie. She would literally die for that kid, so Dylan was floored at her response. Then he'd grasped Anne's intention and discovered her lie – but by then the whole mess had caved in on his head.

The phone rang and he picked it up and swung his leather armchair around to look out at the view. Poppy had helped him build this office and she'd insisted he had the same sort of view that she did, so they could look out and think of each other. Now it just caused him pain. Her office was on the other side of the village, on Cherry Blossom Lane. It was one of the prettiest streets locally. He could imagine her looking across fields very like these, and feeling anguish too. Unless she was wrapped in Jared's arms and happy as hell.

He finished his call and cursed, purposefully ignoring the view and quickly tapping some figures into his computer. He made a mental note to call Sasha and see if she wanted a job. He'd ask her to help him sort out all this mess. He knew she'd bite his head off at first, but it would be worth it if she could persuade Poppy to meet him. Sasha would call him names and probably kick him in the balls, but he'd heard she was still talking to Poppy. How come he was such a pariah? Poppy was ignoring his calls at the moment. So was Billy. Dylan felt the loss doubly.

On that fateful night of the party, Anne had called him, sounding frantic, saying Freddie needed help. She'd pleaded with him to get to her house quickly and said that she couldn't call Poppy and ruin her big night. He'd grabbed his keys and hadn't thought twice about it. He didn't want Poppy's night spoilt either. He knew how important it was, but he also knew she'd drop anything for Anne and Freddie.

When he'd arrived, Anne had suckered him in. She'd kept him there for long enough to be too late for the party, then she'd undermined his relationship. It was his own stupid fault for believing the drivel she spouted.

He'd been devastated when she confided that she was worried about Poppy. She'd been so convincing. She'd tearfully confided that Poppy was keen to make a go of things with Jared, but didn't want to hurt Dylan's feelings!

Dylan hadn't been able to believe what he was hearing, but she'd poked a part of him that had been feeling unappreciated, vulnerable and jealous. Time ceased to exist and thoughts had spun through his mind, reliving every fault in their relationship. Then he'd lifted his chin and grit his teeth. Dylan wasn't 'dynamic' enough for Poppy, according to Anne. Poppy felt she needed a real man, not a boy from her childhood.

He'd been stunned to silence and he hadn't known what to do. That's when Anne finally said she'd been in love with him for years. She'd told him Poppy was probably sleeping with Jared right then – and then she'd leaned over and kissed him.

Dylan was ashamed that he hadn't reacted fast enough to stop Anne straight away, but he'd been trying to digest what she'd revealed. He'd known there were problems in his relationship, but believed they would sort themselves out in time. His heart soared when Poppy was near and he'd stupidly thought she loved him in return. He'd been arguing with Poppy and felt there was something wrong, but he couldn't work out what it was. Anne made him think Jared was the problem. She had been underhand and malicious.

The problem was that part of what Anne said made sense. Poppy wanted wealth and success. What he'd realised over the past weeks was that she was compensating for never knowing where the next meal was coming from as she was growing up. She didn't want to feel that way ever again, and had built an incredible empire to try and make sure it wouldn't. Along the way, she'd forgotten how to sit and smell the blossom trees, even though her whole business ethos was geared towards mental health.

Dylan felt angry that Poppy had had to grow up so fast and feel responsible for her mum, when it should have been the other way round. He also raged at her dad for leaving her. Her mother might as well have been absent, too. She'd done nothing but take from Poppy since she was a child. It was too much for anyone to live through without having serious issues of their own. Having friends like Anne, who had probably been sabotaging her life for years, added to the burden. No wonder Poppy felt the need to lie.

Dylan pictured his own mother, fussing around and shooing them all out of the kitchen for being too boisterous. She'd also been full of cuddles and smiles. There was such comfort in knowing she was there for them. The same went for his dad, too. Dylan's heart broke for the hell Poppy had been through and what she'd quietly suffered, whilst hiding her true self from the whole community. She'd lived in fear of being found out her whole life. He shouldn't have pushed her to bring her two worlds together. It had ripped them apart. Perhaps she'd subconsciously felt the need to keep the two sides of her life separate, after years of second-guessing Anne?

He closed his eyes and propped his chin in his hand, resting his elbow on his desk. Usually the grain of the wood and the feel of the surface calmed him, but today he needed to take action. He'd employ a manager and a personal assistant, and then he'd finally be able to think clearly again. He wondered if he'd ever be happy without Poppy, and already knew the answer. If she wanted a man of action, he'd give her one. He'd show her that he could be successful and happy – and then win her back.

He'd seen Poppy's reaction to Anne being at his side at the party, and that gave him a glimmer of hope. Anne had begged him to let her join him. He still felt such anger at the memory of her deception. She'd said that she wanted to apologise to Poppy face to face for trying to kiss him, and had pleaded with him not to tell her first. She'd used their shared history from school to play on his heart strings. She said a public place might be better to confess the truth, but once again she'd blindsided him and lied, making Poppy believe they were a couple. Even Billy had been duped by Anne's antics, and Dylan had been so furious at Jared's over-familiarity, he'd suddenly wanted Poppy to feel the pain he felt. He'd acted childishly, and now he was suffering for it.

Dylan had wanted Poppy to realise that someone else liked him too, so she'd understand how it really felt to be jealous. He'd realised his mistake within seconds – he'd seen it in Poppy's eyes. But by then it had been too late. He'd tried to get near her all night, but business contacts and her guard dog Billy had kept him at bay. She'd answered one tense call, where she'd told him it was over. It had felt like a knife between his ribs. But he would get her back. He was going to start making that happen today.

CHAPTER THIRTY-THREE

*P*oppy smiled as Sasha and Demi came into the café with their usual fuss and noise. Demi looked as stunning as ever with her dark curls bouncing around her face and her eyes sparkling. She was laughing at something Sasha was saying and they both turned her way, and then stopped short when they saw Anne's empty seat. Then they carried on, putting their handbags on the table, before Chris gave them a stern look and they rapidly moved them to the floor. Chris was a stickler for hygiene and had a pet hate of anyone putting bags on his pristine table tops. He would never admonish other customers, but he treated the girls like his own kids.

'Have you been to the gym?' Poppy asked Sasha. Demi giggled, nudging her shoulder.

Sasha signalled to Chris for their coffees, then turned to Demi. 'Nope. I am not setting foot in that place for a while. I'm finally free of the dashing and dastardly Oliver. Billy has made me see sense.'

'Finally!' said Demi with glee, earning a josh on the arm from Sasha. 'Living with Billy must be brilliant fun. I hope you're both meeting new people and having lots of exciting sex!' she joked.

'Urghh!' said Poppy, putting her hands over her ears.

Sasha tried to look contrite, but it didn't work. 'Does it bother you – me staying there sometimes?'

'That two of my best friends are probably having a lot more fun than I am? Yes. That you seem happy living together? No.' Poppy was getting used to the new set-up, with Sasha staying at the annexe for a few nights a week. Sasha was finally over Oliver, and now Ed was stepping up his efforts to woo Billy back. 'Has Billy said any more about Ed?'

'We are actually off men at the moment and are 'finding' ourselves,' said Sasha primly. Demi's eyes sparkled with mirth. The light in Sasha's eyes dimmed slightly, but she covered it quickly. Not before Poppy had seen it, though. 'It's fun working with Poppy and Billy, but if Billy gets back with Ed, I won't mind being back at my flat more often. I feel stronger now. I've finally realised that I don't need a man to be happy. I think I was just a bit lonely,' she admitted. Poppy squeezed her hand in solidarity.

Sasha looked at Poppy's hand in hers. 'I'd never get in the way if Ed came back. I want the kind of love you had with Dylan, Poppy,' she said, then gasped and stuck her hand over her mouth. 'Sorry! I'm always putting my foot in it. Especially considering the part we played in your break-up.'

Demi was shaking her head. 'Honestly, Sasha. Can't you be a bit more tactful? You always blurt things out without testing them in your head first.'

'The first time she stayed over with Billy, she basically told him she he wanted to steal his flat and invited herself to stay!' Poppy smiled, but the pain in her stomach was worse now.

'Have you spoken to Dylan?' asked Demi, taking her drink

from Chris, who was hovering to hear the answer. Poppy smiled at him and told him to sit down. Anne's seat was a glaring beacon and Chris might as well find out what was going on too. He'd called Poppy a few times, but it had hurt too much to talk about.

'I heard he's working like a demon,' Sasha butted in, earning a scolding look again from Demi, which she ignored. 'He's not with Anne,' confided Sasha, 'And… he offered me a job.'

'What?' Poppy put her coffee down and sat back in shock.

'Why doesn't anyone offer me all these glamorous jobs?' asked Demi petulantly.

'Because you wouldn't leave Allan, and your dad's garage?' said Sasha. 'Plus, I'm way more interesting.' She stuck her tongue out at Demi.

'And more qualified, with the hundred jobs you get through every year,' said Demi sarcastically, making them all laugh.

'But… Dylan offered you a job?' asked Poppy, still feeling light-headed at the mention of his name.

'I loved every minute of telling him to stuff his job offer! Told him I was working for you.'

'What did he offer you?' Poppy was in shock. Dylan had always resisted employing extra staff. Those he did have had all been with him for years. He had always commanded huge sums for one-off items, but hadn't accepted many contracts before. She had seen that hotel room full of stunning furniture, weeks ago, but hadn't had time to compute what that meant. Her brain was so fuzzy right now she was having trouble concentrating on her work. Jared was a distraction. His attentions were getting more ardent, but Dylan and Anne had shattered her. She hadn't recovered from the double betrayal. Even seeing Chris in Anne's chair made

Poppy grimace. She tried to concentrate on what Sasha was saying.

Sasha loved having everyone's attention. She sipped her hot chocolate, making them all wait, until Demi nudged her. 'Oi! Ok. He needs an office manager, like you did, Poppy. He's working every hour of the day and night, and he's not a natural at saying no these days.'

'Oh we all know that,' said Poppy bitchily and Sasha rolled her eyes.

'He looks awful.' She pointedly looked at Poppy's scraggy figure. 'You are both complete messes right now. You wouldn't eat, if Billy and I didn't insist on it, and Dylan is working round the clock to prove to you he's not a waster… like we all thought. Sorry, Poppy.' She hung her head suddenly and Demi looked shiftily away.

Chris gave them both a stern glare and took Poppy's hand in his. 'You need to stop meddling in each other's lives. Dylan is one of the good ones, and so is Oliver.' He looked pointedly at Sasha, whose mouth dropped open in shock. One of the waitresses called over that he was needed in the kitchen, so he started collecting up their mugs.

'That guy Luis is lovely too,' defended Poppy, mentioning the man Billy kept trying to tempt Sasha to date. 'Billy says he's perfect. He runs an architectural practice in town.'

'I'm sure he's very nice, but he's not Oliver,' was all Chris said, as he stood up and smoothly navigated his way past the customers, retreating to the kitchen with their dirty cups.

All of the girls sat in stunned silence. Chris was a font of wisdom and now they were all confused. He didn't say much, but when he did venture an opinion, it was on the money. 'Look,' said Demi. 'Let's forget Oliver for now. Chris is wrong. He's not the guy for you, Sasha,' she added, when she saw Sasha's forlorn look.

'She's right. He's not.' Poppy agreed.

'Ok.'

'Now then,' said Demi. 'What about you, Poppy? You need to start eating properly. And what about Dylan and Anne? Let's clear the air and sort this hot mess out.'

'I don't really want to talk about Dylan and Anne anymore. They're welcome to each other,' sighed Poppy, rubbing her eyes and staring out of the window for a moment, before she caught sight of Dylan's mum's house and turned back to her friends, her heart lurching.

'Ok. Fill us in on what's happening with your mum, then. Is she really coming back to the flat?' asked Sasha, swiftly moving on.

Poppy didn't miss the scepticism in her voice. She chewed her lip, and tried to think of a good way of putting things. Nothing was ever straightforward in her life, but her mum was finally asking to come and look at the flat, which was a huge step. 'For all of the dreams I've had about her coming home, I'm now scared stiff.' She took a deep breath. 'I don't live there anymore and I'm not sure I thought things through. She won't have specialist care there and…'

'And what?' asked Demi gently.

Poppy let out the breath she'd been holding for what felt like weeks, and spoke about something that had been on her mind. She'd kept all of this secret for so long. Being open about it felt strange. Supposing they looked at her like she was damaged goods again? She glanced at Demi and Sasha and knew she had to be honest this time. 'There's a balcony there. What happens if she gets sad or manic again… and jumps?'

Demi's mouth dropped open but she quickly snapped it shut after one sharp glance from Sasha. 'Is she still that unwell?

Poppy sat back and thought for a moment. 'No. She's not. She's on medication and will be for the rest of her life probably – but she's changed lately. She's been using the pods I designed at Green Manor, where she lives, and suddenly she's decided she has a purpose. She wants to assist me, setting more pods up across the country, to help others like her.'

Poppy reached for the fresh coffee Chris had just placed in front of her but she didn't drink it. She had been going over and over the idea in her mind, ever since her mum had first mentioned it a while ago. 'One week she wants to take art classes, the next she wants to work in a cake shop. This is her latest idea.'

Sasha frowned. 'Does she have any experience in cake making, sales, or design?'

'No.' replied Poppy.

'But… Won't it cause you more stress? Having to keep an eye on her, if she becomes involved in your business? It's your reputation. After all, you've spent years…' she gave Poppy a stern look, 'building your brand.'

'Yes, and you can't let your mum destroy your hard work,' said Sasha.

Poppy finally sipped her coffee and winced. It was bitter. She shook some sugar into it.

'I'm actually coming round to the thought that she might be an asset. She's got so much history with mental health issues, she could give me further insight into refining my ideas.'

'They don't need refining!' growled Sasha protectively.

'Thank you,' said Poppy. 'Well, I'm still considering it, but mostly she wants to go and see what I've done to the flat and spend time with Gladys. Gladys is so excited that she's invited Chris, and the three of them are spending a few hours together tomorrow.'

'Well… that could be a good thing, then?' asked Demi, tentatively.

'Maybe. I'm not going to let her become properly involved in anything more until I see she's happy back at home, and has some sort of routine. I asked her to move in with me, but she wants to finally have some space and be on her own.'

'Did you tell her about Dylan?' asked Sasha.

'She already knew. Gladys told her. Mum and I are a lot more open with each other now. Talking to you guys helped me see that I need to stop presuming that I know what other people are thinking. Mostly they are getting on with their own lives and not worrying about me at all. I have to get over my own feelings of inadequacy. They aren't because of everyone else, like I thought.' Sasha took Poppy's hand, then put it down again to scoop up a huge spoonful of whipped cream from her hot chocolate and deposit it in her mouth. Half of it missed and slipped down her chin, making them all giggle, before they became serious again.

'And did you tell your mum about Anne?' asked Demi. Sasha's spoon stopped mid-dip for more cream.

'I did. She's my mum and I needed advice.'

'What did she say?' Both Demi and Sasha seemed to be leaning in closer now. Poppy wondered if this was what it felt like to be in an inquisition.

'She was upset – disappointed in Anne's behaviour – and then said she'd always worried about how obsessed she was with Dylan as a child! I didn't think my mum really noticed my friends.'

Demi and Sasha sat back in shock. 'How did we never see that, then?'

'Because Anne told us all different stories to keep her feelings hidden.'

'Why, though? That's what I don't understand,' said Demi.

'Poppy was already mooning over Dylan and Anne stupidly thought she could steer Poppy away by saying I was into him,' said Sasha sadly. 'She didn't know Poppy was already a goner, had fallen head over heels in love and would stay besotted like a puppy forever.' Poppy winced.

'A bit like your obsession with Oliver,' said Demi helpfully and Sasha ignored her.

'What is it about those Taylor boys? How come you didn't get hooked on one?' Poppy asked Demi.

'She met Allan, and that was that!' Sasha piped up for her.

'I did fancy Miles at one point,' Demi giggled. They all gasped. She held up her hands. 'We had a quick snog when we were at a party once, but that was the same night I met Allan.'

Poppy and Sasha sat there in stunned silence, before they both began to speak at the same time. 'What?'

'What are you talking about?' jumped in Sasha. 'You kissed Miles Taylor?

Demi blushed. 'Only once, and it didn't mean anything. I found out an hour or so later that he'd arrived with another girl, so it was lucky that Allan was there to cheer me up.' Then Demi swiftly changed the subject, asking Poppy about Anne.

'I haven't heard from her at all. Not even a sorry, for ruining my life and stealing my boyfriend,' said Poppy bitterly.

'What about Dylan?'

'What about him?'

Demi and Sasha looked at each other for a second. Then Demi piped up. 'I don't really understand why Anne did what she did. We need to sort this out.' She earned a glowering look from Poppy. 'I know you don't want to talk about it, but we have to. Why did she say Sasha had slept with Dylan? Surely *I'm* more Dylan's type?' Demi joked, earning a swat on the arm from Sasha.

'How do you feel about Oliver now?' Demi asked Sasha.

'I'm finally ok. I've not got so much free time, as Poppy works me hard,' she winked at Poppy. 'And I'm not going to the gym every day to moon after Oliver. There's a new one opening opposite our offices on Cherry Blossom Lane, so I might check that out. Funnily enough, I saw Ollie in the street the other day and he actually stopped to ask where I've been. First time that's ever happened.' She held her head up high.

'And?'

'And what? I walked on by!'

'That's what you need to do with Dylan, Poppy,' said Demi.

Poppy's bottom lip wobbled and Demi reached for her hand and squeezed it. 'I've cried so many tears,' Poppy said. 'Not just for the loss of Dylan, but for Anne too. I thought she was my best friend. I need to learn from you, Sasha,' said Poppy, with awe in her voice.

'What exactly would you learn from Sasha?' asked Demi while Sasha looked affronted. 'Although after mooning over one guy for ten years, it does look like she's finally getting somewhere?' Demi giggled. Sasha batted her with the menu but ended up laughing too.

'We're all moving on,' said Sasha looking sideways at Poppy. 'Aren't we?'

Poppy didn't answer. She still hadn't worked that out for herself.

'Do you believe Dylan was trying to make you jealous, and didn't really sleep with Anne?' asked Demi in a hushed voice.

'I wish I knew,' said Poppy, sighing and resting her heads in her hands.

Sasha shot a worried look at Demi and they both signalled to Chris to bring emergency cake, and lots of it.

CHAPTER THIRTY-FOUR

Poppy tried to focus on her latest job, for a big medical centre provider. They wanted her to design several pods for each of their centres. She found herself smiling more and her stomach fluttered with anticipation about the arrangement. She was also working with Jared on his next project, but had decided to keep the pod side of the business separate from him. He was gradually becoming more important in her life. She wasn't quite sure how it had happened. He'd often turn up at her house after work for a chat about something, or just to check she was ok. He hadn't tried to push her into a relationship since the night at the hotel, and she was enjoying having someone else to take the strain from her. Job offers appeared, as if by magic, in her inbox, every single day.

Sasha's new tenacity had become a real asset to the business. Poppy had wondered if she'd get bored and move on, as she had before with her other jobs, but this time she was jumping in with both feet and she soon had Poppy and Billy working far more efficiently. She'd cut out some coffee and chat times, but had scheduled in creative meetings with agendas, and still let them have the coffee. Poppy knew Sasha was bossy, but was surprised to see that at work she utilised that particular trait in an effective way. She didn't overstep the mark, she respected Poppy as her boss, and Billy, too, and still somehow managed to make them twice as productive. Thank goodness Dylan hadn't got to her first!

The thought of Dylan made Poppy's bottom lip tremble, but she gritted her teeth and tried to be strong. She needed to take a leaf out of Sasha's book and turn her back on those dratted Taylor men. Sasha had yearned for Oliver for ten years – but she'd got over him now. Dylan had called Poppy many times over the last few weeks, cajoling and trying to win her back. She wasn't ready to face him yet. Her heart was healing, but she still knew if she saw him she'd melt at his feet, or jump into his arms. The thought of him and Anne made her want to curl into a tiny ball and weep, but she'd done enough of that recently. She used daily affirmations to stay strong and to pretend she was getting over him. Billy's worried looks and Sasha's enquiries about Jared were both wearing her down.

Poppy walked into her office and immediately smelt the beautiful flowers Jared had sent her the day before. They were wild and fragrant and the card just said 'thinking of you' and was signed with a kiss, nothing else. Next to that on her desk was the little hand-carved box that Dylan had made, with a blossoming cherry tree etched into the surface, to store her secret stash of boiled sweets. She always sucked them when she drew out her initial designs. Tears pooled in her eyes. She heard Billy come into the outer office and say something to Sasha and she roughly brushed the tears away, reaching out for the box and running her hands over the surface, before tucking it away in her desk drawer.

She heard raised voices in the other room and she gasped in sudden recognition – before Dylan strode into her office and attempted to close the door in Sasha's face. Poppy saw Sasha's surprised expression, before she shrugged and backed away. It was a soft-close door, so there could be no slamming in her office, She did have to smile at that.

They stood in front of each other, both breathing heavily as if they had just run a marathon. Dylan reached out to her, but his hand fell to his side when he saw Poppy's dark look. She went and stared out of the window, but for once the scene in front of her didn't soothe her mind.

She saw Dylan notice the flowers and the card sitting next to them. 'You got my flowers,' he stated.

'They were from you?' she wanted to grab the words back as soon as she said them. His face creased in anger.

'You thought they were from him? So you're still seeing him?' he demanded to know.

Poppy span round and tried not to raise her voice. She had a good idea that Sasha and Billy would be straining their ears to hear. 'I was never seeing him,' she hissed. 'But I'm single and can date who I like.'

'Are you single?' his eyes pleaded with hers, but the wall of ice around her heart chilled even further.

'You were the one who cheated, not me.' She fought back tears. She would not let him see her cry, so she bit down on her lip and crossed her arms over her chest and hugged herself.

'I've told you over and over that nothing happened with me and Anne. She tricked me as much as you! When are you going to see that I made a misjudgement, by trusting her? But I did not kiss her back – and I did not sleep with her!'

Dylan walked over to Poppy and took one of her hands, leading her to the couch beside the far wall and pulling her to sit next to him, their knees touching. She started to shake. The feel of his hand touching hers again after all this time made her eyes fill with tears.

'Why won't you answer my texts or talk to me about how hurt you are?' he asked, looking just as washed-out as she did. 'I'm hurt too. You didn't listen to me, you only listen to your friends.' When she tried to butt in, he wouldn't let her.

'I love you, Poppy. I have loved you since we were teenagers and I love you still. I trusted Anne's motives, the same way you did. We had issues at the time – with Jared, and with how little you think of my job – but I've changed. For you.'

Poppy tried to jump up, but he held her hand so she couldn't. 'I never had an issue with your job! I love what you do. I am just built differently,' she protested.

'I can appreciate that,' he tried to joke, his eyes skimming over her lovingly, making her skin heat up and her face flush. She gave him a wobbly smile and he gently brushed her tears away with his thumb.

'I'm ambitious,' she said, sniffing. 'I've always had a drive to succeed and I don't want to have to rely on anyone again.'

'I'm not your mum, Poppy,' he said gently. 'You can rely on me.'

'Can I?' she asked honestly and saw him flinch. She sighed and ran her hands through her hair, realising that she had forgotten to wash it that day. 'I felt that I was trying hard to make a secure future for us and you didn't want to make the same effort.'

Dylan's eyes were blazing into hers. She hated seeing him upset, but this needed to be said. 'I couldn't understand why you didn't want more. I did listen to my friends, but in the end it was my own insecurities talking. I didn't want anyone else relying on me the way my mum does.' She could see a deeper understanding dawning as his eyes misted over.

'Does it make you happier now that I'm so busy that I'm hardly ever at my flat or have any time for a life?' he asked gently.

Poppy looked at his handsome face, that was now creased with stress. She reached out and trailed her fingers across his cheek, making him jump as if she'd electrified him. It had been so long since she'd voluntarily touched him. 'No,' she said honestly. She thought for a minute, and she looked down in shame. 'Maybe... I do like it that you are too busy to see Anne, or anyone else.' Dylan sighed in what seemed like relief and he pulled her onto his lap, where she resisted for a split second, then snuggled under his chin, her face resting on his chest, listening to his heart.

'I was never dating Anne. We haven't spoken since the big argument that night. She's tried to contact me, but I'm not interested in her apologies now.'

She looked up at him at that and he swooped down and captured her lips with his. Her body melted into his and her fingers automatically reached up and desperately tangled into his hair. He groaned and made the kiss deeper and she almost fainted in bliss. There was a knock at the door and they sprang apart as Billy and Sasha appeared behind it, both raising eyebrows when they saw Poppy sitting in Dylan's lap with a flushed face.

'Uh. I take it you two have finally made up?' Billy asked. Poppy buried her head in Dylan's chest with embarrassment and Sasha came in and plonked her bottom on the desk, looking at them, never one to stand on ceremony.

'We need to sort this mess with Anne out.' When Poppy sat up and glared, Sasha held up her hand. 'It's messing with work, relationships and friendships. I spoke to her last night.'

When everyone looked stunned, she waved them all away. 'Anne's completely in the wrong and has gone a bit weird through all this,' Sasha stated, as Poppy stared at her. 'Ok. Apparently she's always had a problem with you two together, but it seems to be all about her ex, Connor.'

'What?' Poppy got up and they all crowded round Sasha,

who seemed to be enjoying being the centre of attention, and didn't seem bothered that she'd just disturbed one of the best kisses of Poppy's life.

'Anne fancied Connor at school but he didn't notice her. When she saw Dylan liked you, Poppy, and also found out how much I liked Oliver...' Sasha said, still blushing at the mention of his name. 'Well, Anne got jealous.' Dylan frowned and Poppy couldn't believe her ears. Had this all been about bloody Connor? 'Connor kissed her at that big party we all went to, as we were leaving school.' Sasha looked at Dylan. 'You know... the school party? The one where Demi kissed Miles?' She grinned as that titbit hit home. Dylan looked shocked. Poppy shook her head. She'd have to tell Dylan about Miles and Demi later. 'So...' continued Sasha, waiting for a mere second for them to catch up. 'Apparently Connor then went off with someone else. Then Dylan was kind to Anne, so she thought she'd pay Connor back by snogging Dylan, but Dylan only had eyes for Poppy. So it was a double slap in the face.'

'I remember that party,' Dylan frowned. 'She draped herself all over me and tried to kiss me, but I moved away. She babbled something about being drunk and we never spoke about it again. I assumed it was nothing,' he said, looking at Poppy. She frowned and he threw his arms up. 'It *was* nothing! How was I supposed to know Connor was behaving like an idiot? Why am I paying for his mistakes?'

Sasha looked uncomfortable, while Billy was stunned. 'Anne's still unhinged if she thinks sleeping with her best friend's boyfriend is ok,' said Billy, then he looked guiltily at Poppy.

Poppy tried to quell her rage and stomped over to her desk. 'Why does everyone think the mention of someone's mental health is going to bring me to my knees? I am not my mother!'

'Finally!' said Sasha. 'We've been telling you that for years.'

'Um, I am still here and I did not sleep with Anne,' said Dylan, moving to stand beside Poppy, eyes flashing at Billy. 'It's about time your friends stopped getting mixed up in our relationship. Now I want to speak to Poppy without an audience, so can you two go somewhere else?' he asked forcefully. Billy tried to look round Dylan, to check with Poppy, but Dylan's face was set and Sasha pulled him out of the room, finally giving them some space.

CHAPTER THIRTY-FIVE

As the door closed, Dylan turned to Poppy and saw that her skin was flushed and she looked deeply upset. 'I had no idea Anne was using me to hurt you, or that I'd upset her when we were kids.'

He tried to quell his anger, but he was questioning why they'd wasted so much time. He really should be back in his office. Nothing was more important than this, but now things were busier, he had headaches to deal with every day. He had client calls, production lines, more staff and a new assistant. He had far more money in the bank, but he'd had enough of that before to be very comfortable. And now he had no time to spend it anyway. He felt like he'd stepped onto a hamster wheel. He didn't know how Poppy did it. She actively sought out more work every day, even though she was in such demand. He was in awe of her, but he didn't want to *be* her. His business was successful without all that stress.

Dylan steeled himself to help Poppy find a balance somehow. He wanted to be the man she dreamt of, but without killing himself first. She was supposed to be an advocate for mental health, but she was definitely pushing him to his limits of sanity.

Poppy slumped into her chair and all his anger suddenly washed away. He went to her and gently brushed her hair from her shoulder, like he'd done a million times before, and bent down and kissed the nape of her neck. She sighed and leant back into him as he stood behind her. He swivelled her chair round until she was facing him and pulled her to stand up, taking her in his arms and feeling no resistance.

He kissed her full lips and she tasted of spice and coffee. A heady combination. He wanted to pick her up and take her back to his flat, but he could tell she was exhausted and, although she was responding to his kisses, she was holding back. He put a space between them and ran his thumb over her jawline. Her eyes were slightly glazed and she looked up at him and smiled, before licking her lips and reaching up to kiss him again.

This time she set his world alight and he had to come up for air or start undressing her at that exact moment. His hands were already running over her back and firm bottom. He had to get a hold of his emotions before he took her on her office desk. He'd missed her so much that he'd had to almost work himself into the ground to stop himself from going to her house, every time she'd ignored his countless text messages and phone calls. He backed her into the desk and took one more of those fiery kisses, before stepping away and running his hands through his hair. His heart was almost beating out of his chest and he felt like he was panting with lust.

'I think we need some air before I do what I've been dreaming of for weeks, and ravish you on that desk.'

Poppy's eyes dilated and she glanced at it as if she'd imagined the same thing he had, but then the phone rang, breaking the tension and making her pause before she picked

MY PERFECT EX

it up. She spoke to Sasha for a minute. Finally she turned to him. 'Hold that thought,' she said to him cheekily. 'But Sasha says I've got a client waiting in reception and I'm not sure seeing that would give them the most professional impression.' She smothered a giggle and blushed.

'I don't know...' he joked, taking her hand and kissing her palm. She shivered as he happily gave her a quick peck on the lips and moved towards the door. 'I guess Sasha will be in here, shoving me out, if I don't leave soon? You were lucky to get her before I did. She's a real asset.'

Poppy smiled. 'She is. She's a pain in the backside, but she's great. She's so bossy that she forgets I'm in charge half the time, but she's surprisingly efficient. Your daft brother stopped her ever looking for a good career. She was too busy mooning after him.'

Dylan rolled his eyes. It seemed it was a popular topic, how daft the men in his family were. Personally, he thought Sasha was perfect for laid back Oliver, but Ollie was blind to her charms, or he had been until she got a proper job and stopped stalking him. Now he'd suddenly started asking how she was. But Dylan was not prepared to get involved in any more drama. His older brother was big enough to sort it out for himself.

He was just about to open the door when Sasha burst in without knocking, and gave him a once-over to make sure he was decent. He laughed and told her he was leaving, which she looked a bit too happy about for his liking. He turned to say goodbye to Poppy, but she was already seated at her desk, head bent over a big notebook. He sighed, but knew now was not the time to draw her away from her work. It was something he'd struggled with before, but from her reaction to him just now, he finally felt air in his lungs and he could breathe at last. She was open to a reconciliation and he was determined that he'd never leave her side again, workaholic or not.

He was going to start delegating within his own operation. Now Poppy had more staff of her own, perhaps she'd be open to doing the same on a small scale, so she could spend some time with him…

She called after him as he was about to step out of her office. He turned to face her. 'Come over tonight?'

His smile was all the answer she needed.

CHAPTER THIRTY-SIX

Just as Dylan was leaving, Jared came in. Poppy winced as the two men gave each other a tight smile and a nod of the head, before stepping round each other. Dylan glanced back, looking Poppy straight in the eye, and told her he'd see her at her house later, before heading out to say goodbye to Billy and Sasha. She guessed he was then going to get on with his own busy day.

She steadied herself on her desk for a moment while she tried to catch her breath. She'd heard from Sasha and the gossip around town about how sought-after Dylan was at the moment. He'd made her forget about her own work, or more importantly, who her next client was, and she could have kicked herself for being so negligent.

Jared was here to talk about a new project they were working on. People were linking their names in architectural articles and design and home magazines, where they were getting great write-ups. She felt the fizz of elation in her veins about the prospect of seeing her business grow. Jared had expressed his determination that their future plans were going to be as perfect as the original project, or even better. *No pressure there then*, she smiled to herself. What a morning!

Jared sat down opposite her and crossed his legs, looking relaxed and calm, but she could feel the tension in the room. 'Everything ok with you?' he asked. She knew it was a double-edged question.

Poppy smiled, her eyes roaming Jared's face. He really was so handsome that it was difficult to keep your eyes off him. He was dynamic and mouth-watering, and she loved working with him. He just wasn't the man for her and he needed to know that.

'I'm excited to get stuck into this new project,' she said, steering the conversation towards work. 'I've got some other clients that I'm contracted to, especially the big sanctuary project I've just agreed to. I know we talked about making more of my mental health pods for communities, but the sanctuary commissioned some and I'd like to schedule time for those first.'

Poppy tried to gauge Jared's response. He was still gazing at her and smiling, so she heaved a sigh of relief. 'If the building project we talked about can start either alongside, or just after that, then I'm happy to see the new contract you've drawn up,' she said with a smile.

He grinned back, staring into her eyes, which were sparkling now. 'How do you know I've already had a new contract drawn up?'

'You never miss an opportunity. And you wouldn't be sitting in my office if you hadn't already mapped the outcome. I've agreed to initial projects, but you want more.'

'You know me too well,' he grinned, raking her face for signs of distress. She made sure she looked happy and carefree. 'What's happening with Dylan?'

She gulped and took a moment to think clearly. She hadn't expected to see Dylan when she'd got to work that morning. Her whole outlook had changed in a matter of hours. Trust Jared to go straight to the question he wanted answering. Ever the businessman, but also a friend... she hoped, crossing her fingers behind her back.

'Uh, Dylan and I are trying to sort things out. One of my old friends went out of her way to cause trouble for us at the party we all attended, as you saw, but she's old news. We're giving each other some room to breathe.'

'Are you and Dylan back together?'

Another punch to the guts. 'We haven't discussed that yet, but I hope so. It looks that way,' she said honestly. She winced as his eyes narrowed slightly, but he didn't jump up and start throwing things around, which was a good sigh. She could see the tense line of his jaw and his tight smile, though, and knew it wasn't what he'd hoped for. Jared relaxed his shoulders and then sank back into the chair as if he was the most chilled-out man on earth, studying her with calm authority.

'Ok. Out of respect for Dylan, who we both work with now, I'm only going to say this once. I think we have a strong connection that could have been more than business and, although I'm not going to go home and rage to the world, it hurts. I was hoping for more, and I thought you might be too.' Jared scanned Poppy's face, but she was holding her breath and tried not to move, she was so scared of what he was saying. Any other time and place she'd have been happy to hear it – but she loved Dylan too much to risk losing him again. Jared was a catch for any woman. Any woman but her.

'If you ever need me. I'm here. You understand?' Jared said.

Poppy blinked back tears suddenly. It felt so good for someone to be finally looking out for her, even if it had to be as a friend. She nodded sadly and hoped it didn't change how they worked together. Would she feel jealous if he met someone else? Probably, but that was something she'd have to get over, and fast. Jared wouldn't stay single for long and she really did want him to be happy. She'd seen the way Libby, the architect, looked at him dreamily, and thought there might be something there, but at the moment he was too interested in Poppy to notice Liv. Anyway she wasn't about to try and sort out someone else's love life, when her own was such a mess. Jared was big enough to do that for himself. She'd made it very clear that she wasn't an option even if, selfishly, that thought made her a bit sad. What woman wouldn't want two sexy men asking to date her?

'I understand,' Poppy smiled at Jared, but suddenly, every bone in her body felt like it was lined with lead. She pulled out her chair from under her desk and stretched her legs. 'I think you are amazing and you're obviously really gorgeous —' At this, Jared threw his head back and laughed and she finally felt lighter. 'But I need to concentrate on work. Dylan deserves to be my sole focus outside of that.'

'He's a great guy,' said Jared, with a sigh, while he stared out of the window at the wild flowers blowing in a gentle breeze. 'It can't have been easy on you lately. I respect your choices, even if I don't like them.' She could see the mischief in his face now. 'I promise to stop asking you to have trysts in hotels with me, but it's good for a man to have healthy competition,' he joked.

'Jared!'

He held up his hands. 'Ok. Back to business,' he said. 'I want to start on the next development in six months' time and planning's already underway. I've taken on board your suggestions from the last houses,' he paused for effect. 'As they are now officially our fastest selling brand.'

Seeing Poppy's beaming smile, Jared got up and gave her an almost platonic hug, which lasted a fraction of a second too long. She was so excited about what he'd just said that she shoved that to the back of her mind.

'Congratulations on doing such a great job,' he continued. 'And if you are signing my new contract, then I'm ecstatic, as it's a partnership deal,' he said as he drew the document out of his pocket with a flourish.

Poppy's mouth dropped open and she gawped, making him laugh again. 'A partnership deal? We decided to keep things separate!'

'I know. But I don't want to have to come back here and beg you to join me every time I'm doing a new build. We are onto something amazing here. I think the future is in housing that becomes part of the homeowners' lives. You saw the trend and made it your own.'

Poppy was still gawping, so he guided her into her seat. She leant back into it, trying to think what his words meant. 'But I work on my designs alone. I love owning my own company, so how would that work?' Frown lines appeared on her brow as she tried to rapidly compute what this could mean for her future. She also didn't know how Dylan would feel about the idea. Not too happy, she was pretty sure.

Jared came and stood behind her, placing the paperwork on the table as she speed-read it. When she sat back up her eyes were glistening with happy tears. 'You know me so well!'

Jared stood back to see her reaction. 'I knew you wouldn't want to leave your business and I realise how important the pods are to you. I'd like to get involved in that too, but I'm needed on other projects. You're already ahead of me, having signed the sanctuary deal.'

Poppy's mind was whirling round with possibilities. Jared didn't want to take over her business, he just wanted to link certain parts of her designs with his houses and industrial builds. 'So you would do the builds, you'd use my designs and technology, and we'd rebrand as a partnership just for those houses? I wouldn't be a consultant like last time?'

'No you wouldn't… and exactly. I want to build bigger developments. The units we design as a team are technical and expensive, so we'll keep those to smaller plots and make them really special… together.'

Poppy wanted to say that she'd need to talk to Dylan about it, but then she remembered she was a strong independent woman who didn't answer to anyone but herself. This was more than she'd ever dreamed of. Her designs could be dotted across the globe one day. With their joint ambitions, she and Jared could become household names.

'I need to show this to my lawyer, but as far as I'm concerned, we have a deal,' she said. She felt like doing a cartwheel, but instead she picked up the phone and asked Sasha to go and buy some champagne, which made Sasha squeak a question back in surprise, asking what the hell was happening. Poppy ignored her, replacing her phone on her desk, and feeling her insides vibrate with adrenaline.

Jared went and sat back down opposite her with a satisfied grin. They then spent the next two hours going over the details of the contract, with her lawyers on a conference call. As they discussed the fine print, they polished off glasses of the beautifully crisp and decadent drink that Sasha had fetched. Meanwhile, Sasha and Billy craned their necks to try and find out what the hell was going on.

CHAPTER THIRTY-SEVEN

Dylan tried to reign in his jealousy but his blood was heating up and his fists were clenched. He worked with Jared by default, and had to show Poppy that could continue, without him wanting to shove Jared's face into the ground. Dylan was the dynamic businessman Poppy craved, not the other guy.

Dylan was pretty sure Jared would also prefer them to stay away from each other. But, to his credit, Jared did seem to know good business when it was in front of him and he grabbed it, no matter what it cost him personally.

Dylan tried to regulate his breathing as he paced along the street to his parents' house. He unclenched his hands, rolled his shoulders and slowed himself down, but then he nearly bowled right into someone. He stepped back and apologised, then realised that the person in front of him was Anne. She brushed her hair out of her face. She was flushed and she wouldn't look up at him. He didn't move, though, so she had no choice but to meet his eyes in the end.

'Anne.' Dylan ground out, knowing his voice sounded

harsh – but she'd caused him no end of trouble. 'I wasn't looking where I was going. I'm on my way to Mum's.'

'Oh…' She looked behind her to his parents' house and then turned to face him. Her eyes were bloodshot and she was shaking. 'Look, Dylan. I've been going through a tough time with Connor and Freddie. I'm sorry I dragged you into my argument with Poppy. It wasn't your fault.'

Dylan felt like he'd just been pronged by a cattle prod. 'My fault? How the hell can any of this mess be my fault? Perhaps Poppy and I should have told her friends about us, and maybe you have a right to be upset about her keeping her mum's health a secret, but she didn't want her relationship with you all to change.'

Anne turned puce and she started biting her nails. Dylan threw his hands in the air as she stared at the floor. He carried on. 'Poppy was right, though. You did change. You saw her as the enemy because she had someone to love and you didn't. It is not Poppy's fault, or mine, that Connor behaved like an idiot.'

Dylan didn't realise how much he had raised his voice until he came face to face with a rather confused-looking Connor, who had just strolled across the road from the shops. Dylan could see a few other people looking their way from the big front window of the coffee shop. He stared at them crossly until they turned away.

'What's going on?' asked Connor, standing side by side with Anne and glancing at her in question. She wouldn't look at him, either. 'Why's Anne crying?' he demanded of Dylan, as Anne started sobbing quietly. Connor put his arm around her protectively, as Dylan looked on in scorn.

'It's nice to see you finally take some responsibility for protecting your family, Connor,' said Dylan, curling his fists again. This was not turning out to be the relaxing day he'd hoped for. 'Perhaps you should both sit down and talk to each other about Freddie and his illness, and how it makes you both feel.'

Anne gasped and her eyes locked with his, but he ignored the pain there. 'It's about time you realised how much Anne has to struggle with on her own, Connor. And you need to tell him how you feel, Anne,' he stared straight back at her and she lowered her eyelids.

'What's he talking about?' Connor turned to Anne. 'Anne copes with everything brilliantly,' he defended.

'Does she, though?' asked Dylan. 'Look, Connor. There are some things Anne needs to tell you. You should take on board what she says and step up and help her. She's only human and you're Freddie's dad.' With that, Dylan caught a glimpse of Anne's scared but also hopeful glance and strode away to leave them to sort it out.

'What the hell?' asked Connor, as Dylan strode further along the pavement.

'I think Dylan's right, we need to talk about Freddie,' mumbled Anne, turning and watching Dylan walk away.

Connor flushed, glanced at everyone in the coffee shop staring at them, and led Anne across the road. 'Let's go and get a hot drink and you can tell me what's going on. It seems like the whole neighbourhood knows what's happening, except me.'

CHAPTER THIRTY-EIGHT

Poppy had longed for this moment so much over the years. Her mum was finally home. She'd dreamed that they would hug and cry and she'd be so relieved that June was home, but instead she had butterflies in her stomach and her nerves were on edge. Was it safe to leave her mum there alone? How would June cope without the constant watchful eyes of the staff at Green Manor?

Poppy had tried to drink her coffee, but she'd wrinkled her nose at the tepid liquid. She made a note to buy her mum one of those fancy coffee machines. June was fussing around and exclaiming about the changes to the flat. Luckily she did like them, although she'd said they would take a bit of getting used to and it didn't feel like home. This was despite the fact that her home, for many years, had been a little room in a medical facility.

Poppy didn't know what had finally caused June's change of heart and led her to say she wanted to come home. She did know Chris had been visiting more regularly, so perhaps he had something to do with the brighter smiles on her mum's face, or the twinkle in her eye? Poppy hoped with all her heart that Chris was the reason. She knew it wasn't for her own sake. She'd been trying to persuade her mum to come home for years. Not just because of the financial burden involved at the start, but also through her own need to have a mum she could pop by and visit, without people watching her every move. Poppy had always had a burning desire to create a safe place for her mum to call home.

Her mum came up behind her and gave her the sweetest hug. She turned and they both grinned at each other.

'It's lovely,' her mum said. 'It's definitely different...' she looked into her daughter's eyes and then poked her in the ribs and laughed, which was the most magical sound. 'I love it, Poppy! I wish I'd trusted you and come back years ago.'

June kissed her daughter's soft cheek and brushed away the tears she felt there. She sighed and led Poppy to sit next to her on the couch.

'I know I was fixated with the way the flat used to be, and didn't want to change anything, but I can see that maybe the old look might not have helped my mental health. This new, brighter home makes me want to smile, not cry. I should have looked after the flat – and you – better. I'm sorry.'

June squeezed her daughter's hand and Poppy felt the tears begin to fall again.

'It's ok, Mum. I know you find change really hard.'

The doorbell rang, making them both jump. Poppy went to answer it, glancing in the little mirror in the hallway and grimacing at her reflection. She quickly shoved on some foundation from the bag she'd left by the door and ran her hands through her silky hair. She hadn't been expecting visitors. No one knew about her bringing her mum home. June hadn't wanted a fuss and Poppy was worried people would scare her away before she'd settled in. But the town grapevine was obviously in good working order. She fortified herself and opened the door.

She almost sagged against the door in relief when she saw Chris holding a box of pastries. They smelt divine and her stomach grumbled. He frowned and scolded her for not eating properly, before following her into the lounge. Her mum was out on the balcony now. When she turned and saw Chris, her face broke into a wide smile. Poppy raised her eyebrows as he flushed, but said nothing, silently handing June the box of cakes. June giggled coquettishly and Poppy almost spat out her last sip of coffee.

'I'm happy to stay here with your mum for a while, Poppy,' said Chris with a shy smile. Poppy looked at her mum who nodded her head.

'Ah... ok. If you're sure?'

June laughed. 'I'm not a child, Poppy.' Poppy looked at Chris, who gave her a reassuring smile.

'Ok, I'll come back later.' She'd known she would have to leave her mum at some point, but she hadn't expected it would be so soon. Her sides started aching and her palms were sweating.

Walking on wobbly legs over to the café, she had to keep stopping as people approached her and said how glad they were that her mum was back home. She shouldn't have been surprised that the local gossip had spread so quickly, but she'd hoped for a little time to get used to the idea herself before everyone else poked their noses in.

Poppy chastised herself for being unkind and pushed open the café door, all eyes on her as she walked to the counter and ordered coffee and a slice of cake from Terry, Chris's kitchen hand. She slid into a table at the back of the shop, head down.

When Terry brought over a huge slab of cake, remarking that she looked like she could do with some energy, she gave him a watery smile. He leant in to hug her and she was left with the scent of chips. How both he and Chris fitted into the small kitchen behind the counter, she could never fathom, but somehow they danced around each other and made it work. She'd heard that Terry was retiring and she'd miss him. He was like a big, much-loved teddy bear and his hugs were known to cure most ills. She took a mouthful of cake and sighed in bliss. Chris really was a magician with sugar. Perhaps her mum would be ok here, with everyone looking out for her, and maybe Poppy could ease off and stop treating her like a baby. She could even start having some fun!

A picture of Dylan floated into her consciousness and she grinned and started typing out a text asking him to meet her at his flat. It was about time she started catching up on some other life skills than those involving responsibility and fear. She was going to get naked beneath or above a sexy man, and she was going to revel in every second of it. The rest of the world could wait.

CHAPTER THIRTY-NINE

Poppy glanced down at the text from Anne and was tempted to ignore it. Anne hadn't bothered to contact Poppy in weeks, and now it seemed she'd decided it was ok to text, and not call. Poppy fumed and was almost tempted to throw her phone in the bin. She held off, though, as it seemed to ring off the hook these days with work calls. She barely had time to catch her breath, but each day was exciting and full of creativity.

Juggling multiple projects made her mind spin, but Billy and Sasha were a godsend. Who would have guessed that Sasha could organise them all so effortlessly? She was still annoyingly bossy, but she had Poppy and Billy's clients eating out of the palm of her hand. They seemed to love her forthright manner. Some found her hilarious and called her a Pitbull behind her back but, just like a Pitbull, Poppy knew Sasha was a softy inside that tough exterior. She was strong but loyal and caring. She was also now handling all of their social media and she had a real gift for it.

Sasha ran Poppy's diary like a dream, and even factored in time for Poppy to run in to see Verity and her shop occasionally, to update her wardrobe for client meetings. Poppy had seen Verity's eyes pop out on stalks one day when she'd had Jared in tow. She'd love to do a bit of matchmaking there, but she hadn't managed it yet. Plus Libby might get her claws out, as Poppy was sure the formidable architect had her sights set on Jared too.

Poppy used the intercom to ask Sasha if there was time in the day's schedule for Anne to pop by. Anne had said she was texting from right outside the building. Sasha's silence pretty much said it all, before she finally said she'd move the next appointment to fit Anne in, and cut the connection. Poppy wondered how many other employers would tolerate their staff cutting a call off mid-conversation, and grinned to herself. Nothing about her growing business in Cherry Blossom Lane was conventional – and she was about to take on another member of staff.

She took a deep breath as Sasha showed Anne in. Sasha hovered around the door, but Poppy asked her to make them some cappuccinos from the new fancy machine Billy had ordered for them, now that they didn't have so much time to swan off to the coffee shop. She nodded to a chair so Anne would sit down. Anne's hair looked freshly washed and bouncy and she didn't have the usual bags under her eyes, although she might have layered on the concealer for all Poppy knew. Something about her appeared calmer than usual, though. Poppy waited to see what she would say, sitting pretty in her own seat, the designer masterpiece that Jared had sent her to mark the successful completion of their housing development and first sale. She hadn't been able to believe her luck when it had arrived. Dylan hadn't been happy. He'd bought her a bunch of flowers and the beautifully hand-crafted cherry tree sweet box for her desk, which she cherished, but she secretly adored her chair. She couldn't believe Jared had parted with his treasured possession.

Now she swung round to face Anne and waited for the other woman to compose herself. Anne was taking in her surroundings and was just about to speak when Sasha burst in with the coffees, obviously expecting to have to break up a fight.

Poppy grinned and reached out for her drink, relaxing back into her chair again and trying to soak up some of Jared's innate confidence. She stared Anne straight in the eye and raised a brow in question. It didn't look like Sasha was leaving, so Poppy asked her to shut the door. Sasha quickly did so, and then perched her bottom on a chair by the big window looking out over the hillside. She made sure she was near Poppy, which Poppy appreciated.

Anne fussed with her hands in her lap and then faced them both. 'I'm sorry, Poppy.' She hung her head and her hair covered her face. She took a deep breath and looked up, biting her lip. 'I've been a terrible friend. You were right about some of us being jealous of your relationship.' She stared at Sasha then gazed out of the window when no-one else spoke.

'It's beautiful. I can see why you both love working here, with views like this. The trees lining the lane as you drive up are gorgeous too. It's like stepping into a fairy tale.' She sighed. 'At school, I had a bit of a crush on Dylan, but he only ever had eyes for you, Poppy. It annoyed me because Connor never looked at me that way. Then when you started talking about Dylan so much, I thought it would break up our group. Sasha was gormless over Ollie, Demi was the same over Miles and you were besotted with Dylan. Where did that leave me?'

Sasha gasped and her eyes blazed, but Poppy remained calm. Her pulse was racing slightly, but she refused to be provoked by Anne's words. Anne had done enough damage.

'So you prevented us from being happy, so we could all be

miserable with you?' asked Poppy, but Anne was staring at the floor.

'What did you do to stop Ollie liking me?' demanded Sasha, who had jumped up and stood confronting Anne. Poppy got out of her chair and laid a hand on Sasha's arm to hold her back. Anne stared at them both.

'I didn't do anything! Ollie never paid you any attention anyway. He was always too busy chatting up anything with a pulse.'

'Anne!' admonished Poppy.

Anne held her hands up in surrender. 'Look. I didn't come here to upset either of you. I admit I was jealous of you both, and even of Demi, too. She's been with Allan for years and doesn't even work at her relationship. Allan will never marry her. He's too busy coasting along.'

'Anne!' both Poppy and Sasha shouted this time. Anne stood up and faced them.

'He uses Demi to keep his job at the garage. He's a waster,' said Anne defiantly. Poppy had to hold her tongue but Sasha stormed out of the room in disgust, before obviously deciding she didn't want to miss the row and returning, plonking herself back in her seat, nostrils flaring. Poppy was glad Billy's desk was now situated on the next floor, or he'd be in there looking for answers too. She had recently expanded to the top floor of the building, and had created a design room there, where Billy worked.

'Look,' said Poppy. 'Let's all sit down and talk this through like adults.' Anne flushed and then her shoulders sagged in defeat.

'I didn't come here to start another argument,' Anne insisted. Sasha was about to say something, but Poppy silenced her with a look. 'I've been struggling, coping with Freddie on my own, and I've got no one to talk to about it.'

Poppy tried to reply, but Anne's words tumbled out like a

torrent and Poppy sat back. 'Connor always assumes I'm fine. He never helps me and my family don't like to interfere. I can't cope with the worry on my own any more. Everyone else seems sorted and happy but I'm left feeling desolate and alone inside. I have to be strong for Freddie, but who's there to support me?'

'Um… us,' butted in Sasha. 'Look, I know you have a lot to deal with, but as you've probably noticed, I'm a mess too, and Poppy is worse than all of us!'

Poppy spluttered and her mouth fell open. Sasha held up a hand to shut her up. 'She's a complete wreck, who's spent years hiding how ill her mum is from us all, so I'm sure she can relate to you trying to cope on your own.' She gave Poppy a hard stare and made her sit back in her seat and stay silent. 'But the way you've behaved isn't ok, Anne. Poppy told some lies, yes.' Poppy huffed that this was suddenly all about her faults again, but Sasha continued. 'The difference is, she didn't try to shag Connor or Ollie, and tell them a pack of lies.' Sasha's stern face told them all she wasn't going to let this go.

Poppy went to look out at the view, hoping it would calm her. 'We've all made mistakes,' she said over her shoulder.

'I haven't!' shouted Sasha. Poppy grinned and even Anne broke into a smile. 'I've been a good friend to both of you,' Sasha went on. 'It's about time you started being honest with yourselves and others. Poppy, you should have told us about your mum and your relationship once it got serious, and Anne,' she took a deep breath. 'What you did was heartless. And Poppy is a nicer friend than I am if she forgives you for trying to sleep with the love of her life…' Both women flushed and stared at Sasha. 'But we know you need help with Freddie. And we also know that Connor deserves a kick in the nuts.'

Anne's eyes went wide, then she doubled over laughing.

'Oh Sasha. Only you could make us laugh at a time like this. I never would have slept with Dylan, Poppy,' her eyes implored her friend to believe her. 'I just wanted to feel attractive for once. I wanted Connor to actually see me as a woman and not just Freddie's mum. I thought hearing on the town grapevine about me with Dylan at the party might have woken him up.'

'Stupid woman,' muttered Sasha and despite everything, Poppy couldn't help but smile. She turned away as Billy burst in. 'Are you ok?' she asked him in alarm.

He was as out of breath as if he'd run a marathon. 'Your next client will be here in five minutes – and I assumed I'd be breaking up a brawl?'

The women all looked at his wild hair and stance and giggled.

'Did you really get that puffed out just from running down from upstairs?' Poppy asked.

'Those stairs are steep,' he defended.

'I'd better get on,' Poppy said to Anne. Sasha, glancing at her watch, shepherded everyone out with a tut.

CHAPTER FORTY

Dylan stopped outside the front door of Poppy's mum's flat, and took a moment to catch his breath. Those bloody stairs would be the death of him. The lift was broken yet again. He'd finally been invited to visit Poppy's mum's flat. He was going to have to bite his tongue when June welcomed him in and gave him a tour. She was bound to be delighted with the work Billy and Poppy had done.

Dylan had only seen the flat for the first time the previous week, when Poppy had invited him over. Finding out just how often Billy had visited had grated on his nerves. Poppy had reassured Dylan that their relationship was back on track, but it still felt like she'd trusted Billy with this part of her life and not him. He would have loved to have made the furniture shine or rebuilt the kitchen for her, but she'd done it all herself, with the help of Billy and his giant murals.

Now he wasn't surprised to see Chris ensconced on the sofa, grinning widely. From what Poppy had said, he'd more or less moved in as soon as June had come home and hadn't let her out of his sight since. A real smile found its way onto

Dylan's face, as he saw how relaxed and happy both June and Chris appeared.

Poppy wound her arms around him, making him start in surprise as he hadn't known she would be there too. Then she rested her head on his back. 'Guess what?' she whispered, taking his hand and leading him into the tiny kitchen, kissing him quickly on the lips and making him crave for more. He'd missed seeing her every day. He'd heard she was practically sleeping at the studio in Cherry Blossom Lane, as she'd taken on so much work. Dylan had been tempted to call Jared and tell him to back off, but he'd known Poppy would erupt at that. She was more than capable of deciding her own workload and would hate him for interfering, however much he wanted to. His own schedule was insane now, too, so they'd barely had time to meet. He'd missed her.

He drew her body closer to him and sighed at the contact. She was about to speak, but he wanted her to know that he'd been thinking about her and he silenced her with a kiss that blew his mind. She responded instantly and melted into his arms. His hands slid into her hair and she whimpered slightly in bliss before they heard Chris walk to the bathroom and they slowly pulled apart. He linked her hands with his and tucked her under his arm, so they didn't lose contact. 'I haven't seen you much lately.'

'I'm sorry about that,' she said. Her voice was rich and heady, and still filled with lust. It was hard for him not to throw her over his shoulder and take her home with him. He wanted to kiss every inch of her body until she was screaming his name – and his name only.

'I told you that Chris is here much of the time. It's something I'm getting used to. Mum's grabbing back control of her life with both hands, but she's forgetting how ill she's been. She's acting like a woman in love,' Poppy sighed.

He gently lifted her chin so she was looking at him and

kissed the tip of her nose. 'Is that such a bad thing?' He hated the selfish feeling that almost overwhelmed him, that maybe Poppy could start living in the present, not the past, and have more time for him. He stroked her cheek and looked into her eyes. 'I think Chris has been waiting for a long time for your mum to come home, so why not trust that he's man enough to take care of her? It's something he's dreamt of for years. Plus she's able to look after herself. She's much happier now she's home.'

Poppy frowned. 'I know Chris has always cared about her, but love…'

Dylan smiled and dipped low for another quick kiss of her soft lips. She looked so adorable in her skinny jeans and soft blue jumper with a delicate pattern along the hem. He assumed it was one of Verity's latest designs. Poppy's hair was shiny and flowing across her shoulders today and he was glad that she'd invited him to the flat in broad daylight and didn't feel the need to hide her relationship from her community any more. He brushed some tendrils from her face and slid his other hand into the top of her jeans, just under her jumper, making her catch her breath while her eyes sparkled up at him. She caught his hand and grinned.

'Chris has loved your mum since we were kids,' Dylan said. 'Everyone knows it round here. I assumed you knew, too?'

Poppy looked out of the tiny kitchen window at the streets below. 'I think I probably did, but I didn't let myself believe. Mum's always been such a mess emotionally. I didn't want Chris to go through what I do.'

'Oh Poppy,' he sighed, pulling her in for a hug and wrapping his arms around her. 'Chris is a grown man and he can decide what he wants to cope with. Perhaps your mum's health will improve with support from a loving partner? She will be able to trust Chris with anything.'

Poppy giggled suddenly and he glanced down at her to see what was so funny. 'Do you know that Terry, who works in the café with Chris, has finally decided to retire?' When Dylan looked bemused, she carried on. 'Mum has offered to work there!'

Dylan's mouth fell open and he had to quickly snap it shut. He frowned. 'Will that be too much for her?'

Poppy jabbed him in the ribs and he winced. 'Now's who's the worrier? I've had a few hours to get used to the idea and I've given up trying to make sense of it. Mum will still have weekly meetings with her old clinic and she has a new light in her eyes. I think it will do her good to mix with everyone again. There's a real buzz about this blossoming romance. It's making me feel a bit giddy and sick, but Mum assures me she's ok.'

'Wow.' Dylan rubbed his face, then realised he needed a shave. Being inundated with work and trying to keep up with a go-getting girlfriend was exhausting. She wanted him to be more like Jared, but Dylan didn't need to work like that. His skills were already in demand and they paid well enough for him to enjoy life. Poppy didn't see that yet, but she'd learn it in time. He'd tried working himself into the ground for money and success, but he'd found his own gentler way worked better for him. He still had an amazing business, but he wouldn't kill himself for it.

Poppy had wanted him to work harder, but what she'd come to realise was that meant they couldn't see each other. Finally she'd understood that his business model, although the polar opposite to hers in structure, still ran efficiently. Making more money was nice, but he had been setting his business up while she was still training and his trade was something he'd studied his whole life. She still had to work on how to incorporate relaxation time into in her own schedule. He wouldn't tell her that just now, though. Sasha was already making inroads into sorting that out, which would benefit them all. Poppy would soon come to the realisation herself. She was one of the smartest people he knew and he was incredibly proud of her. He knew she was in partnership with Jared now, but even that didn't bother him like he'd assumed. He was confident in his own relationship. The threat of Jared seemed to have faded away.

He kissed the top of her head and was trying to slide his hand into her jeans again, when the doorbell pealed. He cursed as she giggled and gently slapped his hands away, blowing him a kiss while she reached for the door.

CHAPTER FORTY-ONE

Anne's face turned a bit pink when she saw the enquiring faces behind Poppy. She shoved the flowers she was holding at Poppy and mumbled that they were for her mum. June hesitated for a second, then gave Anne a wide smile and accepted the flowers, moving into the kitchen to look for a vase and fill it up with water, exclaiming about the gorgeous gifts everyone had been bringing her. As they moved back towards the lounge, Poppy watched Anne's gaze rake over the bunches of flowers in vases dotted everywhere and sniffed the air to take in the scent of vanilla from an infuser on the shelf.

'That smells nice. I remember Poppy saying that vanilla was your favourite scent while we were in school. Poppy tried to make you scented candles from a vanilla pod and some leftover wax once.'

Poppy smiled at the memory and offered Anne a seat near the window. The room was quite full now. Billy, who arrived just after Anne, brought sandwiches from the café but had to stand just inside the door as all the space was taken.

'That candle! It was an epic fail,' recalled Poppy. 'I burnt my hand and our design and technology teacher told us off for messing with the flame. Plus the scorched vanilla smell seemed to linger in that classroom for weeks!'

Anne got up and gave June a quick hug, before asking Poppy if she could speak to her outside. Poppy raised an eyebrow at Dylan, but he just shrugged and raced Billy to grab the spare seat, which resulted in Billy sitting on Dylan's big lap and grinning as widely as if he'd just won the lottery. He winked lewdly at Poppy and she rolled her eyes as Dylan upturned him onto the floor with a bump. She wished Sasha was there to protect her from a chat with Anne this time – but she knew she'd have to face her alone at some point.

Poppy knew that Sasha and Billy were enjoying living together, but she did feel something was wrong. Billy treated Sasha like he had royalty staying, and she was surprisingly gentle and kind to him as well, but they were both a bit over-jolly at times. Poppy had a nagging suspicion that Billy was missing Ed and Sasha still had dreams about Dylan's brother, Oliver, however much she protested otherwise.

She and Anne walked out onto the tiny balcony off her old bedroom and sat next to each other on the metal chairs. 'Everything ok?' asked Poppy.

Anne stared out at the street below, eyes a bit glazed. 'I didn't realise everyone would be here, or I'd have asked to meet at the café.'

'That's more private?'

Anne smiled at last, but she obviously had something on her mind and Poppy steeled herself to withstand it. Last time, at her office, had not been much fun. 'Freddie's next set of treatments is in a couple of weeks. Connor's coming with me,' Anne blurted out.

Poppy gasped and took hold of Anne's cold hand. 'That's great news… isn't it?'

Anne turned to face her. 'I'm here to ask for your forgiveness, Poppy. I know you said we can move on, but I've betrayed you in the worst possible way. I've always been a bit jealous of you. At school, nothing seemed to faze you.'

'Me?' Poppy almost cried out, but managed to keep her voice low at the last minute. 'Why the hell would you be jealous of me? Everything fazes me! However much I love her, my own mother is behaving like a lovesick teenager,' she hissed under her breath, then she leaned back in the chair. 'Mum and Chris are dating,' she said suddenly with a half-laugh, half-cry and rubbed her tired eyes.

Anne sniffed and smiled too, her eyes glossy with tears. 'I heard.'

'I thought you might have,' sighed Poppy. 'Apparently Chris has been in love with Mum for years.'

'I knew that too,' said Anne. 'That's one of the reasons why I'm a terrible friend. I guessed how bad it was with your mum when she went for treatment, but I didn't say anything as I was too involved in dealing with Freddie and my own life. I have terrible depression,' she admitted finally. 'I battle it daily, and I felt envious of everyone who had enjoyable lives and relationships while my child was unwell. Even though I knew you were suffering too. We could all see it, but we chose to be teenagers and pretend it wasn't that bad.'

'We didn't really know how awful it was for you with Freddie and Connor either. We assumed you were coping well,' Poppy admitted.

'I wanted you all to believe that. Otherwise you'd have seen me as a failure, the same way I viewed myself, for not being able to cure my own child.'

'Oh, Anne!' Poppy pulled her into a hug and, after a second's pause, Anne started crying and let herself be comforted. After a few minutes Anne wiped her face and pulled away, her face flushed and her hair messed up. Poppy reached out to tame the wild curls back into submission.

Anne was so proud of her glossy mane of hair, quite rightly so. It was beautiful.

'You're an amazing mum who dotes on Freddie. We can all see that. You have found a treatment for him and he's getting better, so you need to give yourself props for that.'

'Supposing he doesn't get better, though?' Anne whispered almost reluctantly, as if she didn't want to breathe the words out loud.

'Then you'll cope – but you'll also ask for help,' said Poppy, rubbing warmth into Anne's hand. 'The future looks bright for Freddie now and we can all come around and look after him so you can have a proper rest. You need to take care of yourself, too,' she gently scolded. 'So what happened with Connor?'

Anne brushed the tears from her eyes. 'Dylan metaphorically banged our heads together and made us sit down and talk.'

Poppy's eyebrows shot up. 'Dylan did?'

Anne grinned. 'He told Connor to 'man up' as apparently it's a phrase he learned from Gladys,' she smiled. 'He also said Connor should look after his family and told me to stop lying to myself and to you, or I'd lose all of your friendships.' Poppy was dumbstruck. Dylan hadn't told her he'd spoken to Anne – but then she might not have taken the news that well. He and Anne were still a sore subject for Poppy.

'What did Connor say?' Poppy couldn't wait to hear this bit. She glanced into the lounge and noticed they were all silent and listening to the whole conversation too. They quickly began chatting amongst themselves when they realised they'd been rumbled.

'He wants to move out of the area. There's too much history for us here.'

'What?'

'We've decided to move to America, near to Freddie's

treatment centre. Houses are more affordable just outside of town there and he's been offered a new job. It means we'll be nearer to Freddie's doctors and we'll be able to start afresh with a better understanding of each other.'

'*We*? Wow! Poppy sank back into her seat. 'Do Sasha and Demi know?'

Anne shook her head. 'I wanted to tell you first.' Just as she was about to say something else, the doorbell rang and Sasha and Demi burst in. They hugged Chris and June and handed out bags of plump crispy fish and delicious chips with lashings of salt and vinegar, which meant everyone had to quickly stuff their earlier sandwich wrappers under the couch and pretend to look happy about yet more food.

'We thought Chris might like a night off from cooking,' boomed Sasha as they all piled into the lounge. Sasha and Demi began devouring the food as if they'd never eaten before. Even Chris, with June perching on his knee, managed to perfectly balance woman and food. Poppy could see he would never let her mum fall.

Anne ate a couple of chips quickly and then made her excuses to leave, quietly asking Poppy to tell the others what was happening after she'd gone.

'You need to tell them yourself!' Poppy hissed, trying to keep her voice down. The others were chatting happily in the other room and she almost caught her breath as she glanced at them. This was a scene she'd always dreamt of. Everyone clustered around her home, with her mum in the centre. She turned back to Anne and they stood together awkwardly. 'Are you sure this is the right choice?'

Anne's eyes were glazed with unshed tears, but she smiled and hugged Poppy so hard that she almost popped a rib. 'It might not always have been my dream, to move so far away from you all, but having Connor back in our lives is worth fighting for. He thinks it will be less pressure to be near Freddie's specialists and I agree.'

Poppy could see Anne was trying to stand tall, but from the worry lines around her eyes, she knew her friend must have had sleepless nights over the decision. 'I want to give Connor and me the best chance, and I need him to step up and take some of the responsibility for Freddie. I can't do it all on my own.' Poppy was about to speak, but Anne hushed her.

'I know you've always supported me. Sasha and Demi too. But I want to find some freedom from fear and I think being near Freddie's doctors might help. It's possible that Connor and I won't work out, but I think the move abroad is the right decision for my beautiful Freddie. We might even get a dog,' she grinned.

'Anne,' squealed Poppy, making everyone turn their way. 'Freddie's desperate for a dog and you always said no because of the germs.'

Anne grinned. 'That was just me being over-protective. The specialist has made me see that Freddie can beat this. I've got to stop wrapping him up and keeping the world away from him. He's a growing boy and he'll need a new friend when we have to leave here. A dog will help him settle in. Apparently they can help people with anxiety too, so I might discover I'm a dog lover after all.' Poppy pulled her friend into another hug, a genuine one this time, and promised to break the news to everyone after she'd left.

Closing the door behind Anne, Poppy turned to see a lot of expectant faces. 'How much did you hear?'

'All of it!' said Sasha. 'I can't believe she didn't tell us to our faces! I thought we were friends.'

'You are!' soothed Poppy. 'She told me she wants to try and ease the way back into our friendship, so that we can stop feeling awkward around each other. I didn't want her to move to the other side of the world to do it – but we do need space from each other.'

Poppy gazed at the gorgeous faces looking up at her and felt her heart fill with love. 'Anne's ashamed of what she did and couldn't face you two together.' Poppy looked from Demi's teary face to Sasha's fuming one. 'She needs to do this for her own mental health. She's been worrying constantly about Freddie for years and now there is a light at the end of the tunnel with this treatment. Plus Connor is going with her.'

'What?' said Sasha, her voice rising. 'Connor? Are you serious? We didn't hear that bit. He's so unreliable!' Sasha lowered her voice slightly, realising this was not her home and June was getting agitated. 'Sorry, June,' she said. 'It's just such a shock to hear that Anne and Connor are finally back together.'

June smiled shakily. 'It's ok. I'm just not used to seeing so many people at once.' Before they all got up to leave, she held up her hand. 'I'm not going to break down. I'm glad to get an insight into my daughter's life and to see how well she handles her problems, even if she hasn't told me everything about them.' She raised her eyes to Poppy, who blushed. June gave Poppy a hug and she rested her head on her mum's shoulder.

'I'm sorry that you haven't felt able to give me too many details about what's been going on until recently,' said June. 'I'm glad I could help a little, with what you've been through with Anne.' She held Poppy away, to gaze at her. 'Look what you have achieved, though!' She indicated the other people in the room. 'There is so much love in your life, and I'm really proud of you.' Poppy gasped. 'I've been hearing about your business, too,' June's face glowed with pride. 'You're making a difference to so many people's lives, including mine. Just look at this amazing home you've created. I should have come and seen it years ago. It's beautiful. Thank you, Poppy.'

Tears streamed down Poppy's cheeks as everyone hugged her. Finally Sasha, Demi and Billy got up to leave. 'I'm thinking of starting my own business. I'm feeling suffocated by my dad and Allan,' Demi blurted out as she went through the door.

'What?' asked Poppy, trying to grab her back.

'We can talk about it another day,' said Sasha, pulling Demi along the corridor. 'She's not serious, she adores Allan and her dad might cry,' she added. Billy trailed along behind them, and shrugged his shoulders when Poppy sent him a questioning glance. 'Plus her mum might send Demi to live with her aunt in Jamaica if she tries to leave the family business,' Sasha said jokingly, over her shoulder. They all called out goodbyes to Chris and June and left Poppy and Dylan behind.

Poppy sighed and turned to close the door, noticing her mum and Chris had settled in front of the television and were leaning into each other, their bodies relaxed and content. She smiled at Dylan who appeared relieved that all the drama had left with her friends. She winked at him and drew him onto her little balcony.

'Trying to get me alone?' he joked, and she pressed him up against the wall and kissed him to shut him up. It worked. They both had to come up for air, pulses racing. Eyes twinkling in mischief, she lifted her grandad's binoculars off their hook and handed them to him. He frowned and took them from her. She pointed at his parents' house and giggled while he put the binoculars up to his eyes, to see what she'd been looking at. Then he stood back and laughed with all his might. He rubbed his slightly stubbled jaw, looking sexier than ever, and he handed the binoculars back so she could put them in their rightful place. He wrapped his strong arms around her, and looked longingly at her old bed. 'So you've been dreaming of this moment for years – and now your mum and Chris are here to spoil the mood?' he joked. 'I knew you'd been spying on me, but didn't realise you had such a clear view of my front door. If I'd have known, I might have put on a show for you,' his eyes sparkled with mirth. He rubbed his hips suggestively against hers and his eyes went black with lust.

She looked into his eyes and the passion there took her breath away. She pushed against the solid wall of his chest, grabbed his hand and rushed to kiss her mum and Chris goodnight and take her man home, to ravish his body and fulfil every fantasy that she'd ever had.

CHAPTER FORTY-TWO

Poppy woke up and stretched out like a satisfied cat, revelling in the rays of the sun. She'd like to devour every inch of Dylan's delicious body for breakfast, as her hunger for that man didn't abate with time. She could hear him in the shower and all kinds of images of his wet and glistening muscles filled her mind. She smiled at the memory of the previous evening. She hadn't thought once about work or her upcoming deadlines with Jared.

They had certainly made up for lost time. Who needed anyone else, when your current beau was everything you'd ever dreamed of? Jared was driven and oh so successful, but Dylan did things his own way. He was passionate and decisive, but still got results. She could learn a lot from him about balancing work and play. She didn't know why she had been blind to that before. She'd thought Dylan was lazy, but he ran his creative business with efficiency and didn't need to run around finding more work than he could handle.

She loved her own burgeoning empire, but she admired Dylan more now and realised that it was good that they each had their own way of doing things. Life would be very boring if everyone was the same.

Jared would always be looking for the next business opportunity. Dylan was at a stage of his life and expertise where the opportunities came to him. He'd stepped up his workflow to impress her, she realised that, but she'd much prefer him to be around spending time with her, than killing himself working every hour of the day and night.

It was about time she started being herself, too. Her mum seemed happy with Chris and was coping admirably, so the ball of fear that usually resided in her stomach had loosened up. It hadn't quite gone away yet, but Gladys and Chris were doing a great job and had taken her aside and told her to let them support her. They loved her mum, and looking after her helped them in turn too. Gladys was busier than ever, taking June around town to reintroduce her to the community. Chris liked having her by his side too, and proudly showed her off to everyone at the café. It was as if Poppy's family was being reborn. And, even if it was slightly dysfunctional and eclectic... it was hers.

Poppy was proud of how far they'd all come and she wasn't about to hide anything from anyone again. She'd learnt her lesson. She felt weightless with everything out in the open. The only thing that could ruin her new equilibrium would be her dad turning up at her doorstep, after reading one of the many articles about her and recognising her name. She scoffed. As if that would ever happen...

Dylan called out that they should get dressed and surface, after hiding away in his flat for almost two days. She yawned and stretched, grinning as she pictured his slick body, glancing at her little watch and wondering if she had time to jump in the shower with him.

She often walked about the area and chatted to the locals,

and they didn't mention her relationship with the town heartbreaker, or her mum's health, unless it was followed by a compliment. To them she was still the same Poppy, whomever she dated or wherever she lived. A couple of them wished her well, whilst a few others mentioned that they had seen her in magazines, but it hadn't been a big deal.

She rolled over and looked at the ceiling, almost sinking into the plump pillows on the bed. She berated herself for having made assumptions before. Everyone was happy with her relationship, and proud of her. Terry from the café had mentioned that most of them knew she'd helped Anne with the fundraising and supported the café and Gladys. Her breath felt like it had been knocked from her lungs, about that. They were also jubilant to have June back in the community, which made her heart swell with pride.

Poppy pushed herself up and started gathering her clothes, which were scattered across a big overstuffed grey armchair facing the window. She peeked through the deep sage-coloured curtains and saw the sun was shining outside. It was time for a fresh start. She'd made assumptions about her friends, too, and she was ashamed of that, so she now was determined to show them that yes, she'd changed – for the better. She could still be a good friend to them. She pictured Anne and her tearful face and knew it would take time for that wound to heal, but maybe the distance of land and sea would give them both time to reflect on what they really wanted from their friendship. Freddie's health was paramount. Beyond that, hopefully, time would heal them all.

Why the hell she had believed that her friends wouldn't accept her relationship, she didn't really now know. Perhaps it had been the constant worry about her mum clouding her views on everything. She was seeing more clearly now. Poppy didn't need to prove anything to them, because they loved her, faults and all.

Dylan walked out of the shower with a towel slung low on his glistening body. Her mouth went dry and her mind went blank for a moment, before she dropped her clothes back on the chair and walked over to him, never breaking eye contact, and led him right back into the shower.

CHAPTER FORTY-THREE

The next few weeks sped by as Anne packed up her life and organised her move. Sasha and Demi seemed to spend more and more time at Poppy's house or at her studio on Cherry Blossom Lane. Poppy was starting to feel a part of that community too. She had helped Demi find an adult education course on running her own business, and couldn't wait to see which direction her friend went in. At the moment Demi was still working in the office of her dad's garage, but she had tentatively mentioned starting something of her own. It hadn't gone down that well with either her dad or Allan, hence the regular visits to Poppy's studio and office. Billy was still living in the annexe above Poppy's garage and Sasha was there sometimes, but her being there wasn't anything permanent and suddenly Oliver, Dylan's brother, had started popping in on the way back from the gym he owned, even though it wasn't on his route home!

Ollie had confided in Poppy that he was thinking of purchasing the gym complex that had overstretched and shut down, on the opposite side of the street to her office in Cherry Blossom Lane. She didn't think mentioning that to

Sasha would be a good idea for now. She might quit! Poppy enjoyed the interruptions from Demi and Ollie, even though she was busy. Her work portfolio was blossoming beautifully, like the trees outside, and she felt content and happy.

It was as if she'd created her own mini community, where people liked to come and feel better. She kept an eye on Ollie, though, as after years of chasing, Sasha suddenly didn't seem to know he existed and it appeared he now very much wanted to be known. Poppy shook her head at the madness, then grinned. That word didn't feel like a punch to the guts these days. Her mum's mental health was still a concern, but she was far happier, and enjoyed being home. Poppy actually felt that perhaps she'd been the unstable one, not asking for help and believing her mum could never function in the real world. June was not only functioning, she was now flourishing, finally.

Her phone buzzed in her pocket with a text from Dylan, asking her to meet him at her house later. She gazed out of her office window at the hills beyond and grinned. She hadn't seen much of him lately. He'd been a bit mysterious, having sudden meetings that he had to rush off to and not being able to stay at hers overnight due to early starts, but also begging her to sleep at his flat for a few days so they could see each other. They had agreed to take things slowly and spend more time at their own places and with their own friends, but that hadn't happened yet. They were still in the infatuated stage of wanting to be together.

She was pretty sure that having her stay at his flat was Dylan's way of trying to help her find time in her hectic schedule for her mum and Sasha and Demi, out of work hours. She appreciated it, but she missed her own home comforts. Billy was always around at work, but in the last few days she'd heard from Billy that Sasha wasn't at his flat above the garage often either. She hoped they hadn't fallen out. Both appeared happy enough, so she'd have to let them get on with it, although she itched to interfere.

She stretched her legs out and rolled her neck to try and ease her tight muscles, picturing Dylan's strong hands massaging out the aches and parking that thought for later. She buzzed Billy in his office and asked him to come in. He poked his head round the door minutes later and she couldn't help but smile. He was dressed in a fitted black top that moulded his slim body, with a red collar. His jeans were ripped and skinny. He looked like he'd just stepped out of a fashion magazine advertising sexy creative wear. His hair was swept back off his face and he had designer stubble. She beckoned him to come and sit with her and he plonked himself on her lap, making her 'oof,' under his weight. 'I didn't mean sit on me, you idiot,' she joked.

He kissed her nose and perched on her desk instead. 'How's things with you and Ed?' she asked.

Billy gazed out of the window and wouldn't meet her eye. 'We're ok.'

Poppy frowned. 'You sure? Anything I can do to help?'

'You don't need to worry about the work side of things,' said Billy. 'Even if Ed and I sorted things out or didn't speak again, I'm professional enough to keep that at home.' Poppy felt the bite of guilt as this had been one thing on her mind.

'I miss him,' Billy said, gnawing at his bottom lip.

'But?'

When he didn't answer, she pictured Ed and his wide blue eyes and black spectacles. Billy rolled his eyes at her. 'I know what you're thinking. But I'm not going back to Ed. It's been good having Sasha around for a bit instead. But, much as I love her company, and however much of a riot she is to live with, she's so messy! Luckily she's been missing her local friends and family and staying in town more, so I can breathe.'

Poppy smiled and then made him look into her eyes to see if he was really ok. He didn't waver, so she sighed and got up to hug him. 'I hate to think of you being lonely,' she said gently, cupping his face in her hand, as Sasha walked in without knocking and glared at them both.

'I knew you two were having sex,' she raged and then fell about laughing at their confused faces. 'Plus, you're so easy to wind up,' she giggled, then walked over for a group hug.

'Poppy's worried about us, in case we argue and fall out,' said Billy untactfully. Poppy winced. *Could she have no privacy with this lot?*

Sasha laughed. 'Nothing to fret about, Poppy. I think you'd be worried if you didn't have anything to worry about! I thought you'd decided to be Miss Fierce and let people sort out their own mess?'

Poppy flushed and then grinned. 'I am fierce, but I can still make sure my best friends are ok.'

Sasha's chest puffed out at being called a best friend and she stuck her tongue out at Billy. 'She's talking about me, not you, sweet cheeks.' They all burst out laughing and Billy pulled a face at Sasha.

'So you two are both ok?' Poppy asked through her smiles. She really loved these two hoodlums.

'Neither of us are looking for anyone right now and it's been a lot of fun spending time with Billy,' said Sasha, 'but I think we both enjoy our own space too. I might just stay over on the odd night when we all go out.' Billy looked relieved at this and Poppy grinned. Sasha was a handful for anyone, but was still inviting herself to stay whenever she liked!

'And Ed and Ollie?' asked Poppy.

Sasha made a sick face and Billy looked out at the view again. 'They're in the past. Too much water under the bridge.'

When Poppy didn't look sure, Sasha threw a scrunched

up bit of paper she grabbed from the desk at her and it hit her square in the face.

'Ow!'

Sasha grinned. 'I wasn't the school netball champion for nothing, you know.'

'You were the school netball champion because you scowled at everyone and they were too scared to come near you!' laughed Poppy, rubbing her forehead.

Then Poppy's phone buzzed again. She quickly read the message and started gathering a few things to chuck in her bag. 'Can you two keep an eye on things here? I need to go home.'

Sasha gave her a knowing look and Billy picked up their latest client schedule and ran his eyes over it as if she'd already left the room. Poppy winked at Sasha and hurried out to her car.

CHAPTER FORTY-FOUR

Poppy pushed open her front door, half expecting to see Dylan lounging on her couch. She felt the bite of disappointment that he wasn't there. They had agreed to both find some work-life balance, to spend more quality time together at his place, and date instead of always staying in. She hoped they'd made the right choice, after the bliss of being in his bed for three nights solid. She longed for them to move in together, but they had spoken about it at length and decided that it was a big step, and something for the future.

She busied herself tidying the kitchen, putting away some plates that had been left on the sideboard and huffing when she saw a pair of Billy's shoes thrown by her back door. He'd obviously been making himself at home as per usual.

It was raining lightly, but through the haze she saw the redesigned warehouses at the back of her garden, standing tall and proud. She loved the fact that she now had neighbours. Most of the barns had been snapped up by creative industries and manufacturing. It would be a beautiful community to work amongst. One of them was a coffee merchant and they'd opened a small café in part of their unit, for all of the local homes and businesses to use. It was already a hit and brought the wider community onto the site to discover the artisans and possibly become future customers.

One barn filled most of the plot by her back wall, but she could only see the huge expanse of glass that made up what she knew to be the second floor and apex of the roof. The second level had its own deck outside and a small courtyard garden to look out on below. There were tall trees planted along the back fence to give privacy, but they weren't quite big enough yet. She'd enjoy seeing the trees grow, though. Huge cranes had been brought in to manoeuvre them into place and they already reached the level of the barn's first floor.

She frowned when she saw that there was a new area of planting in her back garden. It was too wet to go outside, but she'd have a clear view from her bedroom. She went up to see if she could work out what was going on. Dylan had said he had a surprise for her. Perhaps he'd planted flowers for her? But when she looked more closely, she saw there was a beautiful arch there for climbing plants to grow around, and a carefully crafted bench beside the arch too. She felt tears prick her eyes as she gazed from her bedroom. He'd created a lovers' corner for them. She could tell the bench was his own handiwork. She hoped she hadn't spoilt his surprise by noticing it. He'd probably expected it would be dark before she got home.

Her mobile rang. It was Dylan. She snatched it up, her hands shaking, trying not to let him know she'd seen his secret.

'You're home,' he laughed, and the hairs on the back of her neck stood up at the deep timbre of his voice.

'How did you guess?' she smiled, walking back to the

window to see the archway. She could still make it out in the twilight, and the rain had stopped.

'I bought you a present,' he said huskily and she felt her insides begin to melt.

'I love presents! What is it?' She leaned her head on the cool window pane and then slid the door wide to let the night air inside. The scent of the earlier rainfall on the roses in her garden filled her senses.

'Open the drawer of your bedside table.'

Poppy frowned and turned to open the drawer. She was bewildered to see a box inside, tied with a black silk ribbon. She picked up the box and sat on the edge of her bed, hoping it was something silky and sexy. She put the phone on speaker and placed it on the duvet next to her. 'Open it,' said Dylan.

She frowned when she opened the lid, and saw a pair of binoculars. She felt a bit disappointed that it wasn't the surprise she'd been hoping for, then shook herself out of her mood. Was he thinking of taking her stargazing? 'Look out of the bedroom window,' said Dylan's voice.

She shivered at the sexy tone of his voice and took the binoculars to the window, raising them to her eyes and staring up at the night sky. She couldn't see much, it was too dark. Movement caught her eye in the barn at the back of her garden, as a light went on. She saw a male figure walk to the window. She gasped and focussed on him, almost jumping back in surprise. She heard his warm laughter as he stood there in just his jogging bottoms, body glistening in the moonlight.

'What are you doing there?' she asked in surprise.

'Well, you used to watch me from your mum's house and I kind of liked it,' he laughed. She loved the warm timbre of his voice. 'We've decided not to move in together right now, but I thought about what you said about work, life, balance. We do both want to live here soon. It's your dream home. If we want to be able to have a family in the future and still run our businesses, one of us needs to be closer to home,' he said huskily. 'This is my new manufacturing site.'

Poppy's mouth hung open. She was so shocked at seeing Dylan close by – and half naked, that she couldn't think straight.

'I bought this plot from Jared,' he explained.

'I don't know what to say,' Poppy said. Her brain was racing with possibilities, but the overriding feeling was lust, at seeing Dylan with his top off. She kind of liked looking at him through binoculars. It brought so many memories rushing back. She searched her balcony for a suitable place to hang them, and saw he'd already set up a little silver hook, just like the one she'd had in the flat. She gulped in some air and tears formed in her eyes.

'This way we can work as much as we like and see each other all the time, but still have our own space,' he said. 'There's even a room here that doubles up as a bedroom, in case anyone is working late. The designer is a genius.'

Poppy grinned and bit her lip. 'Don't bite that lip,' he said huskily. She gasped and looked through the binoculars again. He had some too, and was watching her. She flushed and her blood started to heat up.

'I'm coming round,' he said. She almost dropped the binoculars and rushed back downstairs, just as he came in through the big kitchen doors. Those jogging bottoms clung to his thighs and his chest was still bare. She tried to breathe but was finding it difficult right now, with his lean muscles enticing her to come closer. 'How did you get here so quickly?' She was a bit out of puff from running downstairs. She fleetingly thought that she really needed to get to Ollie's gym to tone up.

He pulled her in for a kiss and she melted into his arms.

When they came up for air she felt dazed and wanton. 'Hang on, let me understand. You... and the work unit?'

He picked her up and went to sit on the couch with her on his lap. He stroked her warm face and tucked her hair behind her ear, dotting kisses along her neck and nipping her lip before looking into her eyes.

'I had the idea when we were talking about how we could start a family with such hectic schedules. I know how much your business and Cherry Blossom Lane means to you, and when you took me on a tour of the warehouse units, it seemed like the perfect solution. I've outgrown my current site, but I'm going to keep both for now. I wanted to tell you earlier, but then things got messed up,' he hung his head and his eyes were huge and contrite. Even then, he managed to look mussed up and sexy. 'Plus, I thought I could see you after work and still give you your space.'

She sighed and softly kissed his lips. 'I don't need space from you, Dylan. You were the one that said you thought we needed to spend more time in our own homes. I was happy with you living here.'

'I'd already bought it by then and was having second thoughts about how you'd feel about me working next door, when you'd just got used to us dating again,' he grimaced.

'It's a gorgeous building,' she soothed, picturing the wide windows and huge ceilings. 'You're lucky to have it. Maybe we can both utilise the space for manufacturing,' she mused thoughtfully. 'And how *did* you get here so fast?'

'I built a sweetheart gate into your wall and hid it with the rose arch and bench I made for you, to try and ease the way for you to get used to me being so close every day. I thought it would mean I could see more of you.' He ran his fingers along her collarbone and peeked inside her shirt, making her pulse race. 'I decided we could give each other a secret signal with the binoculars, and have assignations in each other's places.'

'Assignations?' she giggled finally. She shook her head in disbelief. 'You could have just moved in here and had a home office. You didn't need to buy a whole warehouse.' Dylan grimaced, but his eyes were shining with mischief.

'I did also think that we could persuade your mum and Chris and my parents to babysit occasionally, while we run very successful businesses.'

Poppy held her breath for a moment. He hadn't spoken about marriage since before the Jared and Anne incidents, let alone children. It was a lot to take in. 'My mum has only just moved back into her own flat! Plus your mum and dad live miles away too.'

'Mum has been telling me she wants to move into a bungalow after being unwell, and she's also been hinting lately that my brothers and I should all be giving her grandchildren soon. She always stares at me when she says this. Ollie and Miles think it's hilarious.'

He took her hands and his eyes locked with hers. 'I bought the warehouse as an investment, a while ago. Admittedly, I wasn't thinking straight. But if you just want me to move in here while I think of an incredible way to persuade you to become my wife…' Poppy was literally lost for words, so he carried on. 'Ollie has expressed an interest in renting my flat from me and Miles might store a couple of the cars he's always tinkering with in the storage area of the barn. It can be a family business space. I can block the gate back up…' he looked a bit worried now.

Just then there was a noise and they looked up as Billy stuck his head round the door. He'd let himself in as usual, and Sasha was close behind. 'I'll rent your flat from you, if you're looking for a tenant?'

'How much did you hear?' asked Poppy, wrapping her arms around Dylan, her eyes shining with tears.

'Just the bit where the hot man said he'd bought a warehouse at the bottom of his girlfriend's garden, so he could spend more time with her, before he basically expressed a wish to make her his wife,' said Sasha casually, as she helped herself to a bottle of chilled champagne and indicated for Billy to grab four glasses.

'Is nothing sacred in this house?' asked Dylan. Billy ignored him and both he and Sasha stared expectantly at Poppy, who was still in shock. 'Will you marry me?'

She quickly ran back through everything Dylan had said, and how Sasha had simplified it so beautifully. Her heart was racing that he'd stated his intent. 'Of course I will!' She handed him the binoculars that she still had in her hand, kissed him full on the lips, and asked him when he was moving in.

Dylan's whole body relaxed and Sasha and Billy cheered and popped open the champagne, handing them all a glass. Dylan put the binoculars down and turned to Poppy. 'To my future wife,' toasted Dylan, hugging Poppy to him. He put his glass on the side table, picked Poppy up, and only then seemed to remember they weren't alone. He called goodnight over his shoulder to their guests as he strode upstairs with his fiancée. She hid her face in his chest and giggled as he whispered that he was going to practice lots of delicious ways of persuading her to commit to him for the rest of her life.

Billy and Sasha grinned as they watched their friends, then quietly grabbed the leftover champagne. Oliver drove past just at the moment when Sasha and Billy emerged arm in arm from the building, talking animatedly and grasping the champagne bottle and glasses. He slowed down before speeding away again.

Sasha frowned into the night at the car that almost turned into the drive, then pulled away. She shook her head in confusion, then laughed at something Billy had said as he ushered her in, out of the cold.

They sat on the floor of Billy's flat with his laptop, pouring over pages and pages of ideas for the perfect wedding. Then they decided that Poppy would kill them if they did any planning without her. They quickly stashed away the reams of paper they'd printed out, and pulled up the company calendar to give Poppy the next morning off work. That would give her a chance to recover from the evening's shenanigans. More importantly, it would give Dylan the time he needed to drive her to a jewellery shop – and to help Poppy's real life fairy-tale finally begin.

ABOUT THE AUTHOR

International bestselling author and award-winning inventor, Lizzie Chantree, started her own business at the age of 18 and became one of Fair Play London and The Patent Office's British Female Inventors of the Year in 2000. She discovered her love of writing fiction when her children were little and now works as a business mentor and runs a popular networking hour on social media, where creatives can support to each other. She writes books full of friendship and laughter, that are about women with unusual and adventurous businesses, who are far stronger than they realise. She lives with her family on the coast in Essex. Visit her website at www.lizziechantree.com or follow her on Twitter @Lizzie_Chantree

For more writing news, subscribe to my newsletter: www.lizziechantree.com

I really hope you enjoyed reading My Perfect Ex, Book 1 of The Cherry Blossom Lane Series. Book 2 and 3 will be available soon!

If you liked reading my novel, please consider leaving a review. Many readers look to the reviews first when deciding which book to choose, and seeing your review might help them discover this one. I appreciate your help and support. Make an author smile today. Leave a review! Thank you so much. From Lizzie :)

facebook.com/LizzieChantree
twitter.com/Lizzie_Chantree
instagram.com/lizzie_chantree

PRAISE FOR LIZZIE CHANTREE

'Books like this are the reason I love reading.'

'Rarely has a book held my heart in its hands the way, If You Love Me I'm Yours has. An incredibly uplifting romantic story that has had me laughing and crying over and over again.'

'Chantree has a way of creating an intriguing and seemingly innocent plot that slowly draws you in and all of your emotions are set afire – The Ice Cream Shop does all of this and more and I never saw where it was going until the end and, like in all of her books, I shed more than one tear.'

'Take a few scoops of family drama, drizzle it with some hot men, scatter some sprinkles of misunderstandings along with a wafer of romance, and you get Lizzie Chantree's new novel, The Little Ice Cream Shop By The Sea. I really enjoyed reading this and devoured it in a day!'

'Well, what can I say about this book? It's gorgeous, clever, surprising and enthralling.'

'If you haven't had the pleasure of reading one of Lizzie's books yet - treat yourself!'

'I stepped outside my normal genre comfort zone of crime thrillers to read this book; it had been recommended to me and I had my eyes and heart opened. I laughed, I cried and had a precious insight into the life of people who on the surface appear, okay. I have bought another book from this author and started reading it immediately – such exceptional writing. I do not hesitate to recommend this book.'

THE LITTLE ICE CREAM SHOP BY THE SEA

Escape with an uplifting, feel-good romance, set by a sun-drenched beach.

CHAPTER 1

Not again! Genie Grayson wanted to scream and throw her hands in the air. Instead, she stuffed her fist in her mouth and turned away. She'd thought she had her terrible phobia under control – she was a perfectly sane twenty-two-year-old – but the last few weeks had been stressful, and this was her Achilles heel. She looked around furtively to see if anyone had noticed, but there was hardly anyone enjoying breakfast in her family's seafront restaurant.

The evil seagull had dropped a lump of cheese onto her pristine outdoor tablecloth. After flying right into the restaurant awning. It had obviously been at the beer that always ended up in the gutters after a busy night at one of the clubs further down the beach.

Genie rarely admitted to having this issue, as who in the world, other than herself of course, had a problem with cheese? No one who managed a restaurant and ice cream parlour, that was for sure. Not a responsible professional who served food all day and had to be surrounded by the awful stretchy stuff that smelt like her grandad's old socks after a day on his feet.

CHAPTER 1

She knew if she recited the alphabet backwards she'd be ok. She'd had years of practice. She usually got to about W, and then her pulse slowed down and she was able to take a deep breath and move on. She looked up and saw the gull sitting on the wall above the restaurant, its piercing red eyes like lasers. She shushed it away, but it just turned its back on her.

She often wondered if she had an allergy to wild animals. She'd tried to pet one at a zoo on a school trip and got bitten, then her hand had swollen up and she'd been rushed to hospital, even though she'd been fine after a few hours. She'd avoided zoos ever since. She gave the jungle a wide berth too. It wasn't too difficult from her current location on the coast of Essex, but she wasn't taking any chances. Cheese, on the other hand, was impossible to dodge. Not only did she work in kitchens, she cooked when her dad had a day off. Luckily, their bestsellers were their huge breakfasts, and plates of fish and chips.

Genie knew that if she gave into the urge to shove the offending messy table into the road, she'd get herself into all kinds of trouble with her parents, and probably the local council. She was already on their radar for changing all the restaurant's lightbulbs to a deep shade of red one weekend, to create an ambience. She'd had a formal letter the following week suggesting she might be moonlighting as a sex worker. That was slander! She might be a bit busty, and she was down on her luck, but she was too tired to blink some days. She just plastered on a smile and worked through it. Takings really had to pick up, at the restaurant though. They needed more customers.

She had to find a way to calm down and reasonably work out a plan of action, either by talking to her mum, Milly, about their current dilemma, or by finding a boyfriend and having some hot steamy sex to take her mind off things.

CHAPTER 1

While she pondered that thought, she grabbed the tablecloth by the edges with a couple of forks and shoved it behind the counter into the washing basket, quickly re-covering the table with a fresh cloth.

Genie smiled brightly at two school mums who were perusing the menu but her grin dropped as she turned towards the kitchen at the back of the little restaurant. She wondered if anyone would notice if she stood in the middle of the room and screamed. Probably not.

The mums were the only two customers, and they'd already caught her cursing in Spanish under her breath as she wiped down the tables when they'd arrived. They had looked at her in confusion. She'd picked up a 'learn to speak Spanish' course at the charity shop the week previously, in the hope that she might one day travel abroad with friends. She'd also thought it might help if they ever got a foreign customer, however unlikely that seemed. But when she'd got the disc back to the house, it was a homemade knock-off copy and the only vocabulary was swearwords. She hated being conned, so she'd resolutely learned the whole tape, which consisted of about fifty phrases that all sounded mightily dodgy. They were great for easing frustration, though, as no one else knew what she was saying. She hoped. She'd looked up a few of the words, but then been worried her parents would question why she was Google-translating so many profanities. She didn't want them to start to wonder if that council letter had been spot on.

Usually, the breathtaking panorama of sandy beaches and the endless skyline across the road were enough to lift her spirits. But today she felt she might as well go and bang her head against a wall, instead of trying yet again to reason with her parents. The family business *had* to be brought into the twenty-first century. She knew she had a temper and didn't

CHAPTER 1

always explain things clearly without combusting into flames, but they still treated her as if she was nine years old.

All she was asking of her parents was that they let her try out a few new business ideas and a handful of new ice-cream flavours. She didn't want to reinvent the wheel. Their business hadn't changed for decades. They still had the same chairs and tables, and even the menus, that her grandad Gus had installed. Her parents' restaurant, Graysons', offered bought-in, basic puddings, but Genie had seen massive growth in big gooey ice cream desserts presented in glass mugs or tall glasses. She didn't see why they couldn't try this. They had a prime site on the seafront, for goodness sake! She could feel her temper begin to rise again. Then she remembered – their customers. She didn't want to scare them away. She twirled round to face them again with another smile.

Her parents were worried about upsetting her grandad, who ran the ice cream bar. He only offered about six flavours these days. She had spent much of her time with him and her grandma when she was growing up. Her parents had stepped in to take over the business when her grandma had died a few years previously. Her grandad had begun wandering around the small garden at the back of the restaurant and shouting at the plants, raging at the loss of his wife. In the end, they'd explained to customers that he was an inventor seeing if upsetting plants stunted their growth. It was the only explanation they could come up with for his behaviour, which was becoming more and more erratic.

Their regulars knew about Genie's grandma and understood Gus's sorrow and anger, but occasionally a new customer would start to glance around to see if there were spaces to eat elsewhere, which meant even less income for them all. Genie missed her grandma Vera terribly, as she had always let her sit with them after school. Genie would perch on a high stool behind the ice cream counter and Vera would

CHAPTER 1

tempt her with her latest ice cream concoction and cuddle her, while Gus served a steady stream of customers anxious to get Vera's new flavours before they sold out.

With Genie's parents selling breakfasts and lunches, and Gus and Vera on ice cream, the restaurant had worked like a dream. Then her grandma died and Genie's parents had taken the reins, working harder than ever to cover their grief. They looked more frazzled as each year passed. Genie was used to coming home from school to the empty house they lived in, up the hill, as her parents were always working. Soon, she was roped into doing her homework at the restaurant, and then it seemed a natural progression for her to help out. She'd been doing that since she could walk anyway. She loved the restaurant and was proud of her family's heritage. She needed to spread her creative wings, though, and felt that since Vera had passed away, Gus was wilting. She wanted to keep her grandma's spirit alive, and Gus needed Genie more than her parents did right now.

She spent her weekend evenings making batches of ice cream for him to sell, though he kept telling her she should be out partying with people her own age, not keeping an old man company and trying to keep his business alive. He was bored one night and bought two whippy-type machines for simple, smooth ice cream and declared that she wouldn't need to help him anymore. It broke her heart. She could see that he was trying really hard to manage alone, but he was struggling with his memories of his beautiful wife and the happiness she'd given everyone with her smile and her amazing ice cream flavours. He just couldn't replicate them.

Genie had asked him about trying different recipes, but he'd harrumphed and told her that if she thought she knew better, then she could get on with it. And besides, he'd added that there wasn't enough business to try new ideas. He liked his whippy ice cream machines and they did sell a fair

CHAPTER 1

amount of cones, but there was no love in the ingredients. Vera used to sprinkle chocolate chips, lemon rind, tiny bites of apple and many other incredible ingredients into her mixes to make you feel like you were eating a mouthful of magic. Your tongue would tingle and most people came back to order more. People visited from miles around to try her latest flavours. Recently Genie had decided to try to keep the tradition going. After five generations of her family running this business, she was determined to make it shine again, in honour of her grandma.

As far as she was concerned, Gus had given her the green light. She'd always worked hard for her parents and was determined to turn their fortunes round. All the shops along the seafront were looking a bit tired these days. She felt they'd get stuck in a time warp if something didn't change.

She tried to calm herself down. She chanted a mantra in her head that she'd heard on the radio that morning. It was supposed to make you feel zen, but it soon irritated her now she couldn't get the stupid phrases out of her mind.

Her parents had often told Genie she was too bossy for her own good, but then, she'd had to be. Her schoolwork had suffered and she'd failed most of her exams, because she was always helping out at the restaurant or washing and cleaning at home while her parents were at work. Her parents had despaired, but what else could they have expected?

It was why she hadn't yet found a home of her own, even at her age. Her parents had moved into her grandparents' Georgian seafront property when Genie had been just two. The house and the business were their lives. She secretly couldn't imagine living anywhere else, but she'd never tell her mum and dad that. Her grandad had moved into the annex, which was separate from the main house. He'd recently paid a man to put a fence up between the two buildings, saying he needed more privacy. Genie suspected that he

CHAPTER 1

wanted to be able to hide away with his grief. She felt that she couldn't express her own sorrow, as she had to keep everyone else's spirits up. Her dad walked around looking permanently grumpy and her mum often wrung her hands, which in turn made Genie anxious. Genie did the restaurant books, so she knew that they could just about scrape by for now, but how long that would last for, she had no idea. They needed something to change – and fast.

Maintaining the house, her family and the restaurant was a full time job. Although none of the whole parade of restaurants were up to date, they were still quite busy as very few bars and eateries were allowed on each stretch of beach. They rarely came up for sale, tending to stay within a family. Everybody was friends with everyone else, but the décor in each venue was old fashioned, as far as Genie was concerned, and their clientele was getting older too.

That was fine, Genie respected older people, but a few tended to sit for hours, hogging the tables, and they didn't spend much money. She'd almost poked an elderly man's eye out once when she'd thought he might be dead and was checking he was still breathing. Thank goodness, he'd woken up with a start. As an only child, she loved it when there was a mix of ages mingling around. Her dad was an only child too, so there were no siblings to help him run the restaurant. It had fallen to Genie and her mum. But since Vera had died, it felt like the life and soul of the place had gone with her.

The school mums, who were regulars and probably their youngest customers, checked their designer watches to see how much time they could spend relaxing before rushing off to pick up various offspring. It was still only 9.30am, so she wandered over to take their order and chatted amiably, as she did with all their customers, biting back her frustration.

It was hard keeping up a cheerful face with the customers, when she knew that the restaurant's takings were

CHAPTER 1

down again that quarter. The quiet worry that seemed to be with her most days was starting to make itself more apparent. Even if it meant more of her mum's death stares, or her dad's rolling eyes, she was determined to turn the family's fortunes around.

CHAPTER 2

Ada stared out at the beautiful sea view in front of her, but couldn't really take anything in. Tears threatened to spill from her eyes, but she was tougher than that. She refused to feel sorry for herself.

Since her darling Ned passed away last year, she'd been determined to stay in the apartment they had bought together when they knew he was unwell. He'd wanted to come back home to the seaside town he'd been born in. Although it had meant leaving their friends and family behind, he yearned to wander along the sandy beaches and sit and watch the seagulls. He wanted to wriggle his bare toes in the sand and eat melting ice creams as the sun went down.

The months before he went were bittersweet. He had been at peace in his hometown, so she couldn't be cross with him for leaving her alone. She'd never lived here before, though, and the endless beaches and little shops and eateries dotted around were a far cry from her past life, full of interesting people and endless social engagements. Here she had a beautiful home, but her family lived abroad and she could not – would not – let them know how much she was still

CHAPTER 2

grieving, and move home. Here she felt close to Ned. She could run her fingers through the sand and picture him next to her doing the same. The joy on his face, when he'd recounted stories of his childhood in the old fishing town and told her of his summers building sandcastles on the beach and riding the waves with his friends. She remembered it so well.

They had only visited his birthplace once before. But as soon as he was diagnosed with his illness and given such a short time to live, he suddenly craved home.

To her, home was their huge house in America. Ned had been a celebrity photographer and they had moved often, but they had settled down in the States. She had adored the huge rooms with high ceilings and the warmth of the sun that eased her old bones, but here she was, in a new place, a place that wasn't really home for her.

Her sons called her almost daily, but so far, she'd refused to go back. Ned was here with her, she could feel him, even though she couldn't see his kind face anymore.

He would be telling her to get onto that plane and stay with their children, but they were busy. They had careers and families of their own. What would they want with a heartbroken old woman, wandering around their houses looking lost and frequently bursting into angry tears? They didn't need her dragging them down, when they were coping with their own grief. Ned had filled the room with his presence and people clamoured for his attention. He was one of those souls that others gravitated towards, to bask in the glow of his golden personality. She had been well used to it, though, and his gaze always found her in a crowded room.

She knew she could get through this, but she would have to do it in her own time. They would all probably demand that she visit them, or they would descend on her at Christmas, so until then, she had almost a year to compose herself

CHAPTER 2

and to let the outside world think she was recovering. She was an actress. She could do this. She would make damn sure that by the time her boys got here, they'd think she was coping beautifully, rebuilding her life and staying strong. She gripped the handrail of the panoramic balcony on her penthouse flat and gazed through a sheen of tears at the waves kissing the shore. She tried to feel some of the peace that Ned had found here.

Movement caught her eye on the promenade below and she recognised the young woman from one of the breakfast places along the beach. She was looking mutinous, even from this distance, stalking back and forward and muttering to herself. Her hands were bunched into fists and she was brandishing one of them at a very innocent-looking bush, before she swung a kick at a plant pot and then hopped about holding her toes. Ada couldn't help but smile. She had met the girl and her parents a few times and exchanged pleasantries, but Ned hadn't really wanted to eat out. She'd only been there alone, when the isolation had got too much for her. Perhaps she'd go there today and try and chase away her demons. If Genie – she remembered the girl's name at last – was in a bad mood, then they could be grumpy together. She might even have a little chat to the hedge as she walked past, too. It wouldn't answer back. She was pretty sure everyone in her building thought she was an eccentric recluse, so no-one would bat an eyelid to see her talking to a plant.

The little cafés and bars along the seafront were quaint and beautiful and looked as if they hadn't been touched by time, which was charming. Ada did think that they could do with a few modern touches, like softer cushions on their seats for frail bottoms like hers and maybe the odd tweak to the menus as a change from cooked breakfasts and chips. The beach was popular, though, and the street below was often bustling with people. It was just the restaurants that

CHAPTER 2

seemed eerily quiet. She couldn't understand why, as the prices were very low for the huge plates of food that were served. Seaside fry-ups were usually a crowd pleaser. They were too heavy for a little woman like her, though. She wished they offered something a bit healthier. Perhaps she ought to ask for a children's portion, but she always felt embarrassed to do that and ended up leaving at least half her meal.

Maybe if she went for brisk walks along the shoreline, then her appetite would return. She knew she was wasting away here. Her children would be horrified if they could see how much weight she'd lost. She always hid most of her body behind a table when they video-chatted with her. She wore a bulky jumper and stuck a smile on her face and told them she was *fine*.

She straightened her back, which ached slightly from all her tossing and turning at night. She often thought she must be searching for Ned in her sleep, as she woke up feeling like she'd done a workout. She felt the worse for it, not better. Her building had a gym downstairs and a spa, but she'd never ventured in. She used to swim every day at her old home, but now she worried that she'd pass out through exhaustion while in the pool, and hadn't plucked up the courage to risk it yet.

She occasionally wondered if she should just let herself drift off and be with Ned, but she was stronger than that. She would survive this. Brushing a tear from her eye, she turned and decided that she needed some fresh air. In fact, today was going to be the day when that huge breakfast at Genie's restaurant didn't defeat her.

CHAPTER 3

Genie smiled politely at the little woman in front of her, who was becoming a regular. She had beautiful skin, and her soft grey hair was always pulled back into a perfect chignon, but her eyes were so sad. Genie didn't know her well enough to ask her if she was ok, but she could feel the unhappiness emanating from her, even though she always looked up at her with a bright smile.

Today she was working her way through a huge plate of food and had been bravely tackling it for the last hour. She had only got about a third of the way through, and looked exhausted. Genie had once asked her parents to offer smaller portions for different sized appetites, but they had told her not to be silly, their prices were so cheap and no one would want a smaller plate for the same money. Genie secretly thought they overloaded the plates too much. If they would just take two or three ingredients off the breakfasts and add them as extras, they would make much more money. People could still have a hearty breakfast, but the pound or two on each plate for beans, mushrooms, and extra toast would

CHAPTER 3

make such a difference to their bottom line. It would give them a chance to improve everything else.

Genie took Ada the fresh pot of tea she'd asked for and gave her a warm smile. There was something about her that drew Genie to her. She wanted to reach out and give her a supportive hug. Instead, she whipped the plate away as soon as the lady put her cutlery down and was rewarded with a grateful glance. A woman that size probably ate muesli for breakfast, lunch and dinner.

Genie looked down at her own ample hips and bulging bosom and decided that she was going to try and take her nextdoor neighbour's dog out for a morning walk along the shore more often. She'd also try not feel so stressed that she couldn't be bothered to cook a proper meal at night. Her parents loved food that was quick and easy to whip up, but Genie enjoyed fresh ingredients and spent ages scanning new recipe ideas and trying out different flavours at home. It didn't have to take an age to make a meal from scratch – as long as it didn't contain cheese. If it did, she had to put on gloves to handle it. This often caused her to spill most of the ingredients. She'd then have to put on wellington boots to sweep up the disgusting, cheesy tendrils before they touched her toes. Genie's parents had lost a bit of weight recently, but this might have been because they were stressed out about the businesses along the seafront, rather than her delicious evening meals.

She eyed her dad's not-quite-so portly stomach. She was pleased to see he was in slightly better shape these days. He wasn't as grumpy either. Her mum, on the other hand, always made an effort with her appearance and scolded Genie about being such a slob. But Genie didn't have time to spend ages shopping with friends for the latest fashions. Besides, her clothes usually stank of grease from the fryer in the back kitchen by the time she got home, so she had given

CHAPTER 3

up on that years ago. She was clean and presentable at work, with her long dark hair pulled back in a ponytail to keep it away from the food (and cheese) and a fresh blouse and skirt every day. Even that seemed an effort.

She had piercing blue eyes that customers often stopped her to ask about, and long silky black lashes, which meant she didn't need much make-up. Her skin was slightly tanned from working outdoors, even at this time of year. Half the chairs and tables were inside, but the other half were under an awning. This could be swept back at the touch of a button, allowing diners to sit in the sunshine. The British weather was actually good this year, so the awning was open for a lot of the time, even though Christmas wasn't all that long ago.

Genie glanced up from a table she was clearing. Trudie, from one of the other restaurants further along, had popped her head in to say hello. She glanced around to see if they were busy and grinned a hello at Genie.

'Hey Trudie, how's business today?'

Trudie paused to say hello to Ada, which surprised Genie, as she'd thought the older lady pretty much kept herself to herself. Ada greeted her politely and then turned back to her tea.

'We're really busy,' said Trudie. 'And I've run out of milk already. I forgot to send the order today. We've got a coach party in and they're causing havoc, moving all the tables round.' Trudie smiled happily.

Genie knew she wouldn't mind a huge crowd. These businesses were used to being packed to the rafters at weekends, but being busy on a weekday and not having to pace up and down the road looking for customers was a complete bonus.

Genie grinned at the other woman's infectious smile. Everyone along the parade called her Tantalising Trudie, because her hips swayed mesmerizingly as she weaved between tables. Trudie kept Genie sane and was always dropping in for a chat with her or her parents. Genie had tried to copy Trudie's sashay once and had tripped over and almost landed face-first in the lap of one of their male customers. She'd looked up to apologise, and seen Bob from the local council office staring disapprovingly down at her, his face bright red. She wouldn't be trying that move again in a hurry.

Everyone along this parade of restaurants got on so well. It was what had kept Genie going when her own friends stopped coming to the restaurant and she had fewer people of her own age to chat to. Trudie was more her mother's friend than hers, but they still got on really well.

'Of course!' she responded to Trudie's appeal for milk. 'I'm sure Dad ordered enough and we're quiet today, so I'll grab you a couple of cartons.'

Trudie smiled her thanks and pulled out a chair and sat chatting quietly to Ada, who seemed pleased at the interruption. When Genie returned, Trudie jumped up, waved her thanks and jogged back to her own establishment, waving to Genie's dad who had just come out of the kitchen with huge breakfasts for a table of two.

ALSO BY LIZZIE CHANTREE

Romantic Fiction

The Little Ice Cream Shop By The Sea
Book 1
The Little Cupcake Shop By The Sea
Book 2
If You Love Me, I'm Yours
The Woman Who Felt Invisible
Ninja School Mum
Babe Driven
Love's Child
Finding Gina
Shh… It's Our Secret

Book 2 and 3 of The Cherry Blossom Lane Series, coming soon!

Non-Fiction

Networking For Writers

Printed in Great Britain
by Amazon